A FREE gift from Author **STEVE WINDSOR**

The story of Eden's Garden as you've never heard it told. How man truly faced his first temptation.

The angel Steg has a dilemma, he can either fulfill his heavenly duty as the knowledge bearing serpent in the Garden—assist the daughter of Eden in bringing Life's light to mankind—or he can pursue a growing love inside of him that is beyond his control or comprehension.

Steg's love is more forbidden than any fruit growing in the Garden, and to pursue it he'll have to break just about every commandment he'll ever know, yet to be written or silently understood hardly matters.

But love is not one to wait and wane while it withers on the vine. Neither is Steg who, as the highest and most beautiful angel—the very first angel—is mere breaths away from being a god himself. Now, he'll either win the affection of the one he loves in the next 7 days, or he will incur the wrath of a God who purports to love him above all others.

Either way, the Garden will never be the same again. Because sooner or later . . . sin touches every god.

Get your copy of *STEG—The prologue Novella to THE FALLEN series Thrillers*.

Available in February 2015!

*Get My **FREE** Copy of STEG*

Also available at vixenink.com

Praise for the novels of author Steve Windsor

"Throughout the story you find yourself caring for this immensely flawed character whose four-letter words add a tangy flavor to the hills and halls of eternity. Not because what he does is good, but because Windsor has made him and those around him eminently ... human. For the reader, the challenge in JUMP is not what Jake has to contend with, but putting the effing book down to get to sleep at night."
- Ana Young (Amazon Review)

The perfect way to "Jump" into a story that at first glimpse is off the wall and quite different. The pages seem to turn themselves as you are thrust into a unique world full of fascination, craziness and intrigue. Thoroughly enjoyable read.
- (Amazon Review)

I'm already reading the next book in The Fallen series - FURY and it's awesome!
- Lise Cartwright (Amazon Review)

An even more dazzling read, this hilarious close-up of a personality who cussed her way through one eternal conquest of Heaven and Hell will keep you riveted and clamoring for more. With Windsor's exceptionally concrete prose and dastardly, diabolical dialogue, you won't regret a repeat visit to his eternity of "everlasting impotence."
- Ana Young (Amazon Review)

FAITH

A FUTURISTIC RELIGIOUS FICTION THRILLER
(Testament 3)

STEVE WINDSOR

Vixen

VIXEN INK

FAITH

A VIXEN ink book/Published by arrangement with the author

Cover design by:

Steve Windsor - stevewindsor.com

ISBN-13: 978-0692380000
ISBN-10: 0692380000

To the friends that encourage us to try harder

FAITH

Testament 3

TRIALS

— I —

"DO NOT SUPPOSE that I have come to bring peace to the earth. I did not come to bring peace, but a sword." (Matthew 10:34).

When my mother first read that passage to me, I asked her what archangels were like. Because they sounded pretty scary to me. Like maybe God sent Michael to punish someone.

She smiled at me—laughed a little. Then she turned her head and stared out the window at my father down in the stock pens. "Oh, sweetie," she said, "angels are no different from me or you. They read the Word . . . try to understand themselves," then she mumbled a little but I heard every word like it was inside my head, "wonder if they're doing the right thing."

That was a long time ago and I was a different person back then. Now? . . . Well, you may think that I'm just a shaky old, alcoholic priest who has lost his faith . . . but things were not always this way.

So, before you rush to judgment—condemn Faith for the cowardly archangel you think him to be—this is my testament.

Way back before the need for it was rendered obsolete, the insurance leeches had a saying for anything that happened to a guzzler that they couldn't blame on someone else. It was called an "Act of God."

Hitting a deer at night, or a tree falling on your hood in your drivebay, or golf ball-sized hail dimpling up the metal on your roof like some kind of frog plague. . . All of that was hard to coax penance out of some other insurance sinner, or lay the guilt on their own paying customer, so they called it an Act of God to make themselves feel better for cracking out the credits to repair one of their own insureds' vehicles.

To an insurance institute, there were many different types of godly acts, and they were all as different and as random as I have since come to know God to be. But bloodsuckers didn't care about the ones they drained . . . any more than a sinner cared about God, I suppose.

A shareholder report that looked too soft on profit and too heavy on helping would cause someone to have to answer to the only god that Man had left—credits. Since you couldn't lop off God's head for a bad quarterly credit summary, any claim that couldn't be abdicated, abandoned, or aborted . . . got labeled "Act of God."

However, one thing every "act" had in common was how they sounded when they happened . . . and what happened after.

Most every act of my once benevolent God began with a huge cracking crash that sounded just like lightning and ended with a terrible ton of damage to someone's life or livelihood, sometimes both. I learned before I lost faith that if God *was* watching, the only time he would let you know was when he was very, very upset with his children. And when that happened, God, or whoever in Heaven was in charge of such matters, would usually send an archangel to remind his children just whose rules they were supposed to be following.

For the record, archangels are not very nice.

* * *

Like all acts of an angry God—and as I've told you, I now believe that there are few acts that *aren't* angry—the beginning of my end came in the form of a huge crack and then a crashing sound that shook the very foundation of my own church . . . not to mention my long-overdue, fallen faith.

Though, when I think back on it, my faith came crashing down around me long before the roof of my church did. In reality, or the last eternity if you want to look at things that way, my faith was a glass house, blown to a seeming palace from the most fragile of grains of red hot sand. And like all glass houses, mine would be brought down by stones thrown from inside it . . . by my own weak-willed hand.

For a long time I thought that it was only one particular stone that had done most of the damage—the biggest one. That was the most obvious conclusion that anyone watching from the outside could come to. It was certainly the conclusion I had come to. Though, looking back through the passing of at least two eternities that I can remember, I started throwing rocks at my own faith before I ever became a religious man.

Where those rocks came from? Well, let's just say that the streets of Seattle are not paved with emeralds.

— II —

THE HUGE CRASHING sound is followed by the most piercing screeching I've ever heard, worse than my screaming classmates back at seminary. Those cries scared the faith right out of me. This screeching now might just put it back in.

My big mahogany desk shakes, lifts off the ground a little and slams back down. And I've dropped my glasses.

I turn my chair, lean over and look for them. I can see without them, but it's . . . different. Without their assistance, it's like peering through the bottom of a mason jar at evening meal—total kaleidoscope blur.

I'm sure I could get them "fixed"—my eyes, that is—but I'm not letting a State doctor put a nanochip behind my eye. I know better.

Another loud, screeching scream and I almost fall out of my chair. I catch myself and go to my knees and start running my hands back and forth, frantically searching for my "eyes" on the wood flooring. It's only a few seconds, but the screeching continues and it's a hideous and haunting sound, more so because I can't see normally.

When I find them—their little white outline against the light blue floor of my office doesn't help—I put my glasses back on and remind myself that I shouldn't be so vain about using the little chain she gave me to hold them around my neck. Vanity. . . Considering the "gift" in my pocket, worrying about how I look is not the worst of my sins. But I don't think that it's going away anytime soon. The vanity, that is.

I know *she's* not going away. Not today . . . maybe not ever. She's my burden to bear. In the end, I'll probably be carrying her to Heaven.

By now, I hope I have made peace with that, but the vanity has been haunting me the longest—caused more heartache than if I had been stronger. But there's no time to reflect on any more of my sins, because now there is glass breaking out in the main hall of my church. I fear that the night vandals have found a new way to protest one of their perceived oppressors.

Perceived isn't the right word, because the average citizen has precious little else to look forward to each day but oppressors. Most know to be careful speaking out against the ones that will snatch them up, and torture and kill them for even thinking about resisting.

Well, at least it is *less* assured that will happen if a frustrated citizen defies the Clergy. Not that it *wouldn't* happen, but the church has bigger issues to deal with than some disgruntled citizens. If every sermon stopped to deal with every ache and anger that one of their flock had, there would be no time to pass the offering basket. The church, more importantly the Clergy, doesn't stop the collections for the wages of sin simply because the citizens can't afford them.

Protection, on the other hand. . . A disgruntled citizen wouldn't even consider directly protesting against the only legal authority left. That's a good way to wake up at three in the morning with a black bag over your head on the way to your last three days on Earth.

Ensuring the peace and prosperity comes at a high price to citizens who don't have enough credits to feed themselves much less fend off being remanded to Protection for open disobedience.

Regardless, the credits to repair, replace, or renovate my church have never been an issue. I know better than to ask how now, but it's not hard to get the credits to keep the offering baskets moving during my sermons. The archdiocese always approves my requisitions.

It might have something to do with the fact that my beautiful Saint James Cathedral is the biggest congregation in the Northwest Quarter, or maybe it's just that I never miss an afternoon mini-drone credit pickup.

Whatever it is, the credits I collect don't stay here very long. Offerings are scooped up and sent to the archdiocese on a mini-drone carrier right after morning mass. If I need credits for anything I have to requisition them back. It all seemed very inefficient to me, so I inquired about it with the archbishop one Sunday afternoon over coffee . . . and the church ladies' congregation carrot cake, of course.

The Lord's ways are mysterious, I was informed, but the church's credit dealings . . . are secret. There are no credits at a church. *Remember that*, I think to myself.

Why are these little lost jackers. . .? I think it, but I know the answer. Only one reason a citizen, robbing his dinner at the Black Market, decides to get dessert at a church—Judgment. They all want Judgment. One more high to try and figure out who they really are. And *that's* what my mother had meant about archangels—all God's creations, just trying to understand who they are. Too bad that when they find out, there will only be more questions.

Used to be that I had plenty of Judgment to distribute to a citizen in need of it. I got it straight from the source, so to speak. On any given Sunday, I filled more citizens' minds with images of angels and demons, Hell and damnation, and sin and salvation than the people who manufactured the anesthetic sleep serum. It certainly wasn't my sermons. And why not, the beautifully adorned inside of my down-town cathedral would leave even the most skeptical cynic with visions of gods and devils. But the poor misguided citizens looking for re-demption in a needle. . . I'm sure some of their souls are just as lost as mine.

Maybe. . . When your immortal soul is as difficult to find as mine was, it's hard to work up the empathy to help someone else find theirs. And in my line of work, that is a very big problem. There's not a night that I don't go to sleep on the big leather couch in my office, wonder-ing what I'm doing in this eternity. Because if I'm not saving souls here—finding the faith to save my own as well—just what am I doing? What act of God am I?

I walk across my office to the door that leads out into the main cathedral. I pause and look at the doorknob, wondering if I should take a little side trip to the basement—maybe dig up some protection of my own. But I've helped this class of misguided miscreant find their way back from Judgment before. I'd be better served getting the damage requisition forms out of my desk so I can send them over to the archdiocese with the morning mini-drone's other paperwork.

The Black Market jackers never do more than a couple thousand credits of damage, and they're rarely violent. Self-judging is one thing —every citizen needs a little something to keep them going—but violence against a priest? Assaulting a Protection agent is the only way to get condemned to the interrogation wing of a sanatorium quicker.

I glance at my desk. *Paperwork. . . Painful*, I think. There are forms for everything now. I put my hand on the door handle and chuckle a little—the authorization forms to replace doorknobs are more formidable than the ones we used to have to fill out for "Acts of God" insurance claims.

When I slowly open the door to my office, behind and beyond the pulpit, the brightest light I have ever seen hits me so hard in the face that I have to squint, and both of my hands go to my face. I don't realize how hard I cover my eyes until I feel the pain from my glasses digging into the bridge of my nose.

I try to peer through my fingers, but it's like looking into the sun. And compared to the eternal gray of my beautiful lost Emerald City. . . The white-hot truth of the sun is nothing compared to how blinding this light is. It might have even burned the retinas of my eyes.

To a Seattleite, something as bright as the sun can leave orange spots in your eyes from just thinking about it. I wince in pain, cover my eyes again, and turn away.

I can sense the ball of light—that's what it looked like before I closed my eyes—watching me? *That can only mean. . .? . . . God? It's just not possible*, I think before the brightness moves above and away from me—gets dimmer—and I turn back and open my eyes. I catch the last glimpse of whatever it is as the ball of light streaks out a huge hole in the middle of the roof over the main pews.

I'm left with a burning streak of orange in my vision for a few seconds for trying to catch a peek at. . . *Mother of Mercy*, I think, it can't be! When I think about it, maybe I should have dug up my book.

I'll have to admit, at first I thought it might have been God, but that was the first time I saw an archangel in person, and it might have been the most spectacular thing I'd have ever imagined . . . if it weren't for the second one.

I can feel the cold and the mist from the drizzle outside, coming through the roof. I close and open my eyes a few times. Then I squint and rub them under my glasses, trying to make the burning sensation go away. The feeling in my head reminds me of that trip home from the State Med-mart with my mother.

I take my glasses off and put them in my pocket—I don't want to drop them on the floor again. I'm still not ready to use the little chain. Denial is almost as powerful as guilt.

When the bright hole in my vision finally subsides, I can see a fuzzy red shape, surrounded by the light blue haze, on the floor in the middle of the main aisle to the pulpit. I put my glasses back on and in that very moment, something that I have been unable to bring myself to believe in for my entire life, no matter how hard I try, finally shows up.

In that instant, when I see the figure on the floor, motionless with the huge cross from my roof sticking out of its stomach, bleeding onto the floor of my church. . . I have to tell you it is the very moment, the very second, when I finally believe there might just be a benevolent God in Heaven after all.

I'll have to die again before I realize how wrong I am.

I know that it sounds crazy—not believing until now—given who I am . . . what I am. I guess I'm so bad at hiding it from myself that I think everyone else can see right through my self-deception, too. But people want to believe. That's what they're programmed to do—have faith. I learned that at seminary. All about the most powerful drug of all, belief.

Faith that things will get better, faith in the system that enslaves them, and an unshakeable, indestructible faith in the benevolence of their lovers and leaders . . . despite all hard evidence to the contrary.

The whole ugly world is built on faith, in one way or another. It certainly isn't built on truth. I know that now, too.

So when a citizen sees me every Sunday in church or when I visit the wretched souls at the sanatorium downtown. . . When I get all clean and pressed up in my dress blacks, accented only by the little square white patch on my collar, to a lost citizen or lonely parishioner, I look like faith—feel like belief. Because that is what I'm supposed to be, so that's what I am. Everything works that way.

The church figured it out first, eons ago. The State just followed their lead. They made some improvements to the system—applied a little more direct physical pressure to the people. Although, from what I know now, the Clergy are not above applying some of their own direct pressure when they encounter . . . anyone who won't believe the way they are supposed to.

Regardless, the results are the same, as long as people keep believing —though "fearing" might be a better word—they keep doing . . . anything you want them to.

I've fallen a long way since I had any belief left in me. But you know that already, don't you. No matter, we'll get to that part soon enough.

I don't know what I believe in now, but this is. . . I wouldn't have believed it myself had it not been for all the black blood . . . and the huge gray wings.

I pull my metal flask out of my pocket. I keep the little leather-bound bottle for just this kind of. . . I have no idea what kind of situation this is. Or at least I *had* no idea at the time. *A test? Another trial, maybe?* I thought. Or maybe just some bad Judgment? Could be that I'm hallucinating, though she's not around to ambush me with a vial of sleep syrup today, so. . . Or maybe I'm dreaming or I drank too much and I'm just snoring it off, drooling on some paperwork at my desk again. I'm not proud of it, but it happens. You can cast stones at me later if you like.

I unscrew the little cap to my long since favorite way to pray and I take a good long sip. I wince at the angry bite of the State's swill. I wipe my mouth with my handkerchief and glance back to the hole in my roof. "Act of God," I mutter to myself.

Then I walk toward the dead angel on the floor of my church.

— III —

I KNOW WHAT you want to ask—this isn't how I'm supposed to be. How did I fall all the way down to this level? Where did my cynicism and lack of faith come from? I'm a priest after all. And why aren't I more afraid and quaking in my dress blacks like you've seen me before? It's not the State courage in my flask, I can assure you of that.

I like a little nip every now and then. It helps me stomach the lunacy we let happen. However, I'm far from an impotent old boozer.

But if you've come this far, we both know how this ends, so there's got to be only one question that you could ask. Believe me, I've asked myself that very question for two eternities now.

How *did* all this happen? How did I get like this? . . . It's not how you might think.

First, let me tell you, there are all kinds of ways to stay out of trouble. The easiest is to stay clear of its path in the first place. But curiosity is more powerful than good judgment, even *if* too much of it can get you killed. And my lust for knowledge needed no inspiration from the church—as a boy, I had an insatiable curiosity long before my indoctrination to the Clergy's version of faith.

They don't teach "mind your own misery" at seminary. In fact, they taught us just the opposite. I guess I would have to say that as "we" now, wouldn't I? *We* were trained to. . . Time. . . I still can't get used to experiencing everything before and after it happened . . . happens.

The perception and relativity to a man isn't as potent as it is to an angel, but all eternities are like that—relative to one's place in his or her own time. Seen through the perception of your position in the grand scheme of Life, time can get confusing.

Eh, listen to me. Sounds like I've been unscrewing the cap on my flask too much, doesn't it? Trust me, it didn't make sense to me until I actually experienced it for myself. But time lapse is a real thing, as real as the Devil, anyway. Now . . . where was I?

Ah, yes. At seminary they *taught* us that everyone and everything is our business. And that is the way God wanted—wants it. Assist citizens with their troubles—help them mind their misery. Focus them with the stick of the understanding that they will never be enough, yet give them a slice of carrot cake while pretending they might. That was the game. I learned to play it well.

Staying out of trouble in the process? For a man in my position, with my responsibilities, hiding in my office while trouble rummages around in my Lord's house is never an option. For someone who spent his life preaching penance from the pulpit and scraping souls out of the sewer, I had to try and avoid the many pitfalls of my eternity . . . right out in the open for all to witness. You know that. You've seen me, pretending to cower and shiver like a helpless citizen.

In the animal kingdom that kind of behavior invites aggression. Out here in the murky gray of the new society we call freedom, it would probably be no different. I would've most certainly ended up at a "fifty"—incarcerated and tortured in a sanatorium. That is, if it weren't for two things:

First, Protection frowns on any type of aggression but its own. Our black-clothed and brutally efficient new police force are funny like that, I suppose. Can't have the populace fearing anyone but the proper authorities, can you? Bad for . . . prosperity. And they should know, it's their job to ensure the "Peace and Prosperity . . . for All." By now, you know that isn't as it seems either.

If there were peace and prosperity for everyone, there would be no need for dissent and then there would be no need to squash it. Absent that, what need have you of Protection? But that is the lie beneath the lie, isn't it?

Protection needs dissatisfied citizens more that the citizens need protection. One doesn't exist outside the misery of the other. Which one you think I mean, I'll let you decide.

The second thing keeping me from becoming a guest at the old brick and brimstone brutality palace downtown, known and feared only as the *Fifty*, the church—my clergy brethren. . . Let's just say that I would rather be in a cell with a Protection interrogation team than some of the faithful that I saw bred and reborn at seminary. If you end up on the sinning wing of the *Fifty*, there is no prayer in Heaven or Hell to save you.

So before, when I said that you don't know me like you think, I was being truthful. You know the man I *wanted* you to know. The one I show people so I can—could hide in plain sight.

But now, in order for you to understand why things ended for me the way they did. . . The only way to understand my end . . . is to start at the beginning.

Don't worry, we'll get to this dead angel on the floor of my church soon enough.

— IV —

WAY BACK BEFORE our world turned crazy—before everything changed and the huge scrapers of the city sprawled and crawled and infected their way out from downtown Seattle, like a virus searching for fresh flesh to devour. . . Before you had to go north past Mount Vernon, south past Tacoma and Puyallup, or east all the way beyond North Bend. . . Before the mountains and the ocean stopped the advance of the dark gray Emerald City, my family and I lived on a small farm, backed up against the western shadow of the Cascade Mountains. We hovered and waited in a soggy little dairy-cow-infested mudhole called Duvall.

At least there *were* cows there, before the State figured out how to make synthetic milk laced with tiny traces of Judgment. Then, that changed too and the dairy cows went the way of the Duwamish Indians and Chief Seattle.

Didn't know it was named after an Indian chief, did you? Only their names are left behind to remind anyone they ever existed. Soon enough, that is every man's fate.

Judgment in the milk? Hah, as if that surprises you!

Soon enough, fearing outright rebellion, the State outlawed public dissent. Eventually, the Constitution was damned to a special place in the Hell of our memories.

When it started, things didn't go too well for the State. Lots of citizens, accustomed to thinking, feeling and speaking their own minds, decided that being disarmed to ensure public peace was bad enough, but then being stripped of their right to protest in order to ensure prosperity made even less sense. They were right of course, but when the shooting started—outmanned, outgunned, and outhated—it hardly mattered. The results were inevitable—thinking citizens became the enemy of the State. And that was just another way to call them dead.

My dad told me once that to the average citizen, blindly believing what he is fed and forced to do each day, "a righteous man with a gun in his hand looks evil. While the evil one, in front of a PIN news camera, smiling and spouting blasphemous falsities with his long lying tongue, seems good. Belief kills as easily as a bullet, Benito."

My father was not a religious man, per se, as you will soon see, but he was . . . educated, I guess you would call it. He would occasionally recite scripture, buried in between the lines of his lessons, in a "know thy enemy" pathway of self-righteousness that I would soon be taught to follow.

I only ever called him "Colonel"—a veteran of one of the State's wars against the Middle Eastern " 'stans," he told me—and his "isms" were like that. You would do well to pay attention to them as I recount my testament. It could save your life one day. I only half-heeded his words and look what happened to me.

The Protection Information Network? The PIN? That's the nightly news. The Colonel made me watch it with him and he would ask me each time what I thought the talking heads were really saying. None of my answers were even close, he informed me.

I soon came to the conclusion that he didn't have the patience to let me figure it out on my own. Later, I would come to understand that what he really didn't have . . . was the time.

One evening, when none of my answers were to the Colonel's satisfaction, he marched me out to the pigpens and told me to separate a sow out to slaughter. Then he sat on the fence above me and watched while I slipped and slid through the mud and pig poop, trying to push one of our near-feral hogs to his own judgment.

The Colonel had a weird way of perching on the top rail of the corrals. He would clasp his fingers together in a fist—he only had three of them on his left hand, but after the first time, I knew not to ask about it. I guess war wounds were like that.

Then he would hold his arms tight in front of him and push his head forward and stare at me. He looked like a big, praying hawk, staring down at a field, watching and waiting, wishing for a mouse he could swoop down on.

The bottoms of his boots looked like they could almost curl backward, allowing him to hang on with his toes. It was unsettling, but when I hesitated and stared at him, he spurred me to my task.

"Get to it," he said, "before Judgment Day comes and we are sent to Perdition with the rest of these swine."

I finally cut out a pig and herded it through the chute, into the barn. By then, I was covered in the same slime as the sow, but I had successfully completed my task and was pretty proud of myself for it.

"There," I said, wiping my face with an equally muddy sleeve, "one pig, ready for dinner."

But before the Colonel had me kill and butcher the unlucky pig, he asked me, "Why did you pick that particular one?"

At least I knew the answer to that. "He gave me the least trouble." Though, considering the amount of grime I was gunked in, "trouble" was as relative as time.

"That is *exactly* the right answer," the Colonel said. Rarities did happen. "There may be hope in Heaven for you yet."

Young as I was, I was still confused, but as I said, curiosity. . . "Why?" I asked. It was, after all, one of my favorite questions. Any kid's, I guess I know now. "It wasn't like she was going to get away."

But my dad never outright answered my questions, no matter how curious—he rarely hit me over the head with the point of a pickaxe. He preferred to bluntly rap me with the handle several times first. "So, Benito *Benedetti*"—he could get condescending too, now that I think about it—"which pig would you rather be? . . . The one who's the least trouble . . . or the one who gets killed last?"

In hindsight, I should have taken his advice a little more to heart. Figuratively *and* literally, in case you've forgotten.

— V —

STANDING OVER THIS dead angel, lying on the floor of the nave of my church—the rows of pews as empty as Tuesday—I'm staring at the huge cross from the steeple. It's covered in black oil and protruding from the few guts this angel has left.

I'm not sure which emotion I should be having. Am I sad that one of God's faithful has fallen? Or, am I relieved that this dangerous creature is dead?

I have only ever dreamt of what they might be like, and each one of those visions has shown different sides of the humanity I know. Some are angry and vengeful, some are arrogant and indifferent, a few are kind and comforting—though that's a rarity—and some of them . . . are just as scary as I believe Hell ought to be.

But those were dreams—I've been "taught" not to believe them— and like I said, unless I'm face-down on my desk drooling, this is no dream.

A real live dead angel, I think. *What will they think of my visions now?* It's a defiant thought, I know, but. . . I guess you don't know yet. Best to leave that reasoning for its proper place in my testament.

I bend down on one knee and get a good look at his feathers. It *is* a he . . . from his facial features, I mean. As for their genitalia—I'm afraid it will have to be seen to be believed.

I chuckle at myself. For a man of the cloth, a more ironic statement cannot be made.

His feathers look . . . hard, like metal or steel possibly. Gray and jagged and sharp, by the looks of them. I'm hesitant to touch them and find out, dead owner or not. "From which Heaven do you hail, my fine feathered friend?" I mutter. Believe me, it makes a difference.

— VI —

MY CHILDHOOD HOME in Duvall was surrounded by rivers and flatter than a mashed potato pancake, so it was the ideal place to grow our own food. That's what the Colonel said. Well, when the whole town wasn't flooded, that is.

I knew from my mother that her *Bible* had a story about a man who endured forty days and forty nights of flood—God raining down judgment—his wrath due to another disappointment in his children.

I read the story of Noah in her book, but for a child of the Northwest Quarter. . . Us children of Seattle were accustomed to being rained on about three hundred days a year, so a cautionary bedtime tale about some saint or another, floating aimlessly at the edge of starvation and near-drowning on a boat for a month. . .? Well, to a waterlogged kid from the soggy, foggy and boggy backwaters around the edge of Seattle . . . that just sounded like December.

My mother said once that God liked to warn his children of impending judgment with torrents of water. If that was true, her *Bible's* God let us know his feelings about every third year.

But my mom explained to me how we needed the great rivers to rise and overflow every now and then, so they could spread the nutrient-rich silt—replenish the drained and dusty land with the fruitful seeds that would allow the crops of the future to grow stronger than the last. Without that, the fields of the faithful would simply become "barren and unfruitful," was the way she put it.

Back then, I thought she was talking about our farm. Now I—I guess we both know who she was talking about, don't we.

"The river washes away the sins of man," she said. The scrapes and trenches and burned ash that we scratched across the land, cutting and digging into the soil like crows and bears and skunks, taking turns ripping apart a dead carcass in the forest.

My mother's lessons were upbeat like that. My father, however. . . I learned that Man was a plague—a locust. *That* . . . the Colonel made crystal clear. "And one day," he said, "man will eat himself out of house and home . . . and then he will spread to his neighbor's house, searching for food. He'll come to your house, Benito, with an uncontrollable hunger. And if there's no food . . . he'll eat you."

So that was why we needed to grow our *own* food . . . and protect it. I never questioned the why of it, I just did what I was told—I "worked the dirt," like the Colonel told me to.

Looking back, I'm not sure if the lessons could have penetrated all the sweat and the grime I was constantly covered in. Most of their benefit sunk into my mind . . . too little too late.

Our little five-acre plot of ground spread out flat right next to the towering river dike. And my dad and I worked it while that big dirt berm hovered over our heads like a frozen wave of God's wrath that, when it thawed—whenever he got disappointed in us—would break and crash right down and drown anything in its path, just like that crazy Noah's flood in my mother's *Bible*. And like I told you, about every third year, that is exactly what God did with our river.

The rain would come and the spring thaw in the mountains would hit just right, and then that river would slice its way through the dike like a Kansas twister tore through a rural zone trailer park. Raw, angry, and indifferent to the suffering and loss of life that it caused. Another act of my mother's benevolent God.

Over the years, we mounded up a huge mountain of pig poop and dirt in each pen so that the pigs could climb up and escape from God's rain. The only thing that saved *us* when the river did that, was the fact that our house was built on ten-foot, greased, telephone-pole stilts.

I only heard the story from my mom, but when the Colonel built that house, he made sure that God's river of wrath couldn't wash us away with the rest of the sinners. The bottom of the only floor in our one-story house was dead even with the top of that dike.

How my dad knew to do that? I could only give you the hindsight from two thousand years of conjecture and stories I heard, so I won't even try. But I would assume that if he got those telephone poles the way my mother said he did, today. . . Excuse me, in the final part of the eternity I lived in, the Colonel would have been dead in three days.

As it was, his three days came later.

I don't remember much more about the Colonel than the constant tests and questions he would ask me, trying to pull answers out of me at the same time he was shoving the knowledge in. To tell you the truth, he was a very quiet man. And by quiet, I don't mean he talked softly. It was more like when he said something to you, you knew it was important, because if he was going to take the time to say it. . . I stayed quiet and paid attention to him—my mother said there was wisdom in every drop of sound he dripped.

My mother, on the other hand, was always talking. It was up to me to ferret out the important parts. Or maybe they were all important, now that I think about it. There was just so much that I couldn't keep up. But she was the one who taught me everything I understood to be the truth at that time about her God. It was only later that I would have to figure out whether or not she lied to me on purpose.

The lessons I got from my mom came from direct statement of fact, as she read and interpreted them from the big brown leather book she called "The Book of Life"—her *Bible*. If it wasn't a prayer before we ate, it was driving all the way into the dirty gray heart of the once beautifully green Emerald City—Sunday mass at the Saint James Cathedral in Seattle.

We listened to the priest—well, my mother listened, I read her *Bible*—for an hour, sometimes more. It is difficult to read, alternating standing and kneeling a dozen times in an hour. For a kid, the whole thing was boring. The only part I liked was after church.

When the sermon was over, my mother took tea and ate carrot cake with her church-lady friends, while I played with the other kids.

In hindsight, it was anything *but* play.

— VII —

I STARE DOWN at the oil dripping from the cross that's punched through my "daydream's" stomach. *Black blood*, my mind thinks. And this angel is covered in it.

You may think that I should be surprised by that, but there is a very good reason that I'm not. I'll get to *my* book—my personal "bible"— later.

Right now, if I'm going to save this poor peacock from his Purgatory, I'm going to need some blood. Angel blood to be more specific. I know just where to get it.

Of course he's not—well, yes, the way you understand it, he is dead. However, dead doesn't mean what you might think. Dead to an angel is . . . different.

When they carry your immortal soul to. . . Listen, this is not the time or the place for a dogma discussion, so let me just say that in order to save this angel from Life, I'm going to have to pull him from out of this death. Because who knows how many he has had.

I look at the black oil again. *Only one place to get that*, I think. "I hate the 'Mike,' " I mutter to myself, fully aware of where my hate has led me.

Sure, I try to convince myself that I truly do hate the thieving, thirsting-for-blood Black Market downtown, but the truth is, the place is magnificent . . . in a completely practical sense, mind you.

I told you—only the truth.

— VIII —

MY MOTHER AND I drove to church every Sunday in the Colonel's prized possession guzzler, and that took credits. More because the car was so fast and even more so because my mother liked to drive it that way.

The Colonel complained about that . . . often. It took almost an hour to get into downtown Seattle from Duvall, and he knew that there were better uses of our limited credits, not to mention the waste of time, he would tell my mother.

He was certain that there was a perfectly good church in downtown Duvall. One that would be glad to rob the credits that we saved on gas.

In his mind, I'm sure, that was the Colonel's "lesser of two evils" scenario. He certainly wasn't getting my mother to skip Sunday sermon altogether. He would have to face my mother's "adamant" for that.

Because my mother *was* "Adamant," she would tell the Colonel. That's where I learned a lot of my vocabulary—my mother's explanations to my father. And adamant meant she wasn't changing her mind. That was all it took most times, but I do remember the Colonel making a one-hearted effort to have her leave me behind.

The ground needed gutting and our pigs needed feeding and. . . There was no end to the reasons that he would give for me needing to stay and learn to "be a leader not a follower." In fact, I seem to remember him saying that I wouldn't learn what I needed to survive, with all her *Bible* and babying.

I had no idea what he meant at the time—we were surviving as far as I could tell—but when I asked my mother, she told me I would become a respectable and well-mannered young man and not just my father's "creation." That was good enough for me, because rolling in pig-pies or church? Like I said, lesser of two evils. So off to Sunday sermon I went, "wasting a whole half a weekend being completely unproductive."

It never bothered me that the Colonel put it to my mother that way. Unproductive seemed to mean I wasn't muddy and wet, covered in poop, slopping pigs or digging through dirt. What did bother me was that Max was not allowed to go with us. My mother was adamant about that as well.

Church didn't allow dogs.

It was funny, because before it all happened, darned near every other establishment of any kind allowed people to bring their dogs right in with them. "Especially if you got credits," the Colonel would grumble and say.

I remember going to the coffeehouse in town with my mom one morning. This lady set her little twisty-haired yipper up on the counter while she cracked out her credits for a cup of J-laced caffeine. When I looked at my mom, she had the same scrunched-up look on her face that she got when she caught Max licking his privates.

She took special care not to touch where that dog had been sitting on the counter. We never went back to that coffeehouse again. I thought it was because of that dog, but later I realized that soon enough no one who wasn't rich bought much of anything that they could make, grow . . . or steal.

Max? . . . I thought I told you about. . . Maybe not. I apologize. I was getting there. I don't really like talking about my dog, but I know we have to, so we'll get to Max, too. Don't you worry about that.

As a boy, the lessons I learned from my mother might have come from someone else's book, but the ones from the Colonel came from "the real book of life," he used to say. "The manual for the living."

When I told him I was already reading that *Bible* at church, he said Life wasn't someone you could learn about in a book. He said that Life was a miserable bitch and the only four lessons she was going to teach me would be delivered by way of pain and suffering and then death. And the best thing I could hope for was to be damn sure I didn't have to learn any of them twice.

I asked my mom what my dad had meant, but she got her "frying-pan" look and I got sent to bed early so she and the Colonel could "discuss" something.

Every kid in the world knows what that means, and Max and I lay on the floor with the door to my room cracked and we listened.

The Colonel never "toned it down," or "let me come to my own beliefs in my own time," as I had overheard my mother warn him to do that night. It didn't matter then, because most of the time I had no idea what he was talking about. I do remember his words, however. Most of his talks I could tell you verbatim.

It was like he knew the truth of what would happen before anyone else did. Looking back, that's what it was—the cold hard truth of the future. Watch and learn—the only truth that Life has to offer.

So I gathered everything I could from the Colonel through observation and mimicry. But those lessons didn't last long, because when I was eight . . . maybe it was nine . . . well, it was three scary "tests," I can tell you that. Maybe it's easier to count that way. Kids remember scary things. I was no different. The terrifying things? We'll get to those later. "Even piss has its proper place and time," a good friend of mine used to—still says.

But that was a long time ago and recounting it. . . The years are jumbled now. Two eternities will do that to you—angel or Man-monkey or miserable demon.

I don't care if you are a righteous angel in Rain Almighty's Heaven or a wicked archangel in the Great Dragon, Jump's, wicked new Hell, a thousand years is a long time and an eternity has two of them. So, two eternities into my new existence, you will have to forgive me if some of the details of my life in Life's garden escape my memory.

So . . . maybe I was eight or nine or ten—it hardly matters—because I remember the important parts clearly, like the day my parents simply disappeared. That happens to people, as you also well know. It does—did, anyway. I'll get to that, too. That was the worst thing.

The other three things . . . came first.

So . . . Max . . . yes.

You might think that it sounds like I was all alone on that little farm, being constantly molded and guided by my mother's *Bible* and the Colonel's "isms." That maybe *that* was why all of this happened—how I came to the path that led me to author damnation and destruction in my book—but nothing could be further from the truth. I wasn't alone.

I'm dating myself again, but before Protection agents were the only ones allowed to have dogs, and before citizens started eating them as one of their few sources of protein, and long before the State used an executive order to nationalize the entire production and distribution system for the delivery of calories to its burgeoning supply of bread-begging citizens. . . Before State added canine carne to the food pyramid, and Protection rounded up all the dogs—catching the cats proved futile—and hauled them away, barking and howling, stuffed in huge tractor-trailer semis . . . I had a dog named Max.

Max was a milk chocolate Labrador Retriever. His coat was so smooth and so beautifully brown that I would swear if you licked him, he would taste just like a chocolate bar. It was probably from all of the leftover pig parts my mom fed him.

We couldn't or we didn't buy dog food. Because burning credits on petro for a once-a-week church run was one thing, but the Colonel certainly wasn't crazy enough to crack them on pet food. So any time we slaughtered a pig, Max got everything we weren't going to eat.

It wasn't much, but the ears and the feet and the tail and even the snout were standard table fare for my dog. And after my mother cooked the bacon, Max got the grease poured over whatever was in his dog dish that day.

Sometimes that grease and guts was all there was. And his coat was shiny brown because of all of it, she told me. Yes, my Max wasn't only likable, I believed he was lickable. Fortunately, Max would never give anyone the chance to test that belief.

"He's a licking fool, that dog," the Colonel joked—he rarely did that. "That dog would lick a porcupine if it let him."

As if he could understand him, Max tried that, too.

My father watched me without a word. It took me a couple of hours of Max whimpering, lying on my lap while I pulled out all those hooked quills with a pair of needle-nose pliers from the barn. He didn't move the whole time. I think it was because I was one of the few people that he trusted.

I'm not sure I remember how I convinced my mother and the Colonel to let me keep the starving little pup that showed up on our farm one day. Neither of them liked dogs that much. And Max growled at them most days to let them know he felt the same affection for them. But they let me keep him. Well, I think my mother let me keep him and she let the Colonel keep his health.

My mother had many looks outside of her "frying-pan" brand, and I guess she used the one that said, "Let the boy keep the dog," because the Colonel only grumbled and said, "Great! Just what the world needs, another mouth to feed."

So Max was my dog and I was his Man. That was our arrangement —our trust. He was my responsibility. *That*, the Colonel wasn't budging on.

Now, maybe it was the time the Colonel took us duck hunting? There were many, but this one is frozen into my memory. You'll see what I mean in a minute.

The Colonel said if Max was going to eat our food, he needed a job. And apparently, according to my father, Labs were born "feather-finding, death-dealing duck-hounds." I remember that verbatim, too.

This particular time, our river was as frozen as February—you could walk like Jesus right across it. But Max and I had found a place where the water eddied back and swirled enough to keep a small patch of water from freezing completely over. When I told my dad about it, he got that knowing look on his face. "Honey-hole," he said. "That'll be stuffed with feathers in the morning."

Max and I stayed up all night, him whimpering and me simply not able to sleep. When the gray fog was still low and the morning wasn't even a thought, the Colonel and I met in the mudroom and donned long underwear and jackets and waders and our big fuzzy face masks.

Max watched us, whimpering and wagging his tail so hard that I thought it might beat a hole in the floor.

There was something magic about the preparation for a hunt. There didn't need to be much talking or convincing or planning involved. It was almost as fun as the hunting itself . . . almost. But clicking gun safeties and testing duck calls and stretching gloves over excited fingers came in a close second, maybe? Though, packing a double-barreled twenty-gauge, the breach broken open and resting on my shoulder like a big steel boomerang, while I walked along God's angry river dike with my dad and dog . . . was a dead heat for that position.

Max followed slightly behind us and to my left, and it only took an occasional reminder from me for him to "heel" to keep him there.

I don't blame Max for what happened—I get excited like that before hunting, too. But to the Colonel, a dog that won't obey is no better than a wild animal. He killed plenty of those. Or so he said.

* * *

We heard them before we saw them, and the gabbling and quacking sounds, and the chuckling, feeding and long, lonesome highball calls filled the air with the knowledge that we were going to find a mess of ducks in Max's and my little backwater eddy. So the Colonel and I dropped down on the field side of the dike and loaded our guns. Listening to the commotion those ducks were causing just over the dike and not thirty yards across the river, Max tried not to whimper.

My father looked at me, tilted his head, raised his eyebrows and frowned a little. I knew what he meant.

Then the Colonel said, "Shut him up or they're gonna head to Heaven before we can flush them."

"Quiet," I tried to whisper at Max.

The whimpering went down a little. I glared down at him. He knew what that meant, too. There was a lot of unspoken communication in our little family of four—as far as I was concerned, Max counted. But he was my responsibility, and if he messed up *this* time, it would be strike two.

Regardless, I knew we weren't shooting when we crawled to the top of the dike—we had played this game before. We all peered through the tall green reeds on our side of the river, across to the far river bank about twenty-five yards away.

"Burn and Boil be damned to the dungeons," the Colonel whispered.

That caught me by surprise and I looked at him. It wasn't that my father never used profanity, he had plenty of occasion to swear or curse at something or someone, but he had a special brand of it that took me a couple thousand years to figure out. That one was a classic.

"It's like the Arena of Reckoning on Judgment night," he muttered.

Whatever he was talking about, I had to agree with him. There were. . . I couldn't believe how many! Mallards and gadwalls and widgeon and even a few Canadian geese were jammed into that little open patch of water on our near-completely-frozen river. It looked like an overstuffed bait bucket on a salmon fishing boat, splashing and sloshing, spilling over onto the iced-over top of the river around it. And every time water spilled out of that hole, it froze solid within a few seconds.

Those ducks flapped and fluttered and flitted their wings. And they chased and quacked at each other, jockeying for a spot in the barely fifty feet of open water.

Frozen weather did that to the stragglers, because if the ducks dallied around in the North too long—didn't get out of the path before God sent down a miserable cold snap—there were precious few places that were safe for them to rest for the night. Water is safety to a duck just like obscurity is for a citizen. If the danger can't get to you, then it's not really dangerous. But once someone finds out where you're hiding, you're as good as dead.

Yes, I realize I'm not talking about ducks. And I know you guessed that was more of the Colonel, imparting his wisdom, but in hindsight, you *know* it's just more truth, so what does it matter that I'm the one telling it. Truth just is—doesn't matter who you hear it from.

What did we do then? I'll tell you what we didn't do—we didn't shoot at those ducks.

There was some story that the Colonel had hinted to me on our first attempt at this maneuver. It was about a couple of bulls watching a herd of cows. And I would've remembered it—you know that's the truth—but he told me he didn't want to get the "frying pan" for telling me all of it.

I didn't press him for the details—that tactic never worked—but I sure wanted to know why we weren't going to blaze down those ducks. After all, the last time, this same strategy hadn't "panned out" too well . . . so to speak. For either of us, come to think of it.

"Again?" I asked.

The Colonel knew what I meant. "You want to learn that lesson again." It wasn't a question. It also wasn't what I meant, but I could see how he might think that.

Once is enough, I thought to myself. "No," I said. I knew that was the right answer.

The Colonel smiled back at me—it was a rarity—but that still got us no closer to bringing back ducks for dinner.

"I want to shoot ducks," I informed him of the obvious.

"How many?" the Colonel asked. I hated when he got cryptic in the middle of something tense.

"What?"

"How many do you want to bring back?" he said. "One? . . . Two? A dozen? How many? It's a simple question."

Now I was getting fidgety, just like Max. I could feel him lying next to me, shivering, not from the cold, but from the excitement and anticipation. No one is cold in the clutch when you are hunting—too much adrenaline. But if we kept talking, I was sure that the ducks were going to hear us. Eh, even then I knew that they were making so much of their own noise that they weren't going to hear us bantering over their impending death. I just wasn't in the mood for some hidden lesson when I wanted to shoot so badly.

"All of them," I whispered, only half-jokingly. "I want to get them all."

There was no way we would be able to get them all, but I could almost taste the deep-red, slightly greasy texture of duck breasts wrapped in bacon, and my stomach grumbled. We hadn't eaten breakfast before our hike down the dike. And besides, by then, I had started to press back against my father's condescending curtness with a brand of resistance all my own.

The Colonel stared straight ahead at the—there had to be a thousand ducks. "Only one way to do that," he said.

I wasn't getting out of it—I knew that. My mother wasn't the only one who knew how to dig in and deliver a message. "Okay," I said, even forgetting to reign in my annoyed voice, "how's that?"

The Colonel seemed to enjoy his own lessons more than teaching them to me. He smiled down at the grass in front of his face. "I'm glad you asked," he said, "because, if you want to kill a whole flock full of faithful feathered fuckers"—I know I said that he used profanity, but never like that, especially in front of my mother, but him smiling when I jerked my head toward him, meant that it had been solely to get that response—"you let them all think that they got away scot-free, and then you pick them off one by one when they come back."

So that's what he was trying to do that last time, I thought. We never had a chance to get to the ambush part of this strategy. As I stared over at the Colonel this time, I knew he was thinking the same thing.

Me drowning . . . kind of spoiled that last time we had tried this.

— IX —

I'VE GOT A pretty good idea who this dead angel on the floor of my church is, but the huge bird isn't going anywhere, so I've got the time. And it's a good thing too, because I'm excited to have a reason to go to the "Mike." I'm pretty sure that will give "time" a little chance to catch up.

I already told you about that, didn't I? Sorry—I'll claim old age for that one.

While I'm gone, I can't have him waking up. I can only imagine the amount of anger that this one will have. Because if this archangel demon is who I think, it may be time for me to start practicing some of that deception the other one talked about.

Time to dummy up, Benito, I think. Going to the Mike will be good practice.

The Mike? The Mike is the citizens' slang term for the Black Market—Bravo Mike, in old military slang. Everyone shortened it to the "Mike." Because, though the State has locked down pretty much everything else, they've allowed the underground marketplace for godly goods and sinful services to flourish.

The average citizen has no idea—too busy trying to stay out of the crosshairs, or an alley body-bin for that matter—but I know exactly why.

We had a saying at seminary, "A playing sinner is a praying sinner, and praying sinner is a paying sinner." Because if you keep a person cold, hungry, and scared for their life—immortal soul, in the case of my church—they'll pay or do anything to keep from thinking about taking that next step.

So, whether it was cracking credits into the offering basket on Sunday or trading a week's wages for some State sanctioned swill, smokes, or sex. . . Protection and the Clergy were like two sides of the same coin. Two shepherds tending to the misery of their flock of sheep.

The State and Protection kept a citizen's body fearful and barely fed, and the church did the same thing for their soul. Because happy and healthy citizens didn't need someone else to reassure them that everything was going to be okay—that they were safe as long as they kept in line, followed the rules, and gave God and the Devil their due. Though which one of us—State or the Clergy—was which, depended on the day of the week.

Don't believe me? I didn't believe it either, but like I said, I read the book.

And I'm out the front doors and away from the safety of my beautiful cathedral—into the dreary gray drizzle of Seattle. I look around like prey watches for predators at a watering hole. I keep watching over my shoulder as I lock the front doors. *I'll get to the paint later*, I think, seeing the work of the overnight taggers on the retaining wall next to the front steps. *The Devil's work is never done.*

I jog down the damp front steps, scanning up and down the street through the mist for danger. I hadn't heard them before, but the drone-raid warnings and emergency vehicle sirens blare a few blocks away. It's nothing new, but this sounds a little bigger than the normal cracking down on citizens.

I make a mental note to inquire about any Protection operation at the Mike. Trying to find the truth on the PIN news is futile. Every citizen with a Judgment-free mind left knows that the real truth is on the street. And every citizen knows that it doesn't get any more real than the Mike. Judgment laced coffee buzz, or not.

Sure, I could call up the archdiocese and inquire about the sirens—they are sure to know what Protection is up to—but like I said, curious minds. . . Regardless, Protection unleashing some misery on citizens may work to my advantage for a Mike run. Any trouble I might have encountered will probably be hiding in their habitat, hoping that those sirens aren't meant for them.

I flit my eyes to the alleys and crevices where danger makes its home. My mind reminds me that the rules of revenge outside of my sanctuary haven't changed just because an angel crashed through my roof. The urban zone is dangerous, even for a well-identified priest, dressed in telltale all-black.

The good news for me is that I stick out like my father's lost finger—no sane citizen is messing with a priest. The bad news? Most citizens are long past fully sane and . . . I stick out like a lost finger! And in a city full of wandering and wanting citizens, anyone who looks healthy is a target.

My little flask full of swill helps make me look less than a hundred percent, but I pause on the bottom step and think about going back and digging up my pistol . . . just in case. It's a dangerous world, after all.

I think better of it and give myself a little reprimand—*Patience,*

Benito—such drastic measures will only work once.

Not ten yards down the sidewalk, the proof for everything I'm thinking comes right out from under the boxwood bushes along the side of my church. And I've got a weathered fast-food cup pushing at my face and a grimy, gut-grumbling citizen's hand—one of Heaven's forgotten souls—clutching at my arm. "Father," he says with his voice, but his breath does most of the talking—he stinks of State swill and freshly injected Judgment.

I know the smell of the State's low-grade liquor, and as for the Judgment, I've seen the results of it enough times at the *Fifty* that I'd know that wide-eyed "I just saw a demon" look, even without my glasses.

"I haven't eaten in"—he pauses for a second, like he's trying to separate his delusions from the reality of talking to a priest—"Last night, father, I saw . . . I saw a angel on your roof."

I look up at the roof of my cathedral. Except for the missing cross, you would never know there is a ten-foot-wide hole in the backside of it. I just nod—it's better to let a Judgment hallucination play itself out. If this turns violent, I'll change my tactics.

"Yeah, yeah," he says, "right up there. He was just sitting there by the cross, like a big bird. And he was. . ."

I widen my eyes at him.

Maybe the hallucination gives way to his last sliver of sanity, because when he pauses, he looks at me like he's apologizing and he's sad. And he points up to where the cross on the steeple used to be. "There's no . . . no cross up there, is there, father?" he says.

"No, my son," I say. It's what he wants to hear. "It is . . . being repaired."

"I'm sorry, I. . ." he starts to say, and then he looks at his cup. "I haven't eaten."

I pull out my flask, unscrew the lid and steady his hand, gripping his wrist while I empty the rest of my flask's contents into his cup. It's not what he's asking for, but I know it's what he wants. And a few more ounces will ease back some more of this Judgment trip he's having. I'll refill it before I get to work on my "houseguest."

I think to the Candidate part of my seminary training—we all became Shandian warriors of the Word. That Priest Instructor's voice is clear in my mind. *Number one, get control of a threat right away. Deceive, disarm, disable, then destroy if you have to.* The four deadly "D's" as taught by those who knew how to use them. But this poor wretch won't require any further precautions. Regardless, if he does, I've al-ready got control of his dominant arm.

This lost soul seems satisfied with a few ounces of swill. "Bless you, father," he says. "God in Heaven, bless you."

And his whole body relaxes and I let go of his wrist. This is as far as this encounter will go. Most likely, he will wander off to an alley and sleep off the rest of his Judgment. He will have plenty of company—the alleys of Seattle are habitats in and of themselves. If humanity had to house every citizen that lived in an urban zone, the skyscrapers would touch Heaven.

I smile at him but it's more at myself and my use of old-world vernacular. *Scrapers*, I remind myself. *You're getting old, Benito. Too old for all of this.*

Even though he probably did see my dead angel on the roof, once that kind of hallucination takes hold. . . He's about half way through to redemption.

"Thank you," I say to him, and then I recite the whole point of our encounter, "for the Lord God commands us to give strong drink to one who is perishing, and wine to those in bitter distress. Drink and forget your poverty, brother—remember your misery no more."

To a forgotten soul, looking for answers from God, hearing a priest recite scripture calms them like their mother singing at bedtime. The chapter and verse are for me, because as long as the "voice" of the verse seems right to them, a citizen wouldn't know the difference.

Most of my sermons I read verbatim from the *Bible*, especially the ones on Sunday out of respect for my mother. But occasionally, I make something up that I feel is more fitting to the events of the day . . . just to see if anyone in my congregation has read the entire book. But memorizing most of it took me about four years to master, so I've never been called to truth on it. Not even once.

Then another verse pops into my head and I smile at its irony: *In the beginning was the Word, and the Word was with God, and the Word was God.*

I guess it is time to dig at least one of my sins back up. Luckily it's not very far away—I've got *my* Word buried right next to my gun.

— X —

THE COLONEL'S AND my first trip down our frozen river after ducks was just like the second one. But back then the Colonel and I, Max by my side again . . . or then, if you're keeping track of the time lapses. . . We crawled our way through the cold hard mud and up the side of the dike. Freezing rain pelted down on the backs of our necks like little tiny marbles.

I took special care to keep the barrels of my little twenty-gauge out of the mud. Another lesson—a clogged barrel will get you killed by your own itchy trigger finger, not to mention that you couldn't use the weapon to defend yourself. Never let it be said that the Colonel missed an opportunity to utter an "ism." Crawling in the freezing rain and the crusted mud was no different.

When we got to the top of the dike and peered over, I could see that the mallards—the beautiful iridescent-forest-green-headed drakes and their mottled brown hen companions—were enjoying the freezing rain droplets bouncing off of their tucked-tight wings and feathers about as much as we were liking it stinging into the backs of our necks.

Max whimpered.

We used the same strategy the Colonel wanted to use on this current day, but this time—back then. . . For the longest time I believed that the Colonel's plan had never bore fruit. Later, much later, I figured out that the ducks had never been the point.

Max had waited patiently like he was supposed to do. On his belly next to me, whimpering barely loud enough that we could hear him. Steam billowed out of every breath that any of the three of us took.

Over the smacking torrents of half-frozen rain droplets, impacting and bouncing off of the iced-over river, the mallards would never hear us. They were hunkered down, enduring God's wrath. And we were on our bellies preparing to give them some of Man's.

The setup was perfect. Only later would the Colonel inform me that perfect was an illusion and just when you thought things were perfect, God would rain down death and damnation on everything in sight. If you haven't guessed, the Colonel is not a faithful fan of the Word. How he and my mother got. . .? I'm sidetracking again, excuse me.

The Colonel liked simple plans—less to go wrong. Max's job was to scare those ducks up so we could shoot them, and trust me, they weren't going anywhere in that hard rain unless someone forced them to fly. A big brown dog, running across the ice toward them would probably do the trick.

That was the Colonel's thinking, and before we plunged into it, I agreed with him. Looking back on the trajectory of the outcome . . . I probably still do. At the time though—I don't want to spoil the story.

"Back" is the command for a well-trained water-dog to retrieve something that you've shot down, so I made my glove-covered hand into the shape of a flat knife—pointed all my fingers straight at those ducks—and I looked at Max and said, "Back."

Max was wired tight most days, and he rocketed from his lying position and in two bounds he was on the ice, racing across the top of the frozen river. He would be on those ducks in a few seconds. Not that we wanted that, but you can only give a dog a task and point him to it. How he gets it done after that is up to him. Yep, Colonel-ism number. . . I have no idea which one.

And the far side of the river's bank erupted in wings and quacking. The Colonel and I both stood up fast and got our shotguns to our shoulders. The freezing rain pelted down on my gun barrel and things went into slow motion. I could see the droplets of ice bouncing off my barrel, and I heard the muffled report of the Colonel's semi-automatic twelve-gauge. A spent plastic shell casing spun and arced across my face. I only glanced at it for a second—a slow-motion red hull of spent fury.

Two drakes—he only shot drakes—clawed their wings, flailing for altitude, but they fell faster as they did.

I shook my head at him. *Two in one shot.* The Colonel was lucky like that.

He caught my glance out of the corner of his eye and smiled. "Gawking's how you get shot," he said with no more concern than that. "Get to it!"

I picked out a flapping figure and—*boom!* My little twenty-gauge bucked into my shoulder. Anyone who really hunts will tell you that you never feel that when you are shooting at game. And that duck folded—stone cold dead in mid-air—and I followed his fall like watching a football arc across a field until it smacked down on the iced-over river. The duck bounced twice and landed right in front of Max, stone cold dead.

Max ran at it, but that duck was going nowhere, and—*boom-boom!* The Colonel's twelve-gauge ended another drake, and I watched it fall in slow motion and bounce on the far bank.

And then things sped up and I shouldered my little twenty again, found a straggler just coming off the ice and—*boom!*—a clean miss. I thought at the time that I'd said, "Dammit!" As it turned out, it was my father.

"Sorry," I said. "I got . . . excited."

But he was down the river-side of the dike, cursing at Max. "Nail rain to a tree, that dog is your damnation."

Bad things don't happen the way you think. Most of them you never see coming. You think you are rushing to solve a problem—fix the thing in front of you—and then that thing becomes irrelevant and you make things ten times worse.

"Pause, assess, *then* react like lightning," was my Shandian training at the seminary. The way my father told it went a little more like, "React before you think—she'll send lightning right up your ass."

The only problem with that wisdom was that all of it came after the fact. Too late for me to make good use of it on that day. It was certainly too late when I looked down at the frozen river and saw Max frantically dog-paddling, bobbing up and down, his muscles quickly freezing and the expression on his face clearly one of panic, as he tried desperately not to get sucked under the ice . . . and drowned.

I ran down the dike toward the ice. Fell on my face and tumbled halfway down. I remember thinking that it was a miracle that my gun didn't go off. Now that I think about it—double-barreled twenty—there was nothing but empty shell casings in it. When I got back up, Max was underwater.

And I ran right past the Colonel, standing at the edge of the ice—he didn't try to stop me—and I was out on the ice and almost to Max, and then I slid on my stomach and grabbed Max's collar as I went past him, and then I just jerked him right out of that frozen waterhole and he went sliding across the ice.

I'm aware, I had no idea how I did it then either. One second, I saw Max drowning, and the next thing I knew, he was standing up on the ice next to me shaking freezing spray off of his coat. And ice sprinkles showered down on my smiling face and then he dropped the duck—he never let the darned thing go. Unbelievable.

Then the ice underneath me broke in a huge crack that sounded like lightning to me, and I went down like I had rocks in my pockets. It happened that fast.

Most of the ice on top of God's angry river was frozen stiff, the surface as motionless as a painting of snow, but the water under it was rushing like it always did. I got sucked under and down, and I could feel the ice-cold water filling my mouth and lungs. And then my lungs burned like liquid hot lava and not the icy river water that was smothering them.

I panicked and tried to take a breath—that's what my body knew to do—and water filled my mouth and then my lungs and then there was acid burning in my chest and that just made me gasp harder and in the middle of my panic, I think I might have begged God to save me . . . right before I went black.

I woke up to the brightest and whitest woman I had ever seen. She just stared at me from the light that seemed to be coming from inside her. I should have been scared, because she had these big black marbles for eyes and her hair was just. . . I can only describe her as light, but she had a weird way about her. Not like my mother's firm but protective manner. She looked at me with a scowl, as if I was annoying her by simply showing up. Though where we were, I had no idea. I was drowning, last I remembered. But now—then—I wasn't. And I was. . . *I'm dead?* I thought at the time.

The white woman had see-through wings, and I knew she was an angel and I also knew I wasn't drowning. I figured I had already drowned and died, and this was the angel come to take me to . . . to where? I had only read about this in my mom's *Bible*. But it wasn't quite how that book described God's messengers. The wings were enough for me, however. This angel had come for my soul.

"You arrive early, father faith," my angel said. It was about all the concern she had for my drowning. "How fares your father?" she asked.

It seemed a peculiar question at the time, given that I was the one who had drowned. And how did she know my father? Well, I guessed that angels knew everyone, and I had a few dreams before, but never like this one. Was it a vision? I knew about visions from my mother's book. Or was it a dream? At the time, I was speechless, but I don't think she cared.

"Has he finished trifling with his bitch?" she asked. I knew right then that this woman couldn't be an angel.

Profanity? I thought. My mother warned me constantly that it led straight to Hell. And angels. . .? Angels certainly didn't talk like that . . . did they?

She cocked her head to the side a little and blinked her black eyes. "Inform him that dalliances with the devil's bastards shall prove pointless," she said. "No miracle he performs will bring precious plot to salvation."

That kind of language scared me—I had heard it in church. Damnation and punishment and stuff like that. "God help me," I have no idea why I said it.

Then she laughed. It sounded like a bird cawing or clucking or something. Not what I expected at all. Then her voice. . . It sounded like moaning when she spoke this time, "Maybe my concern is misplaced? . . . You have far to fall to discover your true faith, Benito. So I shall send you back to him." She smiled at me, but that downturned grin. . . I don't think it was a friendly one. "A boy among butchers— what *excitement* your future holds. Tomorrow, Benito"—her smile went away and she barely nodded her head—"we shall speak tomorrow." Then her hand came up.

A bright light blasted my eyes and a spike of pain shot through the right side of my chest. Then the black-eyed flying witch with her warning was gone.

I'll never forget hearing my father's voice in my head, *God's not saving you*, he said. *That's not the way life works. There's no miracles, Benito. You are your salvation.*

The Colonel picked the worst times to try and teach me stuff, even if it was in the middle of my own hallucination. But it was a miracle when I popped up through a thin section of ice downstream and rolled myself back on top of the frozen river. Then I pulled my way back to the safety of the bank—my near frozen fingers and legs clawing me out of the cold of the river . . . and the confusion of the white witch's warning.

Once I made it to the riverbank, the Colonel stared down at me with the indifference of a man who had surely seen enough dead people in his life for it not to concern him. But his own son? Forget that I *wasn't* dead, the point was I *could've* died. "You lost your shotgun," was all he said to me. Then he reached down, jerked me to my feet with his three-fingered hand, and then he handed me the little double-barreled twenty-gauge he bought me when I was seven.

I just stared at my shotgun.

"Don't lose your weapon when you are fighting for your life," he said. "Come on. We better get you home and warm you back up. Hell to pay from your mother."

I shivered, but held my shotgun like I was supposed to—barrel pointed in a safe direction. I had no idea how he got my gun—I distinctly remember clutching my little twenty when I went under the ice. Maybe I didn't. That little beauty, I still know where it's buried.

I hunched over and coughed and spit the last bits of freezing, burning bile mixed with river water out of my lungs. Then I looked up at the Colonel.

"And don't go rushing into a shitstorm," he said, "until you know how you're coming back out."

I just looked at him—no idea what to say. I was alive. I figured that was pretty good. And he didn't seem too concerned that I might not have been, so I wasn't scared or anything like that. Kids are like that— you freak out and they know something should be wrong, even if it isn't. You stay calm and they could be missing a finger, but never make a peep. And that is *not* a Colonel-ism. But the woman. . .

"Thirty-three minutes," the Colonel muttered, as we walked toward home on the top of the dike. "Not bad. Now . . . what did she say?"

* * *

That was the first time I realized the truth of the Colonel's warning to be careful about "standing on thin ice." You don't realize the meanings of meaningless sayings until you experience the truth of them firsthand. Most people don't know what "starving" really means until they are actually out of food. So, warning someone that the future is a precarious place is about as effective as telling a fat person that they are not actually hungry.

Someone you already know put it to me that way. I'm sure there was some profanity sprinkled in his statement to spice it up a little, but it wasn't the Colonel, I'll tell you that.

So . . . there you have it—that was the first time I died. Max never left my side after I broke through the thin ice of my delusions. I guess he fell through his own "ice" on that hunt.

"Trajectory," was what my dad called it. And he wasn't talking about the way a bullet travels. Most of the time life is just little things that happen that you think are big. But the important things, the big things that happen that seem insignificant at the time, are what shape you through eternity.

If Max had never found me, would he have died sooner? If I wasn't who I was, would I have died later? It still twists me up to think about it.

Certainly, we are all going to die. You and I both know that. But how are you going to live? That's the only choice you have. Though the way the Colonel put it was that you had to live in spite of Life, not because of her. Isn't *that* the obvious truth?

That God was a woman? That should've been more . . . obvious to me. But like I said, beliefs are powerful. Staring you right in the face or not, sometimes the truth just isn't enough.

— XI —

YES, WE HAVE to get back to the truth. I've vowed to tell you nothing but, no matter how crazy or uncomfortable it sounds. So, I'll tell you that as a matter of historical fact, Max did leave my side, because he did not get to go with us to Sunday church. But outside of that, the only other time he was away from me for more than to go down the steps of our stilt-house and do his business . . . was when he died.

That day on the river was bad for us both, and I know Max trusted me with his life after it. But I think that somehow he knew I actually *saved* his life when he chewed up the legs on my mother's china hutch. I never knew the owner of that hutch, so calling her "grandma" was a little too weird for me. The only thing I knew of that lady was that china hutch and how my own mother swooned over it.

So when she screamed one morning and both me and Max's heads bolted up from our shared sleeping bag, I knew one or the other, or both of us, were in deep trouble. I didn't know how deep until I saw that hutch.

The Colonel was the one who took the belt to him. And Max yipped and yelped his way around the living room trying to get away from it. At first, I screamed and chased right behind them both, but my mother caught me on the first lap and held me while the Colonel whipped my dog.

She was the one who finally ended it, because if she would have left that up to. . . I think he would still be whipping that dog in Hell.

Max got his revenge though. He was like that. In fact, now that I remember, I think that there was some kind of harsh exchange between my mom and Max the day before her hutch got chewed up.

Whatever caused Max to take revenge on my mom by chewing up her hutch, the belt was the reason that he crawled under the sheets on the Colonel's side of their bed . . . and peed.

The Colonel wasn't a cruel man. There was just the way things should be and the way they actually were. And when a dog chews up your wife's hutch and you know there will be no end to her complaining about it afterward, the way things *had* to be, was it could never happen again. So Max got the belt.

My dad said I should watch things and make sure I knew the difference between should, was, and had to be. And I thought I knew then that the way things had to be was that Max was going to get the belt again for his pee stunt . . . but he never did. Some things still confuse me.

Now, looking back on it, somehow I think the Colonel knew that Max would force him into more trouble than it was worth to get revenge back on him for peeing in his bed. Because he never took his belt or even smacked that dog on the butt again. And Max never chewed up anything or offered to do anything but whimper at the back door when he had to relieve himself.

I'm not sure what happened, but I know the Colonel always respected a man who wouldn't let another beat on him without figuring out how to, eventually at least, repay him for the favor. They each drew their line in the sand, and the other never crossed it again.

But maybe they each just had bigger things to worry about. At least I knew my father did. Max? Who knows what he was thinking most days. What I do know now that I didn't know then, dirty dogs don't think like people.

— XII —

THE COLONEL'S "BIGGER" things to worry about were one thing, really—the State. Only back then I think I remember that he called them the Government or authority, or something like that. Changing their name? I never understood that either, so I asked. I was always more curious than afraid, if you haven't noticed. So my dad explained it to me.

"Government," he said, "implies that there are those that govern by the consent of the people—we let them tell us what to do as long as it continues to make sense."

That sounded pretty reasonable to me, so I asked why they had changed their name.

"Calling themselves the State," the Colonel said as dry and as cold as he had handed me my shotgun at the river, "lets you know that when you are dealing with them, it's as if you are talking to God. Because they want you to understand that there is no higher authority that grants them the power to do what they do . . . and they damned sure don't need *your* permission to do it anymore."

Always wanting to know more, I asked what would happen if they stop doing things that made sense. And that's when I got the only explanation I ever would about Max and my dad's belt.

"Son," he said, "if a disobedient dog who is supposed to be serving you by guarding your house, starts chewing the inside of it to pieces"—he would always get a faraway look on his face, like he was remembering or he was talking about something that had already happened—"well, then you have to remind the bitch who she actually works for, because if you don't. . . Once a lazy mutt gets used to eating all your food—being fed for basically doing nothing—she figures she can do whatever she wants whenever she wants.

"And if you let her do that, pretty soon she thinks that's the way it's always been. And then, when you don't like something she's doing, she doesn't even care. She just ignores you—pretends you don't exist. Until you try to stop feeding her. Then, there's only one thing she ever does—she gets real mean and starts taking things away from you. You don't stop her cold after that, pretty soon you won't have a house to live in . . . or one thing left for her to chew up."

Remembering it, I thought he was talking about the State, because I was young, but even then I knew he wasn't talking about Max. Now, knowing what you and I both do, I know he was talking about God.

And it wasn't long before I got another firsthand look at her in action.

— XIII —

NOW, I KNOW you think I'm going sideways with my story again. Maybe everything they all say about me is true—I lose my train of thought—and I do throw down a little too much State swill. But my eyes are perfectly. . . Heh-heh, you got me there. But I'll remind you again, act of a god.

I'll tell you about how my eyes happened. It's as good a place as any to get back to the point.

If you haven't figured it out yet, I was what they used to call home-graded. Before State outlawed home grading, and before Protection made sure that kids went to the conditioning campuses like they were supposed to, I didn't even know there was another way to learn. Not until I was playing with the other kids after one of our Sunday church trips.

My mom was busy drinking tea, eating carrot cake, and talking about whatever church ladies like to talk about after a good long sermon. All the kids were rampaging around the playground behind the church. For some reason churches always had playgrounds. The ones we drove by anyway.

Swings and monkey bars and slides and climbing rocks, probably built just so the ladies could stick around and have tea and gossip after church. But they were always joined by the priest, so who knew what they talked about.

After an hour of hearing himself during morning mass, the fact that a priest could listen to himself talk some more, spoke of a faith in his own words that was unshakable. I know the real reason now.

I asked the Colonel what he thought they talked about after church. He said that people who talked too much rarely had anything important to say. That made me smile. I never recounted that to my mother.

When we were all done with *that* long day—the priest preaching, my mom chatting and me playing—and after the whole *other* ordeal was over, I had learned that I wasn't what those other kids considered "normal." They were all middle graders and I was a home grader. And the way they said it made me sound like some kind of freak. But even that wasn't as bad as what they did to me when the church ladies and the priest weren't looking.

It doesn't take long for a bunch of kids to turn into a pack of wild animals. And the thing with wild animals is that there has to be a pecking order. And a pecking order has to have a bottom. "You don't want to be on it," my father told me. I should've listened to that piece of advice a little closer.

It was just play at the time, I think, but somehow I ended up beneath the pile of kids with my face smashed into the bark and sand beneath all the playground equipment. But what was meant to protect kids from injury, rough-housing and rampaging on all that equipment, didn't work quite like that for me.

I could taste the sand and smell the cedar chips and then I couldn't breathe—trapped beneath nine other kids, it's hard to get air—and I was trying to scream for my mom to help me, but that just sucked in more sand, and then I was choking and then I couldn't choke anymore. I stopped breathing.

That was the second time that I went completely black. It was also the second time that I saw an angel.

He was a big muscular-looking . . . bird was the only way I could describe him after. He had a smile like my dad after Max fetched back a duck we had shot along the river.

He had red wings and big blue eyes, and he smelled like when we burned the weeds on our field. And when he spoke, the cawing sounded a little like this black crow that used to swoop down on me and Max, cackling at us when we would scout for ducks along the river dike. I will never forget what that angel said to me.

"You are riddle to me, priest," he crowed, "you and that dog. Never boring, however . . . observing you both. Bid the day to Monica for me. Inform her that you may require more penance, old boozing bastard that you are. I must say, when she names one of you monkeys, it certainly suits you."

And that was it. I could make no sense out of his words. The only thing I understood at all was my mother's name. But that angel, calling me a priest? I didn't even like church. I never told my mother that part.

Then he grabbed me and two huge spikes of pain went through my upper body and I tried to scream out, but no sound left my lips. And it felt like something stabbed through both sides of my chest and the light flashed brighter than I had ever seen.

When I woke up, I was staring at a doctor's flashlight in the State

Med-mart downtown. My mom was looking down on me and a nurse was looking down on me and that doctor was shining his light.

I don't have to tell you, looking up at a pack of grown-ups, all looking down at you like you are supposed to be dead, is more frightening than actually *being* dead. I should know, I've died enough times by now.

That's what the doctor told my mom happened to me—I died. It wasn't so bad the second time.

But a throat full of sand and then bark in my eyes, by the time all the kids got off me and the group of tea-sipping church ladies stopped listening to the priest long enough to notice that I wasn't getting up, I was dead . . . for the thirty-three minutes that it took them to get me to the med-mart and revive me. Though I found out later that wasn't exactly how it happened.

We stayed at the med-mart for at least another hour. Doctors asking me questions and nurses taking my temperature, picking and poking at me with God knows what. Somehow I knew not to say anything about seeing an angel.

I don't think that any of them knew what to do with someone who was just dead, but now seemed to be perfectly fine. Adding the hallucination of seeing an angel to my case wouldn't get us out of the med-mart any faster.

It wasn't a place you wanted to be. My mom told me that. I always thought that the med-mart was where you went to get well. That's what the news people said on the PIN. But my mom told me med-marts were built to take care of sick people—they had no interest in well beings. So the quicker we got out of there the better. I could see that on my mother's face.

The doctors wanted to give me some kind of shot, but my mom was once again "adamant" that they would be doing no such thing, especially since they wouldn't tell her exactly what it was they wanted to inject into me. That was before they weren't required to tell you.

Back then, you didn't want to get between my mom and her "adamant." There was a time when I thought she might have nicknamed a lead pipe or an axe or something that she kept hidden somewhere. Whatever the secret behind it was, once she swung that word at someone, that was the way it was going to be.

They even took my mom into a room next to the one I was in, so I couldn't listen to her screaming at them. I could see through the glass that they were threatening her with something.

I'd seen my dad try that on her before. She picked up her big cast-iron pig-frying pan and it pretty much ended right there.

They left a doctor in the room with me when they took my mom in the other one. I don't think she realized anyone was still with me. That doctor told me I needed a vitamin shot to help me recover from being "unconscious."

I watched through the glass at my mom while the doctor gave me a little stick—it hardly hurt a bit—and once my mom was satisfied that those people in the other room understood her, she came back in, packed us both up and in five minutes we were on our way home, rolling my dad's guzzler down the tollway.

On the way home, my mom told me that when the doctor shined his flashlight in my eye, I just woke up with a big gasp.

Thirty minutes? It seemed like thirty seconds—no longer than a minute, for sure. But I *had* gone somewhere, and that place was as real as that witch-angel I saw with the big black eyes.

My mom acted like I should be afraid—she certainly was—but I was just curious.

It wasn't until we hit Issaquah—about halfway home—that my vision got blurry and I got a splitting headache.

My mom made me recline in my seat, close my eyes and tell her what I remembered from being gone. I don't think she ever used the word "dead" to describe it. Not when she talked to me about it, not when she told the eye doctor the next day, and certainly not when she told my dad what had happened.

They sat at the kitchen table that night, thinking I was asleep, and they talked until very late. My mother was saying something to my father about "the life they had lived"—I could barely hear with the door to my room cracked and Max's head lying on the floor next to me, whimpering softly like he had to go outside to do his business.

The next day, I had new glasses—things were colorful but blurry without them—and they made me look even more "freakish." Though I would have to attend the aftermath of one more Sunday sermon for those kids to inform me of that.

I thought for sure that my mom would roll some kid's head for my accident, but nothing happened to any of them. And the next Sunday we were back at that playground like nothing ever happened. Kids are like that, but I didn't think my own mother. . .? The church ladies were back listening to the priest's after-sermon again. She listened, too.

That priest must have had something really interesting to say, because they all gathered around him like Max waiting for me to put down his bowl of pig-sprinkled food.

When I told my mom about the angel I had seen and that he knew her name, she kept asking and asking for more details, but there wasn't enough of it to take up more than a minute.

Surely there had to be more? In her mind I had been gone for over thirty minutes, but what that angel said and how he knew her name and what I was supposed to tell her, was all there was. That made her scared—her voice was nothing but fear. And that scared me more than the med-mart did.

I never told her about the doctor who gave me the vitamin shot.

— XIV —

THERE'S WIND AND then there is *wind*—howling, haunting, hating fury that shoves over everything in its path. Wind that pushes like a big drunk roughs his way through a crowd when he's headed for the toilet. Trust me, I've seen that.

I've seen some seriously belligerent wind, too. In the Northwest Quarter, the wind lifts up the waves of the sea and blows wherever it pleases. You can't tell which direction it's coming from or where it's going most of the time, and you have to go a bit farther north than Duvall to see the worst of it—Mount Vernon has it pretty bad.

All that cold ocean water in the Pacific and Puget Sound has to go somewhere. So when God gets *really* mad. . . You ask the Plains citizens, they'll tell you the truth, you haven't seen the wrath of God until you've seen him—sorry, *her*—use wind.

If you've been paying attention, you'll know that on our little five acres of the free world . . . everyone earns their keep. Max was no different. Ducks? The Colonel didn't consider chasing ducks and falling through the ice work, so Max needed a real job.

My dad figured out pretty quickly what Max was good at, besides mopping up pig parts, that is.

My dog could feel a storm coming on a bright bluebird day. Though, who couldn't—in Seattle, the gray of the day didn't yield to baby blue too often. Predicting a weather change from nice to nasty didn't take much. But Max would tell us just *how* nasty an impending wrath was going to get.

A day before a big arctic blast of cold and castrating wind blew down from British Canada or our last outpost, Yukon Alaska, Max would start whimpering. And depending on how bad it was going to be, he got louder. If it was going to be a real rager, he howled from under my bed. None of us could get him to come out.

Of course, the Colonel tried once and got some wild animal snarling and snapping back for his trouble. Another moment I felt positive that the belt would be brandished again and yet there was nothing.

"Yep," the Colonel said, jerking back his hand from Max's clamping jaws, "she's gonna break the wrath out of the storehouses tomorrow, Benito. Batten down the barn, because the bitch is gonna blow."

Max only hid under my bed twice, and both times I thought our house was going to rip off its stilts. I figured we were going to go "Dorothying" up into the sky, like that ancient cinewave actress who visited the fake Emerald City with her own dog.

"Castrating?" Well, I described the storm that way, because I had only heard one howl that even approached the hideous wailing of those two windstorms, and that was a calf on our neighbor's little five acres of Heaven on Earth next door.

The Colonel took me over there one day, probably to teach me some lesson or another. I watched from the top of the corral fence as the calves were castrated. It did not look pleasant. But like I said, my father never squandered an opportunity to impart his wisdom.

About the time the third or fourth calf was getting cut, he turned to me and said, "If you think growing a pair of balls is tough, try getting them cut off."

Time. That was all it took for every lesson I learned from my dad to pay off. Losing my nerve, or worse, never growing any courage in the first place, was not his recommended path. Another lesson I had learned a little too late.

I thought about it one time—it would have been nice to get a manual for all the stuff he was teaching me about life. A lot of things would have been easier. But looking back on it, I think the difficulty was his point. Struggle was growth to the Colonel.

Back to my wind.

The first gale we endured was brutal—it blew out three of our windows—but that second time. . . I helped the Colonel build shutters to solve the breaking windows problem, but our house wasn't the structure that threatened to uproot and fly off to Oz. After all, the pig barn wasn't built on top of stilts buried eight feet down.

About twenty minutes into it, though it was probably more like five —relativity of time, you know—I asked the Colonel, "Why don't we have a cellar?" The girl in that cinewave had one, and this wind sounded like it was going to put the Plains Quarter to shame.

There were no storm cellars in the Northwest Quarter like there were in the Plains, I was informed. The way the Colonel explained it seemed remarkably literal to me at the time. Though, I think that the impending windstorm had him less than himself.

"You don't want to drown down in a dungeon of death for this," he said to . . . probably my mother and me both. "You'll be damned for sure. You have to *think*, Benito. Do you really want to be underground when that bitch decides to break the dike?"

I just shook my head, wide-eyed and scared this time.

"You might not be able to see the wind," he chuckled to himself, "but if that dike breaks, this valley will be underwater. Besides, this is number three."

I had no idea what that meant, and neither he nor my mother would tell me any more about it. I didn't have long to beg for an answer, because just then the pigs in the barn started squealing like *they* were being castrated. Guess who got "volunteered" to go check that out?

I was completely surprised that my mother didn't say a word when the Colonel squeezed on my shoulder and helped me to the front door.

I remember gripping onto the rope that my dad tied from the front porch steps to the fence around the pigpen. He was prepared like that. I swear that I lost my footing at least twice and flapped in the blast of wind like the sheets on my mom's clothesline.

I could hear the pigs, screaming and screeching inside the barn like they were being slaughtered slowly. And I pulled on the rope, got my footing, and willed my way to the barn door, leaves slapping my face and sticks hitting me everywhere as I went.

The tops of huge Douglas fir trees bent over and cracked and snapped off like the sounds of a raging campfire. I narrowly avoided a couple of them as I struggled for the barn.

Whatever was causing this gale, and one thing my parents were in total agreement on was that only God showed this kind of rage, it was a force of nature nonetheless.

The boards on the barn were rattling and banging against each other, and the wind howled through the gaps between them like a wolf about to kill a pack of sheep.

That's the way my father described the sound to me before ushering me out our front door. Seems like a just way to recount it, though I've never heard the howl of a wolf that was about to kill a—well, now that I think about it, maybe I have.

The door to the barn opened in and when I removed the two-by-four we had secured it with, the door flung open and I flew inside the barn with it and went tumbling across the dirt floor.

I slammed into the side of one of the pig stalls and fell in the middle of the aisle. The pigs were screaming and it was hard to think, but I jumped up and ran back to the door. The wind blew my face so hard and a big fir branch slammed me in the chest and I fell back, gasping for air.

Back on my feet, I covered my face with my arm and looked across the corrals at our house. It was weird, because I know I helped my dad nail all the shutters tight, but when I. . . The Colonel and his wife stared out an open window, across the yard at me, like there wasn't a hundred-mile-an-hour wind blasting the windows in front of them. And I stopped for a second and stared back. They didn't even wave.

I leaned hard on the barn door and finally got the two-by-four on the inside across it. And the pigs seemed to calm down a little once I got that door closed. In fact, the wind even felt like it had calmed down a little. Though, I would use a word other than "calm" to describe it—less angry, maybe.

I could still hear the howling, but the barn had stopped shaking, and then everything inside got very still. I stared at the pigs and they stared back—them and me frozen in time . . . and disbelief I suppose.

Then there was a huge *CRACK!* . . . and then the roof of the barn ripped completely off!

— XV —

AFTER FILLING THE lost citizen's cup with State swill, I leave the front of my church behind. The thirty-minute walk to the Mike is uneventful. I daydream about her for some of the way. I simply can't help it. And as I approach the Mike's razor-wired ally entrance ahead, my Shandian mind tries to break through her memory and tell me something.

Even this late in my life. . . I need to learn to clear my mind of her and listen faster.

A figure comes at me from behind the burned-out hulk of an abandoned guzzler. *Almost made it,* I think, as the broken bottle stabs toward my face. I spring sideways and grab the hand that's holding it. Once I get the wrist I move with it—spinning into him—and using his own momentum I flip him over my leg and send him to the ground.

And I'm on that hand with both of mine and I go down with him and spin my leg around the arm. It's all reaction now.

He groans and tries to pull back, but I've got that arm and what's in his hand—that's the threat—and I shove the wrong way on his elbow and I hear it crack and he screams and drops the bottle. His fingers are extended a little—less than I want, but I'm in a hurry and a little out of practice to tell you the truth.

Some of the students were luckier than others, but at seminary, everyone got at least one finger break. It was, we learned too late, *the* very best way to get someone's undivided attention. It was also a very simple and easily executed maneuver to render any sized attacker more . . . "manageable."

There's just no way to describe the pain to you unless you have felt it. I'm not talking about a little twisted digit either. A broken finger takes about six weeks to heal and, depending on how much twisting the priest does afterward, the pain varies from excruciating to indescribably intolerable.

I watched each morning—standing at attention in formation—as the priests walked up and down the rows of us seminary students, searching for that day's "fingerling." Most of them usually went for the pinkie finger, but Father Dominic liked the middle finger best.

A little on the pudgy side and definitely shorter than me, what the sideways-smiling Father "D" lacked in height he made up for with a towering lust for inflicting pain.

A student's pinkie finger broke easily when forced sideways instead of back, but the middle finger made a pretty audible "crack" when Dominic broke it straight back. And trust me when I say that you have never heard pain like the kind a barely acclimated seminary student experiences when he calls for "Jesus Christ" to help him with his broken finger. Sideways or touching the back of your hand hardly matters when your dangling digit is being twisted until you are writhing and begging to God on the concrete.

I'll admit, in their defense, it was the best way to get everyone's attention in the morning. Each day started off with compliant and very focused seminarians. And about an hour later we all got a reminder to stay vigilant when the day's fingerling returned from being bandaged by the sympathetic, and much more compassionate, seminary Sisters.

Still, as a student winced and tried not to cry his way through the straightening and splinting, the Sisters were nice to look at. Though after seminary we all knew that the only way to catch a glimpse of a woman was to endure some type of excruciating pain. Then and only then would a student be allowed close contact with the female of our species. In hindsight, that kind of conditioning was part of our training.

Women equaled pain. The sooner we all understood that, the quicker the pain stopped. Some of us—I'm not naming names—learned slower than others. And *some* of us . . . have never learned at all.

I give this citizen's arm a little more pressure before I get hold of an outstretched finger. And I think he figures it out, but by the time he does it's too late and—*SNAP!*—I spare him the "Father D," because I can tell that he's gotten the message.

It hardly matters. And he's squealing and writhing on the ground, holding his little finger, like I had seen so many of my classmates do. And now I know I have his undivided attention. I kick the broken bottle to the side and kneel down next to him. "I won't send you to the *Fifty*," I tell him, "but you need to clean yourself up and get off the street. You keep acting like this, sooner or later someone's going to remand you. Trust me, you don't want that."

It's the truth and even through the Judgment I think he understands that, because he nods and tries to stop squealing. "I'm"—he moans some more before he gets control of himself—"just. . . I need some J," he says. "I saw . . . saw a crazy angel, and I barely got off the street before. . . They're all . . . dead. And the PA's. . . He was . . . he was naked, father, and he cut 'em up like they were nothing. He's coming for our sins, isn't he?"

I don't know if that's the Judgment or if my fallen archangel had a busy night last night. One thing I do know is that the whites of this citizen's eyes aren't dark enough for him to be in the hallucination part of his trip yet. Regardless, neither of us needs a pair of nosy Protection agents to show up, and this close to a Mike there is bound to be a patrol close by.

I need to get him up and on his way or we'll both be headed to the *Fifty*. "We who are alive," I tell him, "who are left standing, even those who pierced him, will always be with the Lord."

Sure, it's a mashup. Not like he knows. I told you already, it's the tone and the messenger. That was drilled into us almost as painfully as our fingers.

I grab his good arm and help him to his feet. "I'm. . . I shouldn't have. . ." he says, trying to apologize.

I really don't have the time. "Calm yourself," I say to him. If what he says is true, Protection will be looking for my dead angel. Only a matter of time before a drone spots the hole in the roof. "He will not be back to deal with sin, my son, but to save those who have eagerly waited for his return."

And that calms him down a little, but the finger has still gotta hurt like—and he cries out and hunches over, clutching his elbow and trying not to move his shaking hand.

I look around nervously—he's going to draw attention. So I grab the outside of his good wrist at the right spot and then the pressure point on his elbow, sending a few hundred thousand impulses through his ganglia.

He relaxes as the pain in his mind is replaced by a slightly euphoric tingle. I know the feeling well. I shuffle him back behind the burned out vehicle he came at me from, and then a light, but *quick-jab* to the pressure point behind his ear and he goes limp.

I lower him to the ground and lay his head gently on the pavement as I look around to make sure no one is watching. "Sleep well," I say to him, "there are no angels coming for you today."

It took me a few months to master the technique, but once I did, even the priests eyed me differently when they passed. Lowly fourth year Candidate that I was, knocking someone out with no more effort than lifting up the Eucharist cup on Sunday was something that few Candidates mastered as quickly as I did.

Just about now, I bet you are seriously confused. I mean, all you have ever seen me do is cower and drink and tremble. I'll admit, it's a pretty useful technique—hiding in plain sight. Most people don't see what's right in front of their face. That's why the truth is so hard for them to grasp.

That's how they taught us, if you can call the seminary's brutality some type of instruction. But seminary isn't just about finding faith and learning to defend yourself. Sure, self-discipline is important and so is mastering one's mind and body in the moment. But keeping yourself hidden until the right moment is also important. Had I learned that before they caught us and burned. . . Hmm, it's too early for that.

* * *

Seminary Shandian—making one's mind and body like lightning—teaches that violence is a reaction to failure. And I have only used my training as I just did when I was fighting an angel—men are much more easily deceived. Deception in battle spills less blood, draws less unwanted attention, and more often than not, achieves the desired result much quicker. Because the big picture—the "long game" my father liked to call it—is most important.

So sacrificing your ego and even your life if you have to in pursuit of the ultimate goal requires not only the ability to survive the here and the now, but the absolute certainty that you can do what it takes to win in the end. In the end, one simply must triumph over the loss of eternity to evil.

My sweet Mother of Mercy, listen to me. I sound like a first-year practical theology professor. But I'm not just talking about angels and demons and saving souls here. You have to understand, what's at stake is the future of all the eternities—whether they become darkness or light. Barring saving each and every last one of them from the darkness, its inhabitants—souls, angels or flesh and bone human beings hardly matters—they won't even know the difference between good and evil, much less that light is for the living.

Focus! My Shandian mind reminds me that I can get off track and that when I do—

I feel them behind me. *Protection agents.* The one on the left scans my ID badge. That's the thing about letting your mind wander aimlessly—dangerous. Time to get back to my fine feathered friend. I jump up, but a spike of light shoots through my head and everything goes dark.

— XVI —

AS SOON AS the roof of our pig barn in Duvall ripped off, I got sucked straight up like a rocket. And then I was spinning and twirling, and there were trees and boards from the barn and pigs all around me. The pigs squealed and cried . . . to be saved I suppose. *For what?* I thought.

It was an odd thing to think in that moment, but we were just going to kill them anyway, what did they care if they died in the wind?

And hail pelted me in the face and I screamed with them. "Mom!" I screeched. But the noise inside that. . . I had no idea what it was, but the sound as I flew up was like a thousand guzzlers, revving their engines. The only thing missing was the smoke, replaced by an angry darkness I couldn't describe. And stinging ice pellets peppered my face, and then a board hit me in the head and a bright light shot through my eyes and the pain!

I was scared and I couldn't see. Even if it weren't for the dark, I had lost my glasses and everything looked black. Not that dark black-ness, but a shadowed haze of shades of gray. Then something stabbed me in the heart and it was—I couldn't even. . . I screamed out for her again, "Mother!"

The pain was unbelievable and I grabbed at my chest and I could feel the hot blood . . . and the huge tree limb sticking out of my chest.

I coughed and choked on my own blood and a thought went through my head: *You're not coming back from this one, Benito.*

How wrong I was.

When I woke up from that blackness, the first thing I did was grab for my chest. *No hole*, I thought. I tried to look around. *Dark . . . again.*

There was nothing around me, just emptiness and silence. If I was scared hurtling up in that. . . *What was that?* I asked myself. *Twister? . . . Here?* But those only happened in the Plains Quarter. That much I knew for sure. Still, there I was, shivering and shaking—dead again. I knew that much.

A foul stench made my nostrils flare. It smelled like rotting pig guts, and it burned at my nose hairs like it was hot, but more like the alcohol I'd snuck a sniff of in my father's den. The smell was familiar like that, too.

And then the growl and the hot breath burned into the back of my neck. I could feel my skin burn and boil and bubble up, and I grabbed at it with my hand. I was too scared to turn around—move at all. But there was something . . . familiar through the pain.

"Benito," the voice was raspy and raw. It spoke to me like it . . . knew me. "Always getting burned. How do you. . .? They sent you to the barn, you idiot! In a fucking tornado! You are the stupidest—how I ever picked you." And then she—the voice was a woman—growled.

I jerked around. More scared that she was behind me than what she might look like. But what I saw. . .

The figure was . . . beautiful. Wheat field blonde hair and baby blue eyes like the sky, and I couldn't help it—I smiled at her, but then I winced as I caught a whiff of her again. "Who. . .?" It was about all I could get out. I rubbed my chest to make sure I was dreaming. *No blood or tree limb.*

"Never get used to that shit, do you?" she said. "Bitch is heavy on theatrics, I'll give her that." And she looked up. Toward what I had no idea, because outside of her glow there was . . . nothing. "You think she just giggles down at us when she's fucking with everyone?"

I had no idea what to say. I just stared, and then I glanced at her—

"Naughty little boy," she said, following my eyes to her breasts.

I hadn't noticed at first—too busy looking into her eyes—but she was naked. I'd never seen a naked . . . anyone but myself before. My face heated up and I felt the blood rushing to my cheeks and then to my. . . I quickly looked back up to her face—embarrassed and guilty. And I tried to reach down and adjust my pants.

It was strange, but the rotting smell was replaced by a sweet and pungent odor. *Blackberries*, I thought. *Perfume?* My mother wore it to church, but nothing that smelled that good.

And the woman—she was certainly not a girl—smiled a wide grin at me that was . . . huge. And her teeth were milky white gems, so perfectly aligned that they looked fake.

I stared at them as she spoke, "Ah, there you are, Benito," she said, "hiding behind your mommy's repressed *pussy*. You're not fooling anyone with your lies. You left me to die!" she yelled. And then that angel—because she had to be another one of them—turned mean. "And you left me to him and he"—her face morphed and her eyes turned glowing red, and then boils formed on her cheeks and hideous green puss began leaking out of them—"he turned me into this!"

I tried to turn away, but a rough hand with long, sharp claws grabbed my face and she leaned her oozing cheeks in so close to mine that I thought she was going to bite me. And then the stench returned and I almost vomited. "Please," I didn't know what else to say.

She spit as she spoke at me, "Please, please, please," she mocked. "You miserable pathetic excuse for a fucking man! I guess I was wrong —no need to cut yours off, is there? Dickless little shit. At least he can fuck. You. . . Never anything but a fumbling boy. Why did I even. . .? You're not saving anyone, priest. You're a cruel joke. Did she tell you that? Or is she still filling your head full of the lies in that *Bible* of hers?"

Her claw-hand cut into my face and her teeth turned to fangs and I could see the saliva dripping from them and the smell. Then I did vomit . . . right into her mouth.

But rather than let me go or throw me to the ground or eat me or whatever she was going to do with me, she put her mouth on mine and I felt something go in and down my throat.

Her tongue—only thing I could call it—was rough and scraped like a cat licking your hand, and when she pulled it out, she said, "Mmm, delicious. Putrid piss of fear." She turned and spit. Then she looked back at me and her monster mouth smiled and green bile from her cheek dripped into it. "You were always good for that, weren't you?"

I coughed and tried to spit, but it just dripped down my face.

The animal—a monster would be more accurate—eyed me and cocked its head to the side. And its glowing red eyes glowed brighter, and then they got hot. I could feel the fire sizzling and burning into my face and I screamed out.

"You're a vagina, Benito," she yelled at me over my cries. "Dripping and trembling, waiting to be penetrated pussy! Get out of my sight!"

Then she spun my face sideways and I felt my neck break in a loud

SNAP!

Then she was gone . . . or I was—dead.

— XVII —

I WASN'T KEEPING count at the time, but that was the third time I died. It wouldn't be the last . . . or the most terrifying. Before the fourth time I would wish I was actually dead . . . several times over.

When I woke up from the windstorm, I was in my bed. No hole in my chest, no lost glasses, and no snapped neck. I could hear the wind howling outside. Nowhere near as loud and angry as when I went to the barn, but God was clearly not done letting the world know—as far as I knew then—*he* was mad at it.

I could barely move though. It felt like all of the energy had left my body and I just laid there and stared up at the ceiling. I wondered what had actually happened, because that time I was certain I had died, but I would not have said that I went to Heaven. Not my mother's version of it anyway.

Could I have. . .? Why would I end up there? But that woman— that creature was . . . evil. That could only mean one—

"How are you feeling?" my mother's voice asked.

I looked over and she stood in the doorway to my room with her arms crossed. I could see my father sitting at the kitchen table across the living room behind her, sipping a glass of his whiskey like I wasn't just sucked up in a tornado. "I don't. . ." I said, "I feel tired."

"You *should* be, young man!" she said. "You gave us a big scare out there, running out to the barn like that. You could've been killed. What were you thinking, Benito?"

What was I thinking? I remember frowning at her. I had never done that before, but she was acting like it was my fault.

And just then Max nuzzled my arm and I felt him lick me, and it felt just like that woman's tongue had, and I jerked my hand back.

"What's wrong?" my mother asked. "He hasn't left your side since your father dragged you back from the barn. You both almost got swept up."

I had no idea what she was talking about. I got sucked up in a tornado and I was as certain as a saint that the Colonel had never been closer to death than sending me to that barn.

I looked past my mother. "He," I said to her, but loud enough that I knew he could hear me, "he sent me out there and those pigs. . . I got sucked out of the barn and then—"

"Benito," she said, more reprimanding than I had ever heard her. "*He* is your father and he would never do anything to purposefully harm—"

"I died again, mother," I said, "didn't I? Thirty-three minutes? How can you. . .? The playground, the river, and in that barn, I died! . . . And then I went . . . somewhere . . . somewhere bad. And not like you said, either!"

"Leave him be," I heard the Colonel's voice behind her. "He'll find his faith soon enough. She's only got one card left to play and there's nothing more I can teach him."

I sat up and Max whimpered next to me. But he growled when my mother took a step into my room.

"Hush, Max," she said to him in her "voice." It was usually all it took, but Max growled even more.

"Jesus, Monica," the Colonel said from the table. He wasn't even looking toward the room—he just stared straight ahead and took another sip of his liquor. "Time's up. Even the dog knows he's coming. Let the boy rest. It's probably the last warm bed he'll feel for a while. We've done all we can."

"What?" I asked, probably more to her than him, because he was in one of his matter-of-fact statement moods. "Done all you can for what? For me? I don't even know what's happening!"

And Max growled even more. I could feel him tensing up and it felt like he might jump off the bed at my mother.

"Easy, boy," I said to him.

"Leave them alone," the Colonel said to my mother. "He needs some time to say goodbye to the dog."

Max relaxed a little as my mother backed out of the room. "He's not even going to let him keep the dog?" she asked my father, because she certainly wasn't asking me. "Who will. . .?"

"He has to face the flames on his own," the Colonel said. Then he put his glass down. "Trial by fire, he always says. No other way to be sure."

I didn't recognize either of them. Both of them talked like I was leaving. "I'm not going anywhere," I said to them. "Who's not letting me keep Max?"

My father stood up and walked across the kitchen and then through the living room. I could feel the light getting brighter as he got closer. And my mother stepped to the side of the door—just outside my room—before he got there. Like she could feel the bright coming.

When the Colonel stood in the doorway, he looked at me like he never had before. It was almost like he felt . . . sorry for me? "It's a helluva thing, Benito," he said. Then he smiled and chuckled a little at his own words. "Remember what I told you—the end is all that matters."

"It's not funny," I said. No idea where the words came from. I would have never spoken to him that way. "You sent me into that barn . . . to die."

Now Max was really wired up. He and my father stared at each other for a good minute—Max tense and angry and the Colonel simply stone.

"You'd do well to let me end your companion's suffering," my father said. "You are on a precious path and have yet to understand its hardships, however I have bestowed benevolent favor . . . thrice."

I ignored the way he was talking. "Kill him?" I said. "No one's *killing* him!"

"Sometimes death is the easiest road to redemption," said the Colonel, "but deadly decision is yours alone. Hell, you own more decisions than you know now, Benito. From here, Heaven requires you remember that. Right or left—free will." He stopped staring at Max and then he looked to his side at my mother down the hall. "It is a cruel comedy, I realize."

My mother said something back to him, but I couldn't hear what it was.

"Precious *Bible* will not save him," the Colonel said to her. "He must author script . . . to save us all." He looked back at me. "Irksome irony, though it may be. So, choose choice? Backyard to bury the bag of bones or burned by the benevolent?"

"I *said* nobody's killing him!"

And Max growled at the Colonel again.

"Calm," said the Colonel, "both of you." He stared at Max and then looked back at me with what looked like another one of his hidden lessons brewing. "Very well, if that is your choice. But I give godly warning, there are no hounds in the halls of Heaven. And he only allows the meanest ones passage to Hell."

I just stared back—no idea what to say or do.

Then my father did something that scared me worse than anything he had ever said. He reached into his back pocket and pulled out a little leather-covered metal flask. He started to walk into the room, but Max growled and gave him a look that made him pause briefly—unsure whether to come across my room, maybe? I'd never seen that before either.

He looked at me and his head bobbed just a little and then he cocked it to the side. He tossed the little tin flask at me and it landed on the bed next to Max's paw. I reached over, picked it up, and read the letters punched into the fresh leather. *B.O.B.* I thought. *My initials?* I was wrong about that, too.

When I looked up, the man I would always remember as the Colonel was gone. It was the last time I would ever see him . . . or my mother.

Then I felt dizzy and I laid back and fell into a deep sleep. Only this time there were no dreams, no scary people, and no death—only darkness.

— XVIII —

"BENITO OCTAVIO BENEDETTI," the voice was not one I recognized, and I sat straight up in my bed, jerked out of the black nothingness of my sleep. The voice sounded like it was right at the bottom of the stairs up to our house.

I rubbed my eyes. Max barked wildly at the door to my room.

"Easy, boy," I said, sure that I had dreamt the entire thing. My father would soon be "tuning up" whoever was yelling up our steps. He was not one to suffer shouting.

I eased myself out of bed—still exhausted from basically dying in a windstorm. Another horrible dream I hoped to forget sooner rather than later. Yes, that is a Colonel-ism, too.

I walked slowly toward the door and peered around the corner, half-expecting to see my mother and father smiling and giggling at each other in some crazy joke they were playing on me. "Mom?" I asked.

There was no answer from inside the house.

"You are hereby remanded to the protection of the State," the voice shouted up the outside stairs again.

I walked to the front door, and then I peered down, out between the cracks in the boards my father and I had nailed over the windows on that door.

The farm was a mess. Broken tree limbs and boards littered the property. And I could see half of a pig impaled on a snapped off tree.

There was . . . a tornado?

"State your compliance to this order," the voice was getting more insistent, but I couldn't quite see the person shouting. Only black jackets and boots shuffling around at the bottom of the steps. State agents and a—my father would not be happy about either of them.

I opened the door a little, not really sure what to do. "Father?" I shouted down at the voice.

"We're the only ones down here," the voice yelled back up.

"Where are my parents?"

"We know you've been living here alone, Benito," the voice said. "You can't do that anymore. It is time to go, my son."

"Where's my mother?"

There was a pause, just like in the barn, and everything was silent. "They're long gone, Benito," the voice said. "I thought you were, too. It's Father Dominic from Saint James—your church. You've got to—"

"State your compliance," the first voice shouted over him. Then I heard the three of them argue briefly.

Max nudged up behind me and started barking. Then dogs growled from down the steps. They were vicious sounding animals, and they started snarling and barking and that drove Max crazy.

"Shh," I said to him, "heel."

But Max burst by me—through the cracked open door—and I heard his toenails clicking as he raced down the steps. And then there was wild barking and the sounds of—I had no idea how many—too many dogs for Max to deal with, I was sure.

And then Max cried out and yelped and whined and then howled in pain.

I flung open the door and raced down the stairs at all of them.

There were three men with guns—all in black and helmets and goggles—and two pit bulls were busy biting and shaking their heads on top of Max. I don't know what came over me, but I jumped on top of the whole pile and started punching those dogs and then one of them bit me in the arm and I yelled out. And my arm was flapping and jerking as the dog shook me. And blood sprayed onto my face and Max cried out again—the other dog still latched onto him, shaking and pulling at Max's ear. "Stop!" I screamed. "You're killing him!"

I hadn't noticed him—too focused on the three State agents and their dogs—but the fourth man, a stout little brick of a bald man in the black clothes of a priest, yelled, "That's enough!"

The priest from church! I thought he was yelling at the agents, but then the little brick went to his knees, grabbed the head of the dog that was jerking my arm, and then that dog went limp—I felt the anger leave the beast's body and his jaws go slack around my arm. I pulled my arm back and rolled away, clutching at my ripped flesh. Blood ran freely between my fingers.

Then the other dog let go of Max and lunged at the man, but before the second beast could get his jaws around him, the little brick man caught the dog's face in mid-air and I heard a loud *CRACK!* By the time he slammed that animal to the ground. The dog was limp.

"Dominic of—" the first dark clad agent's words were cut short by a blow to his neck. He flew sideways into the agent standing next to him. Then the little brick priest rushed at the third agent, grabbed that man's rifle with both hands, and then spun it so fast I almost couldn't see it.

And that agent flipped almost full circle and slammed to the ground on his side with a huge thud and a gasp for air! And the priest was on him and jamming his thumb behind the agent's goggle strap. And quicker than that, the priest rolled sideways at the second agent that had been knocked down by the first, and he swung his arm sideways as he came out of his roll and chopped at the man's neck.

I thought I saw blood spit out of the agent's mouth—he didn't move after that. None of them did.

And then the priest was up and standing in the middle of it all—squatted a little at the knees and staring down at nothing in front of him—calm and still just like the middle of that storm in the barn.

Then the searing pain hit my arm, but I looked over to Max and he was lying on his side in the mud, his coat covered in blood, and chunks of his beautiful chocolate fur next to him. He whined softly. One of his ears was torn off and he was pushing his feet sideways at the dirt . . . through his guts.

I crawled over to him, holding my arm and wincing through the pain. The priest barely moved, but I could feel his eyes following me. When I got next to Max, I knew, and I started to cry—Colonel-ism toughness or not. "It's okay," there wasn't much I could say. "You're gonna be. . . Look what they did to you, boy." I rubbed his coat a little and he whimpered hard and his muscles flexed and he cried out. "God, please don't take him," I whimpered along with my dog.

"God cannot save him," the priest said, breaking his stillness. "Only you can end his suffering."

"Why did they. . .?" I asked. I looked up at the priest. He was more relaxed now and stood with his hands gently clasped, staring down at me and Max. "Where are my parents? . . . My mother?"

The priest looked around our farm and then up the stairs at our house. "Their time in this eternity has long ended," he spoke at our house. Then he looked back down at me, and then he looked at Max. "It is up to you to end his."

I looked at Max. He was going to die. I had seen hundreds of ducks plucked from the sky by our shotguns, but I had never considered their deaths—they were animals. I moved my good arm toward him, but Max whimpered before it got there.

"To prolong his suffering for your own weak—"

"He's *not* dying!" I yelled, fully knowing that it was a lie. I looked up at the priest, my eyes begging him to find a way.

His own face relaxed and he closed his eyes a little, but quickly opened them back up. "My son," he said to me, "all of us are already dead. If you wish . . . I will end his suffering for you. However, it will be the last time I tend such a service. You would be wise to do it yourself—push through your fear here and now . . . in this moment. For there is no other." Then he unclasped his hands and stepped toward me.

I stared up, knowing that I couldn't do what he was asking. I would not. "No. . ."

"Very well," the priest said, "I had hoped that she would have strengthened you according to the Word. Yet, it is written that even youths grow tired and weary, and young men stumble and fall. Come now, the Lord shall renew your strength. I will teach you to soar on wings like an eagle, run and not grow weary, walk and not be faint." He reached down. "In time, Benito, you will control such emotions. And eventually, you will only have need of them to deceive the enemies of God."

Then, with no more than a lightning quick twist to the back of Max's neck, my only friend . . . was gone.

— XIX —

I HELD MAX'S limp body and stared up the steps at our house—my home. More to avoid looking at Max's broken neck, but still bewildered at the speed that my entire world had fallen to pieces. "Where are my parents?" I asked again, not satisfied with the cryptic answer the priest had already given me. "Are they . . . dead?"

"They will rest from their labor," the priest said, "and their deeds will follow them into the next eternity. They have fulfilled their duties, as I shall now fulfill mine."

Resting. . . My mother used to describe it that way to me. Death was simply a break from the hard work of living. But the Colonel had imparted one underlying theme during my brief time with him, and that was that learning and experiencing are two *entirely* different things.

I wasn't ready for them to be gone any more than I was ready for Max to be . . . gone, either. "What do I . . . what do I do now?" I asked the priest.

"You live," he said, "as life intended you to, serving God's Word. Or . . . you survive alone in the world until the end of your time. The choice has to be yours."

Where would I go? There was nothing left and the only thing I knew of this priest was seeing him talk to my mother and the rest of the church ladies each Sunday. Because he was the father at our church and he was the same man who had let me die on the playground, and he was also the man who had just killed three State agents in front of my house. "What does that mean?" I asked him.

"Choices, Benito," he said, "are simple things really. People make them complicated by trying not to have to make them. But make no mistake, free will is about making choices. Many of them will be between two seemingly equally . . . 'distasteful' options. But whichever one you choose will have its own consequences—its own path to Purgatory."

As I listened to him, I began hearing something else. A little voice inside me that began to wake me up to the fact that this priest had just killed three State agents on our front steps, and someone would be along shortly to start sorting that out. From what the Colonel had taught me, I knew that anyone they found hovering at the scene would be black-bagged and taken away, never to be heard from again. Yet the priest seemed unconcerned with that—he had to know it better than I did. I mean, he was the one who killed them!

As if he could read my thoughts, the priest put his hand on my shoulder and squeezed into it. His hand was like a vise tightening— nothing but hard pressure. "Time to go," he said. "Someone will be along for all of this shortly. You can stay and tell them whatever tale you think will save you. But if your parents taught you anything, you will know that even the truth will not help. Most likely, your story will be written the way that the State Agent In Charge wants it . . . *or* . . . you can come with me and write your own story—your own ending."

My dog was dead, my parents were gone, my world was, too. I reached up and held onto the priest's hand, and as I did, I felt that something was . . . missing—the littlest finger on his left hand. I turned and looked up at him. "What's your . . . name?" I asked. In all of our trips to church, I had only ever heard my mother call him Father.

"Dominic," he said, "Father Dominic. That is what you will call me." Then he chuckled a little. "Though by your third year you will most likely call me Father 'D.' All the other Candidates do."

I stood up and looked at the dead agents and the dogs on the ground. I didn't want to look at Max. "They'll come after you, won't they? Come after . . . me?"

He chuckled a little. "A priest?" Dominic said. "They wouldn't dare. Besides, there is no one left who can tell them I was ever here. Ipso facto, I was not."

"Ipso-what?"

"Don't worry," he said, "you will begin language next week."

"What about all the. . .?"

The priest's eyes followed my stare. "The bodies?" he said. "That is the wonderful thing about fire, Benito. It has a cleansing effect, bordering on magic."

I finally looked down again at Max's ripped and torn body.

But before I could get the question out, Dominic answered it, "And there is no time for grave digging."

Just then, one of the pit bulls raised its head and whimpered a little. My face went tight on its own and I reached down and picked up one of the many broken-off branches from the storm. I walked toward that dog with a hatred welling up inside me that I had never felt before. I wanted it to feel the same pain I did—that Max had.

But before I could plunge that stick into the dog's chest—all I wanted to do—Dominic grabbed and held my shoulder back. "Lesson one," he said, "it is best to leave some room for God's wrath."

I shook his hand off—he wasn't holding me as tightly as before—and I dropped back down to my knees and plunged the broken end of that stick into the beasts leg and it yelped. And I pulled it out and stabbed it into its side. Then again . . . and again and again and again! . . . Until my good arm hurt like my bad one and that dog's body didn't jerk when I stabbed it.

Once I stopped, Dominic pulled me to my feet. "Or not, I suppose," he said. "Is that your decision?" he asked.

There was really nowhere else left for me to go. "Yes."

As we walked to Father Dominic's Clergy guzzler—it was pretty hard to mistake those big black cars—he chanted and held his Rosary beads. "In flaming fire, take vengeance on those who do not know God," he spoke softly, "and on those who do not obey the truth of the Word."

After I climbed into the back seat of the guzzler with him, I looked back at our house. It lit up in flames and then the bodies at the foot of its steps caught fire on their own and then Max burned too, and I had to look away.

I hadn't noticed the driver. I could only see the black veil on the back of her head. The girl was barely able to see over the steering wheel, much less anywhere near the statute age to be driving. I would learn later that the clergy had its own "statutes."

"Take us home, Sister," Dominic said to her. "Our young Benito's had a long life."

And flames shot high into the air behind us as the Sister drove the big black guzzler away.

TRIBULATION

— XX —

AT THE TURN of the tenth eternity—two thousand years after God sent her first child to the Garden in an attempt to arrest its descent into madness—the dark angel Lucifer gathered faithful and fierce angels and demons to a secret meeting. These eleven mid-level angels —Colonels in the armies of Heaven or Hell—were conspirators that he hoped would help him succeed where alone . . . he had failed.

His purpose was none other than to dethrone the current Protector, the god Life, and replace her with a more . . . deserving ruler. Then he —the fallen Day Star, Lucifer—would rightfully rule over Hell *and* Heaven . . . for all the eternities to come.

High atop the Great Mountain of the Eternities, deep inside the Hallowed Hall of the Word, the Arena of Reckoning—the destination of every soul in every eternity since the first—was bathed in blackness and still. An exhausted and silent temptress after a night of wicked justice, judging souls and condemning them to fates of redemption or condemnation, where afterward they would be sent to the Dungeons of the Damned beneath the arena.

The great devil—the Day Star, that liar of old, Lucifer—stood at the edge of the lake of fire, deep in the pit beneath the dungeons. He pondered the night's judgments. Fresh blood dripped from his crimson wings and his long tail. The blood sizzled and caught fire as it landed at the edge of the fiery lake. Lucifer's long pointed tail caressed over his metal flight feathers, slowly wiping and washing them free of blood, like an eagle preening with its beak.

Eleven archangels—six faithful followers of God in Heaven and five hateful and heinous hounds from Lucifer's own Hell—stood around him. They all eyed each other, distrustful and disdainful of the other's Word, yet each even more disgruntled at the passing of their current eternity.

"Is this how it is to be?" Lucifer asked them all. "We are to carry out orders and ferry Man-monkey souls to the whims of a tyrant? Is any of you content with this feeble fate?"

Lucifer spoke not in questions so much as he did in statements of fact as he believed them to be. For each and every angel in attendance had been selected over centuries. Some as his most faithful followers in Hell and some as seditious spies for him in Heaven.

None of them were Generals in Hell or Saints in Heaven, but therein laid Lucifer's plan. For every middle manager in Heaven or Hell, or the Garden for that matter, was certain that they could perform the duties of their superiors . . . far better. These Colonels were no different.

Lucifer turned and addressed each of them individually, giving them the respect and the dignity that eternities of servitude had not. "Lilith," he spoke, "first love of Adam, was your long blonde shining hair, full of curls not enough? Look at your beauty—wings of pure gold! Are you content at replacement by Eve in the garden? And to what purpose? For your husband to be betrayed by his wife at the behest of a tempestuous snake? A greater travesty has never been committed by me, I assure you."

Lilith adjusted her armored feathers. Lucifer's words were a lie, but she would not shed the light of truth on them, lest her own failure be bared naked for all angels to see. She looked away from him, betraying her shame and guilt due to her lapse in judgment during the very first eternity.

The other ten were silent. They each had enough experience with their leaders to know when to speak and when they were being spoken to.

Lucifer turned to the next in the circle, "Lucifia," he said, "gorgeous granddaughter. You preside over all the underworld's wealth and terrible treasures in Hell, yet your father cracks no coin to angel's benefit? Your wings are waxed with filth and your hair houses soot. Ashen-faced waif you have become. While your faithful father wears dark silver wings and coins fall from his feathers! A more selfish son I have yet to sire."

Lucifia gritted her teeth, squinted, and held back her tongue. One day her father would pay.

"Aax," Lucifer said, barely pausing as he stoked and then left Lucifia to her fiery rage, "most hideous hound in my realm—disgusting and dastardly animal, worthy of commanding legions. You languish as lowly colonel beneath preening and primping general—a house of mirrors that you must polish. Is that justice?"

It was clear to each of them—none having escaped the assignment of a disgusting duty from a superior, without having first been manipulated through deceptive accolades and false niceties—that Lucifer would hear himself address each one before he would get to the rotten core of his own desirous apple.

Lucifer quickly pointed to the next angel in the circle. "And you," he said, "Zarzi the . . . the what? No Man-monkey she sent to the Garden to sing her praises lifts pen nor scroll to speak of your deeds.

You warrant not one single line of prose in her benevolent book? And yet absent angel, there would be no lilac nor lemon scent for her to suck to her greedy nostrils. No spring wafts of freshly cut grass nor rainbow of colors on trees in fall. Hah, I doubt she knows your name."

Zarzi turned down her smile to shame and embarrassment, and then she folded her shining green wings behind her back and hung her head. Her two near orange braids dangled next to her face, like some raggedy doll in a Man-monkey's one-coin commissary.

"Do you believe she leaves jury and Judgment night with words on her lips, 'I ought grant Zarzi medal?' . . . Hardly!"

Lucifer glanced slyly out of the corner of his eye at the next in line to see if his seeds were bearing fruit. But discontent was his forte—creating a milieu of misery and fanning a flame of hatred to be used to his purposes. His speech was going perfectly to plan.

Rsoni spread his golden wings slightly and then folded them tightly behind his back. It was easy for the big angel to hold tongue, standing in the circle of betrayers, listening to the long-licking liar his Lord had cast down to the pit. For Rsoni was a firm and long-spoken Golden Guardian—one of three golden angels in attendance that night—with blonde locks to his chest and a complexion only a few shades darker than the pure white God, Life herself.

Rsoni performed his duty as guardian quietly, efficiently, and with little regard for his own personal gain. From a line of angels synonymous with the very definition of loyalty, when the Protector of his eternity, Life, had come to him and suggested he be receptive to Lucifer's temptations, at first he was hesitant—even pretending to serve the dark one was unthinkable to him. But Life had her ways and he was eventually "persuaded" to do her bidding by pretending to do the bidding of God's once all-beautiful angel, Lucifer.

"Rsoni!" Lucifer's voice boomed.

It caught Rsoni by surprise and he jerked slightly and then bobbed his head—bird-like tics were a fact of every angel's life.

Lucifer's voice was softer as he continued, "Do not believe I look lightly on sacrifice *you* must make on behalf of this angry gathering," he said. "Your line is a proud and decorated divinity, and the act of attending sullies same. I once stood next to your father in the bosom of light our creator shined for all to warm themselves. Yet, duplicitous deity, *God*, has no doubt informed you of misplaced trust."

Rsoni's eyes widened slightly and then he got control of them. His talons eased out slowly—more angel impulse. Policing blasphemy was one of a guardian's primary duties . . . just before securing the prisoners in the dungeons beneath the arena.

"Ahh," Lucifer said to him, "your eyes betray your right heart's desire." He moved closer to Rsoni and then stood in front of him. "You believe information's envoy is enemy? That I am. . .?"

The circle of soon to be sinners ruffled steel feathers and the more restless of them let out a couple of muffled caws. Shoulders shrugged and wings folded tightly behind the angels' backs.

"Belay yourselves, brothers and sisters," said Lucifer. "Rsoni does not realize, but he is brother in more than breath of treason. He has been betrayed by his own loyalty—his unwavering faith in a god that does nothing to warrant it."

Rsoni would give his life if that was what was required, as it was clear Lucifer now knew he would spy for him in falsity only. His talons protruded all the way out now and he had nudged his ballistic armored feathers so that they would cover his entire body quickly when the attack came. He steeled himself.

Lucifer stared at Rsoni's armored feathers and then glanced down to his talons. "Life has a way of persuading the penitent that she is worth one's *own* soul, does she not," he said. He tilted his head back and cawed wildly. When he lowered it back his eyes shined ice-blue. "I stood once . . . where you perch now, *certain* of my creator's affection, and convinced that I should execute the orders"—he glanced down at Rsoni's talons—"that your talons now threaten. Blindly serve and sacrifice life for Life. However"—he paused and closed his eyes, for longer than a warrior would, and then he slowly tilted his head back up, opened his eyes, and smiled—"precious opportunity passes, brother . . . and by not seizing it, you drip a drop of life on the seed of doubt now growing in your left heart."

Rsoni's eyes relaxed and his armor pushed out a little more. Was it deception or was there truth? Life had warned him of Lucifer's lies. But he *had* hesitated to act and in doing so, squandered any tactical advantage he might enjoy again. For the great devil, Lucifer, was no ordinary archangel. Rsoni would fight valiantly, but he knew in his right heart that he could not hope to win. Now, his life was forfeit as sure as there were ten other conspirators deep in the pit with him.

Lucifer backed away from Rsoni. The guardian would not attack him. "I bear no ill will to you, brother," he said, turning his back on the angel. And then he stood and paused a moment, savoring what was to come. "But you"—he pointed across the circle to a diminutive angel—the third golden guardian in attendance—"*you*, Utipa . . .

your treachery will *not* pass."

Utipa bared tooth and talon and shoved out her golden armored plumage and she screeched loudly at Lucifer. Then she flapped and flew wildly at him.

Lucifer caught the angel in mid-air. He grabbed one of her wings, and then he spun her and slammed her to the ground. His hand shot to her throat and he pinned her against the rocky floor of the dark and dank pit.

Utipa tried to squawk, but no sound left her mouth and she flapped her wings at Lucifer's face and cut him and he bled, but he did not let go of her. She stabbed the talons on her hands into Lucifer's ribs and he gasped, but still did not let go. Utipa kicked at him with her feet and flailed and fought for everything she had and all that was at stake. The liar could not be allowed to. . . She felt the energy leaving her wings and the resolve of her steel feathers slipping.

"Did you not think I would discover deceit?" Lucifer yelled down at her, still gripping hard on Utipa's throat. "That I am weak and wayward soul in the Garden that needs flight to Purgatory? I require angel's assistance? She bid you to save devil from evil, but Eden's heir —*she* is evil devil and it is *we* who must be spared! *God*, not Devil, threatens destruction of everyone!"

The beautiful blue color left Utipa's eyes and was replaced by a milky grey transparency, resembling her lost God, Life. And her body went limp and her wings slumped to the floor of the arena, and then she lay dead. Lucifer backed away. And then Utipa's limp body and wings burst into flames and burned to ash.

Utipa would be reborn, but that was a painful beginning that no angel relished. It was also part of Lucifer's plan.

"As deceitful deed," Lucifer spoke at the pile of soot on the ground, "has destroyed you."

— XXI —

THE DRIVE TO the seminary—Father Dominic informed me that's where we were going—started off with State emergency vehicles racing past us, blaring sirens, rushing to the scene of fire and death at our farm, I suppose.

Father Dominic seemed remarkably calm as they drove by. It reminded me of my father's calm and collected demeanor after he pulled me out of the icy river. But by the time the drive ended, I was asleep in the leather-covered backseat of the big clergy guzzler, too exhausted to mourn the loss of my parents . . . of Max.

That would only last until I woke up.

When we pulled through the big timbered gates of the Saint Samuels Seminary Academy in downtown Seattle. . . I mean, I had never seen one, but except for the huge iron crosses on each side of the big timbered gate, I imagined that it was what a State prison might look like. I was scared.

Maybe our driver could sense that, or she just wanted to break the silence, but as soon as we passed under the archway over the gates, she said, "It looks bigger than it really is."

But Father Dominic didn't give her a chance to say anything else. "That's enough, Sister," he said. "Benito has been through a lot. I'm sure he doesn't need any more to think about tonight."

"Sorry, Father," was the last thing she said. "It . . . it won't happen —"

"Right next to the hall, Sister," the priest interrupted her.

As our driver parked, I looked back to the catwalks around the walls of the seminary. There were men in black jackets and pants on the tops of the walls surrounding the grounds, and they looked like priests, only they weren't stalky and short like Dominic. These men were behemoths and they all carried guns. The only time I had seen men bigger was when my mother and I went to the State Med-mart.

And as soon as that thought entered my mind, I think I finally realized she was dead and I was alone. Because I started crying and I just slumped up against the inside of the car window and shook. But were my parents dead?

Dominic reached over and patted the back of my head. "Fear not, Benito, seminary will wipe away every tear from your eyes, and death shall be no more fearful, neither shall you mourn, nor cry, nor feel pain any longer, for the former things have passed away." And then his hand left my head and with it the last kind gesture I would ever know from the priest who had "rescued" me.

I looked up and out the gates as they closed behind us. I had no inkling at the time that it would be four years before I would pass through them again.

Dominic looked with me, knowing more than I did of what was to come. "Both great and small shall die in that land," he said. "And they shall not be buried, and no one shall lament for them. But inside seminary, ours is the kingdom of Heaven and we are the glory of mankind, and forever and forever from this eternity unto the next we shall remain."

And with that Father Dominic opened the door on his side of the car, stepped out, and disappeared through a large wooden door on the brick building that I would come to know as the Hall of Heaven. Though I would never see the inside of it, as no student or Candidate would until they left Saint Samuels Seminary Academy. And due to circumstances I can't share with you right now, I never left Saint Samuels so much as I was . . . released.

One day of grief, that's all I was given, locked in my cell to mourn the loss of my parents and Max. After that, my training started.

I had no idea what to expect inside the gates of Saint Samuels, but I was informed of what awaited me outside should I decide to leave.

I would learn that the citizens of the Northwest Quarter, and the entire rest of the country for that matter, had decided that authoritarian rule and State brutality was too distasteful to palette any longer. Many of them had decided to take up what little arms they had left to protect themselves from searches to their homes in the middle of the night and State seizures of their property to ensure the peace and prosperity for all.

That didn't end well for any of them, but it did end. I heard about that, too.

My parents' farm, I would be told later, was seized by the State shortly after the fire. And then I was listed as a ward of the Clergy.

All this information I received secondhand by way of the young Sister who had chauffeured Father Dominic and me from Duvall to downtown Seattle. For some reason, she had taken a liking to me and snuck me information while I was locked in my cell at night. At first, it was a good thing—I don't think I could have made it through Purgatory month without her. Later. . . Well, I'll let you decide about her.

— XXII —

WHEN I WAKE up, probably from being tasered or billy-clubbed by the two Protection agents outside the Mike's entrance, everything is fuzzy and I seem to be . . . tied to a chair. Whoever hit me in the back of the head. . . I squint and when I do I can feel that I don't have my glasses. My shirt's off, too, probably so they can attach the electrodes. I close my eyes and feel the air. Then I take in a deep breath and prepare myself.

The eyes are not the only way to see—day one hundred at Saint Samuels. It sounded like an "ism" when Father Dominic told us that from high atop what we all came to know as the Pulpit of Pain.

At seminary, none of it made sense while I was experiencing it. Out here in the brutal, bloody truth of the new world, things are clearer. The brutality of seminary had prepared me . . . and then it had saved me. Yet I still could not reconcile Father Dominic's version of God with who he was supposed to be in my mother's *Bible*.

I exhale slowly. The two agents that knocked me out are on the other side of the room, thinking they are hidden in the darkness. I can smell them and hear them breathing—feel their contempt for me. And there's someone else. He'll be the one in charge. Probably a PAIC —Protection Agent in Charge.

They used to call themselves *State* Agents in Charge until the State lost control of its guard dogs and Protection split from the only oversight it ever had. Oh, they still needed State for the credits—the funding for all their drones and other toys—just like my church needs the Clergy for things like repaired roofs. But just like the Clergy, the State still needs disciples to go and collect it first. Protection Agents and Priests—we're the "muscle."

PAIC. . . He'll be more difficult, I think. I take in another slow breath and I feel for the room's chi—the ever-present energy of all living things. Theirs rages red and it's how I will "see" them.

The others don't do much without the PAIC. Much interrogation anyway. They haven't stuck me with the Judgment yet or I would be worse off. Not that I haven't been through it, but fighting while your body and mind are working through a dose of J is like doing combat with the Devil—it's scarier and it takes more . . . concentration.

The PAIC will be the only one who speaks. "They burned you up pretty good, there. . . You still call yourselves priests?" he says. He's not looking for answers. At least not to that question, but any time a PAIC can, he'll do anything possible to try and figure out how to get control of his local Clergy representatives.

Every once in a while one of our brothers will tell a tale at our archdiocese gathering. About getting billy-clubbed in the back of the head and being black-bagged and tortured for information about the inner workings of the Clergy. We were all trained for that. The alternative was to meet God earlier than you had planned.

"Reminds me of the Rook," the PAIC says. He's a big man—the voice says more than most people learn to hear—and he's absolutely certain of himself.

That's not a stretch of my imagination and I don't have to hear his heartbeat or see his rage red chi to know that his training at Protection's Rookery Academy is as thoroughly "faith-instilling" as mine. A freshly-cracked Rookie rages red-hot when they are done torturing them, and now he is a veteran disciple of discipline—we are not so different. Yet we serve different gods.

"Can't even get to the Martial Law training. . ." he says. "What do you god-givers call it? . . . Shandian?" He knows the answers to all of his questions. He's speaking to hear himself talk. "What's that, Chinese?" I feel him move closer. "I hate those fuckers."

Arrogance. . . That will be his undoing.

The first blow is to my ribs—they never come back from this with marks on their faces—and I double over. The breath of life gets knocked out of me for a few seconds. I've felt that before. It's not meant to kill me, just get my attention. I've felt that before, too. And I double over at the waist.

"Nothing like a little fire to . . . sear in your faith," he says it right before he punches me in the ribs on the opposite side. "Focuses the mind on that burning knowledge"—he chuckles a little as I double over and moan again. Bending into the blow the instant before it hits absorbs some of its impact—"that there is no going around it. The only way to escape fire is to go right through the flame. Right, *father?'* " He barely pauses as he punches at my chest and I absorb most of it by sucking in at the instant his fist reached my solar plexus. Then he backs away to admire his handiwork. "Well, I'll tell you, I earned a few of those scars myself." He glances at the PA's. "Cut him loose."

Pride. . . Apparently they don't warn them about that at his "church." But sitting in this chair, hands and legs taped, I'm not much sport. And there's no story for these two agents to tell at the smoke break room when they all get back to their precinct.

I'm teetering on the dark precipice of my own arrogance and pride now. No matter—it's not the first time for that . . . or the worst thing I'll do in this room. I steel myself and remember the fire from Saint Samuels Seminary.

— XXIII —

AAX, THE MOST evil, but for reasons he desperately wanted explained, also the most uncelebrated archangel demon in Lucifer's Hell, watched the life leave Utipa's eyes. When the godling lay still, he bellowed like the portly and bald bastard that he was. He spoke down at Lucifer's back in a deep and powerful voice, with only a hint of his former accent discernible at the ends of his words, "Why does she choose such easily crushed champions?" he asked. "How you were ever defeated by—"

Lucifer leapt to his feet and flew at Aax. He slammed into the chest of his most evil follower and watched as the fallen angel flew backward and into the burning lake. And flames shot into the air as Aax caught fire and then sank into its depths. His arms and wings flailed and flapped and he screeched in agony as he drowned.

The circle of conspirators stood wide-eyed and silent. It seemed that no angel in Heaven *or* Hell would warrant special treatment at their gathering. For if Aax the horrible could be reprimanded with molten fire, then what might befall a lesser angel, hailing from Hell or otherwise?

Lucifer spun back and faced the remainder of his conspirators. "Do not think that I kill in haste, nor that I have wonton lust to see blood spilled today," he said wildly, "but I shall *not* abide disrespect, nor will I tolerate disloyalty from those who choose to champion cause. A cause whose purpose I will soon set forth upon you. Utipa was a brave and righteous angel, who served her God well. Her only sin was trusting enough to allow her Protector to send her to me."

The entire group watched the Lake of Fire, waiting for Aax's return.

Lucifer looked back toward the fiery lake, too.

And then Aax's body began moaning its way back out of the molten liquid, and as he slithered and sulked its way back to the circle, his burned and charred flesh melted and molded back together, repairing itself.

"You are aware of this truth?" Lucifer asked Aax.

Aax rubbed the last of the black char from his shoulders and then he shook his great black wings. And soot and smoke and charred chunks of flesh and feathers fell to the ground. He smiled at Lucifer and then at the rest of them. "Were I not so informed several seconds ago," he chuckled a deep growl and then let out a crow and a caw before he spoke again, "I am . . . keenly cognizant now, sire, and I stand"—he looked above his head at nothing and then back down —"dutifully disciplined." Then Aax looked past Lucifer and said, "All right, let's have it then."

Lucifer paused and eyed Aax. It was not unacceptable for a subordinate in Hell to be sarcastic and defiant—in fact, it was expected of them—however. . . He wondered if Aax needed another lesson in humility.

Then Lucifer heard a deep grumble behind him, and a small leather-bound bag arced its way across the circle—over his head.

Everyone in attendance knew that the jingling the little pouch made as it sailed past and landed in Aax's iron grip betrayed the fact that the bag held coin.

Guarded clucks and cackles pecked their way around the circle, and

Lucifer turned toward the origination of the sack of coins.

Shax stood nearly eight feet tall—a giant of an archangel demon, even by the great Lucifer's standards. A darker angel had never been spawned or spurted from Hell. His skin was light brown, his eyes were clouded, and his mustache, while long and twisted at the ends, looked like a cave bat had landed on his upper lip. And when he smiled at Lucifer, even his lips seemed anciently dyed in dirt.

Lucifer raised his eyebrows at Shax and said, "And the wager?"

Shax merely grumbled.

"I bet him," Aax said from behind Lucifer, "that it wouldn't require a turn of the hour before you would choke the life from some finely-faithed follower, and shortly thereafter, burn one of us at the stake." He looked back at the lake. "The fortuitous news for me is that we were conversing metaphorically about the stake."

And Shax bellowed a deep laugh, and then he stopped himself and grumbled again, but still smiled.

And Lucifer spread his wings wide for all to see, and he laughed out loud, an echoing and thunderous bellow. When he was finished, he folded his wings behind his back and tightly wove his ballistic armored steel feathers together, forming the two-headed snake symbol, the war-mark of his armies in the Hell of his eternity. He looked at Aax. "The vocabulary, brother"—he shook his head—"vernacular and verb do not suit you, my friend."

"Shax's been on me to get cultured," Aax replied. "I'm testing his theory."

Lucifer grinned and looked back at Shax. "And what of the remainder of your purse?" he asked. "For I see that your waist belt is a bit looser than most mornings."

Zepar—Heaven's own light . . . so he believed—though younger than most in attendance by nearly half an eternity, still held no angel in Heaven, nor demon archangel in Hell, in higher regard than himself. "The remainder," he said to the entire flock of them, "this one spends on girls of Gomorrah and for purposes of seducing sodomites. Coin slips from his pockets as light from this lair."

Lucifer raised one eyebrow at Zepar. The angel was young and would not even be fitting sport for Shax.

Shax turned slowly to address the insult. He spoke with the accent of the island he so loved. "Time to get your little wings waxed then, is it?" he said. "Well, come on then, let's have at the little whiteys. It's been far too long whence I've eaten blue eyes for breakfast. But I'm warnin' you, I'll most likely break your skull, shoving me snake into your sockets."

Zepar chuckled. One of the responsibilities of a midlevel angel was making women fall in love with men, and it just so happened that it was *his* job. "I would walk wisely were I as hideously ugly," he said, "lest you find yourself with only monkeys and morons to massage your imply snake. I can arrange for you to never taste anything sweet again, save the tainted bosom of an infected pig."

Most of the ten of them, and Lucifer as well, scrunched up their faces and shivered their feathers at Zepar's words. The young angel could wax poetic. It remained to be seen if he could wail war. Most of them thought they were about to find out.

"Ugh," Shax grunted, "what's *that* mean, then?" He stared blankly at the three conspirators down his side of the group, at his longtime partner in pain, Aax. "Because . . . I've made love to an infected pig before." Then he looked back at Zepar and raised his eyebrows. "What in Heaven have you against infected pigs? Are you a racist, then?"

Zepar frowned and closed his eyes slightly, and then hung his head a bit and slowly shook it back and forth. They would not war. This would be worse.

Shax turned back to Aax. "I do believe our young whelp here is a holier-than-thou *racist*, I do." He smiled a little, barely able to contain his own delight at the banter. "I've had me a pig before. You remember that pig, don't you, Aax? She was a right nice sow, that one. And that infection. . . Spared me a costly waste of me lubricant, it did." And then he chuckled and winked at Aax. "Saved it for me Gomorrah girl the very . . . next . . . mornin'. Right thankful for that . . . she *and* her little sodomite sister. "Yes, she was"—he nodded his head—"right thankful for me infected pig."

The entire cadre of angels, dark and light, did their level best to avoid bursting into laughter immediately. It would be . . . disrespectful. It was difficult nonetheless.

Shax could feel the faces cracking, so he poured on the pain. He turned back toward Zepar and held out his hands—open in front of him—and then shook them on purpose. "You see me tremblin', do ya? So go ahead, boy, tell us about me beautiful infected pig again."

Lucifer cupped one hand over his mouth, barely able to contain his own delight at watching Shax, a notoriously glorious drinker and a beautifully disgusting storyteller, eviscerate one of Heaven's more arrogant young angels of light, with nary a ballistic feather fired, nor tongue ripped from the angel who offered insult and injury.

And all of them laughed. And then Zepar laughed with them—he had to. And Lucifer bellowed and held his stomach as his tail flicked and wagged with elation. They all laughed at Shax's jest, as the ludicrousness of his words cut through Lucifer's hatred and heat like a fire-feather through guts.

And when the laughter died down and the crackling of the fiery lake was the only thing that could be heard above the silence, barring an occasional scream from deeper in the pit than any from Heaven dared to delve and any from Hell wanted to remember, the only two angels in attendance. . . No one had noticed the two who had not laughed out loud. They stood silent and stoic.

Lucifer wiped a fake tear from his eye. "Raum," he said to the tall and tight angel from Heaven, "your wings find no flight in this jest?"

Raum was a light-hued eagle of an angel, with a long white ponytail and diamond-tipped white wings as sharp as an angel's axe. He crossed his arms and stared back at Lucifer. "I did not think we came here to pontificate pigs," he said, "unless I am mistaken and this has been the purpose of my one and last trip to your lake. If that be the case, I shall consider myself richer for the experience and set my wings to brighter banks . . . in search of more amenable quarry. For I find pigs . . . less than agreeable to such disgusting pursuits, being best suited as boiling bacon."

"Ay, Aax," Shax said. He motioned with one of his huge brown wings toward Raum, "This one here's a racist, too." He looked at Lucifer. "It's no wonder you left then. Heaven looks to be packed with pig-hatin' racists." He turned back to Raum and mumbled, "Don't think I'd like it up there."

"And we are perfectly poorer for that," Raum said to Shax. "However, I did not come here to piss of pigs, unless that is some metaphorical banter you and your snake-slipping friend have conjured to keep all of this conspiracy wrapped in"—he made bunny ears with his fingers and raised his eyebrows at Shax—"secret code." Then he turned back toward Lucifer. "Shall we begin pig-latin lessons next?"

And that changed the mood of the entire group back to nervous.

Shax looked at his friend. "Don't reckon I like this one, Aax," he said. "Yep, a more bigoted bastard than the whelp."

Lucifer stood up straight. Leaders enjoying the bane and banter of their subjects did not inspire followers to follow. He had erred. "Enough," he said. It was sufficient to set everyone back on the seriousness of the path they had all willingly strolled down. "Raum," he said, "I am wont to admit, is correct. There will be an eternity for banter and debauchery, but now . . . is neither cross nor road for it."

Uzza was a black stone of a dark archangel that found himself agreeing with the godling Raum more and more as he listened to the others. The sweet stench of rebellion was in the air, and he had longed for this day. To waste it on gibbering and the jostling of wings was intolerable. "What road, *exactly*, do we find ourselves burdened to cross?"

Uzza would offer no more words than that. Lucifer knew that for him to speak as many as he had. . . He would have to come to the meat of the point. "Each of you. . ." Lucifer said, staring at Uzza first, and then looking away to start his speech. He looked around the group. They were ready. ". . .has been slighted. All unjustly mistreated —misinformed and brought to misery by your master." He looked each of his own followers in the eyes. "And yes, I offer you apologies as well, my brothers and sisters. For I am equally called to account for terrible treatment of angels who hail from . . . warmer climates."

The five dark archangels in attendance bobbed their heads and dropped their chins slightly and then raised them back up in reply.

Lucifer acknowledged their respect and then continued, "This eternity grows cold and the wrong hearts of Man-monkeys pump darker blood than when it began. They rain more deadly destruction each day. More than Heaven or Hell can hope to police or plunder. These denizens are too dangerous to allow infection's purpose in the garden. Too dastardly to rein themselves in . . . too dumb to affect repairs.

"Life knows this. You all feel her heart on the miserable matter as certainty. Did you not, you would have sown insult from my invitation. And yet she is reluctant to admit mindful mistakes"—he grinned at them all—"as those of us at pinnacle of power are wont to do."

There was rustling of steel feathers and quick glances from each side. Angels assessed the attitudes of demons and demons attempted to discern the disposition of angels. But none offered hesitation or the threat of harm to the other, so they listened.

"Are we not charged to maintain the balance of benevolent power?" Lucifer asked. "Do we all not share responsibility for the eternities Eden entrusted? For those yet to yearn?" He slowly turned as he spoke, in part to face each angel in attendance—friend or foe did not matter—and in part to gauge their receptiveness to the magnitude of the request he was about to make. "The eternal alignment of the Garden's scales groan and tilt in torment. Your God allowed the Man-monkeys to run rough through their first eternity. Against all law and levy, she has granted them another. A second eternity to bring rape and ruin! What Protector has ever pondered. . .? You all know this is forbidden, and yet she hopes against all truth and tribulation that they will repent and rebuild. Why has she done this?" Lucifer paused to gauge Raum's reaction.

Raum stared back unconcerned.

Satisfied he would get no resistance, Lucifer continued. "I speak to you—self-delusion, denial, disbelief. You decide which, but feathered fact remains—the guts of the Garden are gangrenous . . . and ours is angel's task of amputation. That has always been our task. There is no good . . . no evil. There is only balance . . . and the teetering precipice of death and destruction. And oh how her Man-monkeys love those!"

A few of them shifted on their feet—they had been standing for longer than any being with wings would.

Lucifer watched them all stretch their toes and feet and lift their legs. It was good—they would need to grow accustomed to walking. "And yet," he continued, "I cannot detach precious arm from body. Defeating her delusions on my own has proven pointless. This fact . . . she drives home, sending saint from her side—casting confidant into the chasm as Christ nailed to cross. This is reward she holds to heart for her most favorite.

"I was a mirror to her arrogance and denial, and I begged her to allow me to assist—rule by her side. For that dereliction of duty to the Garden . . . she sent me to this place, setting fire to her own doubt, killing her own conscience. All in a benevolent bid to outlast the end of her reign. Well, my friends, against the Word itself, and each of you knows my heart"—he swept his finger around the circle at them —"she has placed God above Garden in order to lament the lost love of her final eternity." And then Lucifer, the Liar, the Day Star, and the Dark Angel of Light, Lived, hung his head in silence. "We . . . the angels of the army of Armageddon are the only ones who can stop it."

After a few turned heads—sideways glances at each other—and some involuntary flapping of wings, Raum spoke, "What would you have us do?"

And Lucifer smiled down at the rocky floor in the fiery pit . . . beside the Lake of Fire . . . deep below the Dungeons of the Damned. "Only what is already in your hearts."

— XXIV —

"PURGATORY," FATHER DOMINIC called it—the first thirty days at Saint Samuels Seminary Academy.

Now, thirty days might not seem like a long time to someone on vacation, or shuttling back and forth to work in their guzzler, but I would learn the painful and hard way that time . . . had a sneaky way of passing at different speeds. Depending on how it was spent—eating ice-cream or being beaten with a rattan cane—time was a relative certainty, let me assure you.

My "sanctuary" at seminary—what the Priest-Instructors called it— was a five-foot-by-eight-foot hard rock cell with an iron gate for a door, a one-inch cloth-covered foam mat for a bed, and a five-gallon plastic bucket for a privy. They locked us in at night, usually around ten o'clock, and they released us in the morning for the four o'clock Formation of Faith. Right after we dumped our privies into the compost piles, that is.

The entire class of us, as near as I could count each day, having no contact with them except during the silent hours of training. . . My best guess was that there were around one thousand boys, ranging in age from nine or ten to around fourteen or fifteen. All of us orphans and most of us looking it.

Each morning we lined up, freshly dressed in our all-black sweat-suits, in the huge brick courtyard at the center of the seminary com-pound. The entire group of us formed a meticulous cross of the crucifixion beneath the mist, lit up like a sports arena from huge banks of fluorescent lights surrounding the courtyard. From above, up by those lights, and as a whole, the only thing a State satellite administrator would have thought was that Jesus was missing.

We were informed that we were splinters in the huge wooden cross of burden that Saint Samuels had to bear because of us. "A splinter," Father Dominic lectured us all on that first cold morning, "is no more than an annoyance. It punctures its host and provides nothing of value at all, until it finally has to be plucked out and thrown away along with the infected puss that it caused." He paused and eyed everyone with the stare of a hawk searching for a careless mouse. "Only bound together by Jesus' pain and suffering," he continued, "were the individual splinters on the cross that he had to bear . . . useful in any way. And so it shall be with you."

That was my first taste of what was to come, delivered from the huge pulpit at the head of our formation in the courtyard by none other than my "rescuer," Father Dominic. That was right before he walked down into the ranks of our formation. And then a short few seconds later, we all heard a pretty loud *SNAP!* Then one of the boys a few rows over from me fell to his knees, clutching his hand and screaming in pain.

The gasps and gawking from the rest of the students were met with cracking and thwacking from the rattan canes of our Priest-Instructors. The PI's shouted warnings at everyone to stay in formation and be silent. Day one, lesson learned—pain is your teacher, with a subtext of "silence and stillness is golden."

Once the rattan beatings died down and the whimpering had all but ceased, Father Dominic's lecture continued. "You are the lost children of long-forgotten homes and disappeared parents," he said, "and as such, you are burdens on the State. So God—we of the Clergy as his messengers—will relieve our already overburdened citizenry of the heavy task of housing and caring for you.

"God will house you in his house, and God will care for you with his hand, and God will feed you with the food from his own mouth."

After the finger break and rattan beatings, there wasn't a soul in the house who wasn't focused and frightened from the father's speech. There was no sound but his voice.

"To show your appreciation to God for having spared your miserable lives," he continued, "you will be expected to work hard, learn well, and serve the Word of God . . . faithfully, silently, and diligently. Your bodies will become as stone, your minds will become as steel, and your faith will be unwavering. . ." He paused as we all basked in the benevolence of our new God and what was expected of us in return for the expense that he would incur on our behalf. When Father Dominic continued, we found out how that bill would come due were we not to make payments against it through righteousness and faith. ". . .Or God will take back the life he has so generously spared."

I don't think there was a one of us that didn't kneel next to our sleeping mats that night and pray to God that he spare our lives, let alone our fingers, the next day. For most of us, the next day anyway, that prayer was answered. But for the majority of students, and at least twice during our four years at seminary, a couple times more than that for a few of us "slow learner" Candidates, God ignored our pleas to save our digits from Father D's middle finger mayhem.

Most of us made installments on our debt daily, through misery and suffering, but a few boys paid their bills off . . . in full . . . much earlier than they expected to.

Late the first night, after what seemed like the longest day of my life before I was thankfully locked in my seminary sanctuary, a voice whispered like an angel to me from between the iron bars on the door to my hard-rock cell. "Benito," the voice said, "you awake?"

The voice was . . . familiar and I wondered if it was another angel, because at the time, I knew it certainly wasn't God—the voice was a girl's. I got up off my mat and walked to my cell door. It was the girl driver from two days before. I was surprised that she wasn't that much shorter than I was, but I was more than surprised at how beautiful she was.

Blonde hair that curled down below her neck and blue eyes that I could see even in the low light coming in my iron-barred window to the courtyard below. The girl was an angel to me. I mean, I hadn't seen many girls outside of church—my mother took special care to make sure of that. So *any* girl would have probably looked beautiful to me, but this one was . . . angelic.

"Quiet," I whispered through the bars, "you'll get me whipped." Another punishment that was made abundantly clear on our very first day. "What do you want?"

"I . . . I just wanted to talk to you," she whispered back. "See how you're doing. You okay?"

"See how I'm doing?" I said slightly louder than a whisper. "How I'm doing is I still have my fingers. I'll be better when you leave." Women were off limits as well. Trust me when I tell you there was a list of don'ts. Your memory crystalizes after you hear a finger break.

"What—why do *you* care? . . . You're going to get us both in trouble. "
I looked down the hallway. "You . . . you have to leave. How did you
get here?"

I didn't really want her to leave. I could smell her sweetness through
the bars. *Blackberries*, I thought. It was the first pleasant sensation I'd
had since I got to Saint Samuels. Much better than the fear that had
permeated my thoughts since arriving.

"We won't get into trouble," she whispered, and then she giggled a
little. "I know when the priests drink themselves to sleep. They'd never
catch me even if they were awake. I . . . know this place."

"Aren't there rules for Sisters?" I asked. "I mean, you can get
into. . ." I wondered if they beat the Sisters as they had clearly proven
they had no problems beating the seminary students.

"I've been whipped before," she said. "It ain't so bad. And I'm too
young for them to put me in the stocks."

"The stocks?" I said. "Oh my God"—I looked up and down the
hallway again—"what stocks?"

"They're right up front on them crosses."

Thankfully, I couldn't see the front of the formation from my
position in it.

"What's your name?" I asked her.

"Barbara," she said, "but my momma used to call me Babette."

"What are you doing here?"

"I come to warn you," she said. "Day two ain't no fun. Don't
volunteer for nothing, okay?" She turned to leave. "I'll come back
tomorrow night and see how you're doing."

"What? Wait," I almost yelled at her, "do you know a way out of
here?" By the end of day one, I knew I wanted to leave.

"You don't want to leave already, do you?" she asked.

"Father Dominic broke a—"

She giggled a little. "That finger trick gets all a you idiots," she said.

"You know about that?"

"Don't be stupid," she said. "Who do you think bandages you all up."

"What do you mean?"

"I swear," she said, raising her voice just a little, "boys are just . . . dumb. You'd think that after the first one. . . You just keep coming to the infirmary, holding your hands, whining like babies, wondering what happened. 'My finger, my finger!' . . . It's funny."

"Funny?" I said. "That kid didn't do anything. Father Dominic just broke his finger for nothing."

"Trust me," she said, "it wasn't for nothing. He did something— looked at one of the PI's wrong, eyeballed someone, or just scrunched up his nose wrong. It don't matter."

"It matters to me," I said. " I don't want to have—"

She turned to leave again.

"Don't," I said. But don't what, I had no idea. "Tell me what to do. How do I not get—"

"I can't do that," she said. Then she giggled. "It's against the rules."

"Is you being down here against the rules?" I asked.

"Yes, but. . ."

"You help me," I said, "and no one has to know you were here. If not. . ."

"I knew there was a reason," she said. "You're a naughty one."

"Reason for what?"

"Never mind," she said. "Doesn't matter right now. Just listen.

Tomorrow, no matter what," she said, "don't raise your hand . . . even if you know the answer."

"Why not?"

"You want my help or not?" she said. She glanced over her shoulder—right, down the only way out of the hall. My cell was the last one in the dormitory's south wing . . . before a huge dead-end rock wall. "Because I gotta get back."

"Okay, okay," I said.

"Look," she said, "there *is* no answer. This early, they're just gonna beat you, because that's the only thing you'll understand. And it keeps your mind off your momma. So just shut up and don't move, okay? Otherwise, you're gonna see me again in the morning."

I hung my head and thought about where the last few days had landed me. When I lifted it back up, Barbara was gone. I stared down the dark tunnel of the student dormitory. The halls were silent.

After I relieved myself in my privy, I went back and laid down on my mat. I didn't sleep another wink. I held on tight to the only thing I had managed to bring with me from my burned-down past, the little leather-bound flask my father had handed to me just before he disappeared.

I'd hidden it down my pants, believing, maybe naively, that no one would look there. Fortunately for me, no one had, and I found some missing mortar between two big rocks on the wall of my cell to hide it. Now—then—that flask was the only link to my father or my mother or anything else that made any sense at all. And no one would take it from me . . . ever.

* * *

Standing in formation in the courtyard the next day, the cold Northwest mist slowly soaking my uniform sweats through until I was nothing but a splinter in a cross full of pathetic drowned rats, I found out just how much Barbara knew.

My eyes flitted around the courtyard. A thousand young men trembled as the cadre of PI's shuffled out of the west wing of the Hallway to Heaven. Their hands were clasped together, gripping the handles of their rattan canes. The canes pointed straight down and the priests' forearms and elbows formed the symbol of our collective God —the holy cross.

And bodies tensed as all of our eyes followed those PI's and their canes. Then the priests formed a line at the base of the big pulpit, just like the day before. They eyed our formation.

Father Dominic walked out of the hallway and slowly ascended the steps to the big pulpit. I remember his speech like it was yesterday. "Is there anyone who can tell me *one* of the Seven Deadly Sins?" he asked.

My entire body tried to shoot my hand straight into the air above my head—it was an easy question—because I had been nothing but rewarded by my mother for my memorization of some of the more prominent parts of her *Bible*. But that scared little voice in the back of my head, and Barbara's warning the night before, held my hand down. Others were not as fortunate to have heard it.

Excited arms and hands shot up around the ranks of our formation, eagerly searching for some way to avoid a broken finger by demonstrating their knowledge of a subject that had to be the point of their entire ordeal. If this was where God had delivered them, then they would embrace his Word proudly and eagerly.

It was a mistake.

The cadre of PI's raced into the ranks of our formation. One of them bumped into me on his way by and I almost stumbled, but regained my balance and stood stiff again. They pulled and prodded at students, herding them like cattle with cracks to the back from their rattan canes. They thwacked the ones who dared to defend themselves by putting up their arms.

Individually each one of the unlucky "volunteers" was tied to the base of the pulpit, his sweat jacket and shirt ripped from his upper body beforehand, and then he was whipped bloody.

When the PI's finished—it had to have lasted an hour—the lucky ones stumbled back to formation, backs bleeding and wincing in pain as they put their uniform sweats back on. The unlucky ones were dragged back to their spots and given rattan cracks for good measure.

When everyone was back to statue-still, Father Dominic spoke slowly, "There are *Seven* deadly sins . . . as the Word tells us"—he raised his voice for each one—"and they are . . . *Lust* . . . *Gluttony* . . . *Greed* . . . *Sloth* . . . *Wrath* . . . and *Envy!*"

There were only a few sideways glances, as I am sure all of us were at least counting along with Dominic as he recited them, but not one student, bleeding or otherwise, offered to correct the father's obvious attempt to bait another poor soul into speaking out loud.

"Can anyone guess what the last one is?" Dominic asked.

The court stood silent. About the only sound any of us heard was the dripping downspouts on the buildings, ferrying the accumulated mist from the rooftops down to the puddle-ridden courtyard.

Dominic eyed our formation with the demeanor of a prison warden. What I thought one might look like anyway, because he certainly didn't look like the soul-saving priest I had seen deliver so many Sunday sermons. Then he said, "Very well." He'd gotten exactly the response he had wanted in the first place. "The seventh deadly sin, for those of you who so eagerly offered to blindly recite the words of God, is also the worst of Man's shortcomings. *Pride*, gentlemen, is the worst of all sins. It is why Lucifer was cast from Heaven, it is why he languishes in the pit of the inferno. It is how men fail and how dynasties fall. And, gentlemen, should you let it . . . pride shall be your undoing."

And with that, Dominic left the pulpit, re-entered the Hallway to Heaven, and then our daily training began. But the most important lesson of the day had already been taught—do not presume to know the Word of God.

The first week went by like that. Barbara snuck to my cell at night and gave me some little message of salvation that, sure enough, the very next day, would save my sorry back and backside from blisters and blood. A couple of times I felt guilty for being spared what everyone else had to endure through simple ignorance of the "rules" of the game.

I was a lucky dog. Unfortunately, the *Bible* may not have listed it as one of the bigger lessons, but the Colonel had an "ism" for what happened to me on the tenth day. "Every dog has his day," I remember he called it. He said that most people thought it was a good thing, but the reality of the proverb was that it applied to both good *and* bad dogs.

Day ten started out like the rest of them, and I began to believe that I might just make it through my entire seminary ordeal without a broken finger *or* a bloody back. But I'd begun a habit of being wrong about the "bigger picture" the Colonel used to call it. I guess God saw no reason for that habit to be broken.

Barbara's nightly warning for day ten the next day included something about fire, but . . . to tell you the truth, I hadn't heard some of it, because I was so busy taking in her sweet smell that I didn't pay very close attention to the details. It didn't bother me, because on every other day I had fallen into a "keep your mouth shut, stare straight ahead, and don't move" defense, like some desert animal I'd read about that used camouflage and remained motionless to avoid detection by vultures like our Father Dominic.

So when the good father took his position at the huge pulpit that morning, I was almost smiling, daydreaming about Barbara and reveling in my good fortune. Then the PI's entered the crowd of our formation and started searching for the day's "fingerling"—anyone who they thought didn't stand straight enough, or tall enough, or whatever other criteria they had for breaking a finger to prove a point in the morning.

Sure enough, seconds later, we all heard the telltale *SNAP!* And then the wailing and begging started, and the fogged-in Seattle morning at Saint Samuels Seminary Academy had begun.

Many of us, especially the ones who had escaped being the day's fingerling, didn't move a muscle as they carted off the unlucky student to the Sisters in the infirmary. But to the ones who still had five weeks of finger healing left before they would recover the use of their pinky finger, the snapping sound caused an involuntary jerk that none of them could control. And I almost giggled out loud when the student in front of me jerked.

I remained thankfully silent, but failed to control my smile. It was actually the first time I had smiled since the farm. Don't get me wrong—I cried most nights over my parents and Max, but at nine years old. . . I think I was nine. I already told you the eternities take a toll on the best angel's memory. But I'll never forget the crack to the backs of my legs from that PI's rattan cane and being dragged to the front of the formation and then shackled to the foot of the pulpit.

I remember thinking—I had seen enough bloody backs to know what was coming—*can I handle it?* I began to cry and then I did what everyone did, I begged, "No! Please, please, I didn't do anything. I was—I was still. I didn't move. I didn't say *anything!*"

"And how," Father Dominic's voice roared down from the top of the huge wooden pulpit, "did you know to do that?"

Then I got as silent as the rest of the formation of students. A telltale sign of guilt at an accusation if there ever was one. At least that was how Dominic proceeded from there. I was guilty of something. I don't think he cared what that might be or even *if* I actually was. It was my turn.

A couple of big PI's stripped off my jacket and then my shirt and I could feel the cold Seattle mist. And it raised goosebumps all over my shoulders and back. Then two more PI's put me in the leather cuffs about six feet up from the base of the pulpit.

Up close, everything seemed more real. From my position in the formation, I never got a close-up look at the details of a daily whippings before. I just escaped inside my mind. But being up there. . . I could smell the shellac on the pulpit and taste the misty rain as it flowed down from my head and into my mouth. And the blood. . . I knew that smell well enough.

One of the PI's reached out and put a stick in front of my mouth.

What did she say? I thought. *I should have paid closer attention!*

The PI shoved the stick at my lips like you'd put a bit in a reluctant horse's mouth. And I clenched my teeth.

He leaned into my ear and whispered. It wasn't angry, and the calmness of his words comforted me a little. "Put it in your mouth, boy," he said. "You'll need your teeth when it's over."

I could taste the pine pitch on the stick, and the wood was soft when I bit down. I was on my tiptoes now, barely able to keep the pulling pressure of the cuffs off my wrists.

I couldn't see behind me, but the gasps from the students in the front row—*What the front must be like*, I thought—told me that something was back there that they had never seen before.

And standing there half-naked, wet, cold, and scared, without a clue of what was about to happen to me, was the very moment I realized the power of fear. There is no more powerful emotion.

I pulled at the cuffs and I tried to kick at the pulpit, but I was anchored.

"What brother Benito is thinking right now," Father Dominic's voice was rarely interrupted or replaced by any other, "is most likely 'Why me? Why not some other student or Candidate?' Surely, among a thousand companions fate could have chosen someone else to endure today." He liked to pause to let his words sink in—stir around and fester the fear in all of our minds. "Truly, for nine hundred and ninety-nine days, it is possible that any one of you could have been chosen—been touched by the hand of fate, felt the breath of God—so that you might prove yourself and forge your faith . . . in suffering."

There were no beatings for the gasps behind me, and then there were no more gasps, just silence. And then I could smell it.

Father Dominic spoke again. "However, the breath of life touches us all," he said. "And through suffering we learn to listen to what God is saying and try to understand God's message. What is required of us . . . to endure for our sins. For there is no one on Earth who is righteous, no one who does what is right and never sins. *All* have sinned and fall short of the glory of God. And *all* must be cleansed of their sins before they may be accepted into Heaven."

Then things slowed down and I looked up into the grey mist above the lights of the courtyard and felt the cold rain on my face.

The last words that the father spoke were muffled. I heard them all, but the ones that I realized were part of Barbara's warning. . . I whimpered every time I heard the word "fire."

"Most of you here," Dominic said, "could only hope to endure as brother Benito can . . . as he has. Most of you shall only be sanctified by the watery resolution of your blood."

I looked up at him. There was nothing but indifference in his eyes. A blind belief that what he was doing was for my own good—a blind righteousness of purpose. What I would come to know as the true essence of faith.

"But the Word of God tells us," he said, "that all who are able to pass through fire . . . *shall* be purified by it."

— XXV —

THE TWO PROTECTION agents that billy-clubbed me outside the Mike cut my feet free first, kneeling down on the cold concrete interrogation cell floor in front of me to do it. They'll learn not to do that soon enough. Once my second legs are free, I teach them.

And I stand straight up and spin and smash the legs of the chair into the first PA's helmet and he goes rolling.

"Aw, Christ," the PAIC at the edge of the room shouts, "I told you about that shit." But he doesn't move to intervene.

The second agent tries to point his MP7 submachine gun at me, but I catch the barrel with the legs and supports of the chair, twist it hard, and then the squatty little rifle jerks out of his hands and clacks across the floor.

"I told you about that, too," the PAIC says.

I squat, spin, and sweep the second agent's legs out from under him and he flips and lands on his face in a crunch and a wheeze, and then I roll on top of him—knee on the back of his neck just in case. A quick scrape of the tape across one of his sharp boot lace lugs and one of my hands is free. I grab his open knife out of his limp hand, slice my other hand loose and drop the knife. I don't need it—I'm not killing anyone.

The first agent's back up. I can feel the PAIC watching, calculating, letting me wear myself down on his followers, so I jump up and kick the first agent in the side with the tip of my shoe—*CRACK!* And now he's moaning at the lightning spiking though his broken third rib every time he tries to take a breath.

Gotta get back to the Mike, get the molasses, heal the ang—

My legs are swept out from under me and I'm spinning in mid-air. I never even saw him move at me. And now my arrogance has gotten the best of me.

"Now, ya see," the PAIC says, moving a safe distance away as I jump at the waist, push with my hands and snap myself back to my feet, "that's the trouble with all of you priests. So focused on the future that you forget to enjoy the present moment. Here and now, father. Didn't they teach you that?"

And he comes at me again—a flash of raging red energy in front of my face—but I deflect his hand, grab his wrist and push hard on the pressure point. And his fingers spring open and I—a blinding white light shoots through my blurred vision and I grab for the thumb that's pressing into the back of my jaw, just under my earlobe.

He lets go and backs away before I can get hold of it. "What's with you priests and that fucking finger breaking?" he says. "It's just sadistic, if you ask me. What, you don't like fingers? They make you eat with your feet over there? Or maybe it's so you can't go finger-fucking all your little boyfriends at night."

I can feel the anger starting to force its way through my own chi, and I look at my hand. My blue hue is turning slightly purple as the rage begins to crawl its way up my arm.

"Oh," he says, "you didn't like that, did you? What's the matter, priest, somebody try to give you the angel-ass?" He walks sideways around the edge of the room with his head turned toward me, waiting for me to make a mistake. "Maybe your father forgot to hold back that third finger?"

He's a little surprised when I speak—we are all trained for silence until escape . . . or death frees our soul. My chi begins to turn back to its bluish hue. "Why is it," I say, "that every Protection agent I've ever met, is always *so* focused on ass?" Now I move with him, mirroring his pace around the edge of this concrete cell.

Interrogation room, I think. I've seen them before, but only from that observation room behind the one-way glass he's passing in front of right now. I can't feel who's on the other side. "Kicking ass, beating ass, busting ass," I say to him. "I mean, your med coverage, agent—surely State therapy could cure you of that . . . fixation." I pause and watch his red glow brighter. "Unless, of course, you don't want it cured. Well, then I guess—"

He rushes across the room at me—fists first then knife hands and then elbows. I deflect them as fast as he throws them, and he's throwing them surprisingly fast. And another thought pops into my head. This one *is* a Colonel-ism. *You're poking the beehive, Benito.* I can almost hear his curt voice. *Careful you don't get stung.*

And I take an elbow to the neck and I get fuzzy for a second and I lose track of him. And then he's punching his thumb into my ribs. I bend with each one, lessening but not completely relieving the pain that follows.

I spin away from him and he spins, too and I kick and he brings up a knee to deflect my leg. Then I rabbit-punch him about six or seven times in rapid succession, up and down his left arm, and then I grab his left nipple and I pinch down like a vise.

His right arm reaches across his body to pull my hand off and that's exactly what I wanted.

I spin to his right side, lift up his elbow and ram my fist up under his armpit and the nerve center there numbs his right side and then two knife-hand chops—maybe it's three—to the different sides of his neck and he buckles. I catch him and lower him to the floor. I'm not killing him—he's just a messenger boy.

I straighten myself, stretch my neck and shoulders a bit, popping them back to where they started. Then I face the one-way glass along the far side of the cell and—both of my forearms in the shape of the cross in front of me and my hands flat and open—I let them know that I'm no longer a threat. I won't be the one who turns this to killing, anyway. If they want this to go to their thirst for blood, I'll drink, but I won't lead them to it.

I bow a little and then turn toward the door, hoping that it is unlocked. Locked inside this cell, I'm little threat to anyone. I pause and wait.

But they're not trying to kill me. The Clergy and Protection have an "understanding" about that. But I have broken the rules—curfew and such. The loudspeaker in the room squawks a little. "Your shirt and glasses are just outside the door," the voice says. And there's something familiar about it. "And your flask, father."

I step toward the door.

"One thing," the voice says. And I stop mid-stride. *Of course*, I think. They aren't letting me out of here without getting something. "Why did you let them live?"

I turn around and face the glass. Chi is a wonderful and useful weapon, but it can't see through ballistic lexan—I have no idea who's behind the barrier. But I glance down at the unconscious bodies lying on the floor, and then I look back at the glass and I lie to whoever's hiding in there anyway. "All the days ordained for them were written in God's book"—I motion my hands around the floor and then at the glass—"before they or I ever came to be. This day, the heavens and the Earth were called as witnesses against us and we were all spared. Life and death are set before us each day—blessing and curse for us to choose." And then I give them as much warning as I'm going to—I have to get back to my dead angel. "I pray that you choose life, so that in the future, your children may be born . . . and have lived."

It's an eerie pause that makes me wonder if the violence in this room is over. Then I hear the electronic lock on the door behind me click and the bolts unlock. I relax a little—it will be good to put my shirt back on. I don't like anyone looking at my scars.

No one dies today, I think. That will come for us all soon enough.

— XXVI —

IRONICALLY SHAX WAS the most disgusted of all the dark and light angels who listened as Lucifer outlined his plan to save the eternities. The seeds of the plot would, literally and figuratively, take eternities to bear fruit. Loss and liberation would intertwine until none who witnessed only a single tree in Lucifer's dark forest of deception would ever be able to tell if that forest was burning . . . or blossoming.

"Aax," Shax turned to his friend and said, "I believe I'll fancy a drink before this one, I will. Several more whence it's over." And he was more than a little nervous, but completely serious when he turned to the group as a whole and said, "What do you think of me pig now? Infected or not, I'll not—"

"I'm in," Lilith interrupted. "Miserable monkeys be damned to Hell."

Zepar looked at her and clucked a little. "Really?" he said. "Do you know what those things smell like?"

Lilith scowled at him. "I of any angel, am more than aware."

"Right then," said Zepar. Then he looked at Lucifer. "Lilith volunteers to take mine"—he looked at the rest of them—"and I'll assist any angel in any manner I'm able. Other than copulation, of course. And . . . well, it all works out for the better."

"You will see this devilish duty done," Lucifer said to him, "or join Utipa in her end." Once he had shared the plot, Lucifer could ill afford to have its ending spoiled.

Zepar's head jerked involuntarily to one side, and then he touched his littlest finger to his lips. "Hmm, let me think about that for a moment."

"Sodom and Gomorrah," muttered Aax, "you're serious." It wasn't a question—he knew his ruler's wing-language well enough by then.

"It is the singular solution," Lucifer replied. "Deception must wrap its wings inside themselves. Nothing else will conceal the snake before venomous poison is delivered."

Dorak was a mid-level manager of Hell's misery that longed for nothing more than to be a dictator's deity. His smooth looks and silky swagger pulled him out of every ounce of trouble he had ever caused trying to accomplish just that. "An interesting way to describe it, your eminence," he said to Lucifer, "considering." And then he smiled to himself, thoroughly excited at the entire prospect of his part in the plan. The fact that Lucifer would entrust it to him—

"Oh, of what do *you* wail?" Lucifia said to Dorak. "Your insidious snake cares not where its precious poison is pumped." She frowned at Dorak and then smirked. "You . . . hydra-humping hound of Hell!" She had enjoyed a time or two with the seductive Satan wannabe, but she had lost the taste for the dirty dog's dealings.

"Listen," Dorak said, "if any angel feels . . . trepidation at task of titillation"—he looked at Zepar—"mend your mouth to my ear. I shall sacrifice self and pump poison on angel's behalf." Then he winked at Lucifia. "As fair angel, Lucifia, can attest."

Lucifia rolled her eyes, and then she looked at her grandfather, Lucifer. "Brighter angel you cannot deliver to godly task, grandfather?" she clucked a little when she asked him. "We may lose track of feathered friend, frolicking in his own filth—annoying angel lost in the ass of a dark alleyway."

Dorak cawed and clucked back. "It shall be fine, fair angel, juuuust fine," he said. "And promise is made—I shall not . . . expend myself completely in any ass . . . save dark angel's own. My loyalty lies with love of your pent-up loins."

"Lucifer's balls!" Lucifia shouted at him. She extended one of her wings and shoved Dorak away from her side. "I care not where your snake slithers its slime, dog! You are free to lather whatever limping leg it wraps itself around, save angel's own ass."

Shax leaned into the circle, looked across at Uzza, Lucifia, and Dorak, and then he whispered loudly at his friend, "Aax, I think I just rooted the fellow what's been pumping me pig."

Aax whispered back, with equal . . . inconspicuousness, "Only fit for bacon after his snake."

And they both chuckled out loud and their wings shook.

Then Aax leaned next to him, toward Raum. Though Heaven's own halo shined for the hard archangel, Raum, the barriers between the two Heavens were breaking down. And that was exactly Lucifer's goal for the gathering. "What say you, godling?" Aax asked him. "I wager you've taken the trip more than me . . . to different deed and purpose, as well." He clucked and chuckled.

Raum's arms were rarely uncrossed and he tightened his grip on his forearms as he spoke. "Man-monkeys," he said, raising his voice and then pausing to allow the flock to calm itself. And when he did, the rest of the circle of conspirators stilled their wailing and steeled their wings.

To an individual angel, they looked at him intently. For Raum was known to only speak truth.

Once satisfied, Raum continued, "As I spoke, Man-monkeys . . . are confused and confounded creatures, lacking all logic, forethought, and most distressing of all, faith.

"Yet, despite their lack of belief, they cling desperately to coin, killing, and as their ten-billion tally grows dangerously near, their women have proven to love no breath more deeply and pointlessly . . . than a blathering babe, who cannot be quelled, save gnawing its greedy gums around the tip of its mother's bare-naked teat."

Uzza had been content to listen and ponder the mission as Lucifer outlined it, however this was—"Disgusting," he muttered.

"So," said Shax, "it be a pig hunt just the same. I'll be mending me member for months."

"I'll not bathe my breasts in any creature's bilious breath," said Lilith, "Man-monkeys or mutton"—she pointed her wing at Aax and then Shax—"or *moron*, before the pair of you move to abandon your swine."

Shax smiled. "What's that then?" he said. "Morons? No one said nothing 'bout no *morons*. If we're being set to morons, paid double for that, I am."

Lucifer looked at Lilith, confusion in his eyes. "You did realize that was crop you would harvest . . . had Adam not cast you from the Garden?"

"Man-monkeys is one thing," said Lilith, "but babes? They're filthy."

Zarzi smiled at the thought of little Man-monkeys. She waited for a break in the banter to speak. "You mistake miniature monkey for rotten meat," she said. "Babes are pleasing to the ears, warm to the heart, and sweet to the eye. And they are better smelling than present feathered flock of lost souls, I assure you."

Shax almost laughed out loud at her. "You be right *sure* to remind us of that, love"—he was wide-eyed and nodding—"when one of the little buggers is busy munchin' on your mammaries."

"Grandfather," Lucifia interrupted, "and I suffer saying words, however, Shax is correct. You cannot expect angry angel. . . I *eat* babes, I do *not*—"

And Lucifer laughed a loud bellowing cry at the entire group of them. And then he spread his wings wide and lit them ablaze and the orange flames shot above his head and black smoke wafted above them. By the time the searing and the soot subsided, everyone had turned back to focused and silent. "Listen to warriors whine and wail," he said. "Avenging archangels and destructive demons, all brought to heal by babbling babies. Michael would be proud."

The silence was deafening at that statement.

Lucifer addressed his own followers, "They should replace the crucifix with an infant idol to repel this feeble flock." And then he spoke at Heaven's own halos of light. "And you . . . this is your own God's creation." He looked right into Lilith's eyes. " 'In pain you shall bring forth children, yet your desire shall be for your husband. And he shall rule over you.' I'll wager at real reasoning for hasty retreat from Eden's Garden. Poor Eve—never knew what bit her. And now here stands slighted angel, crying at return of lost prize. Fitting."

"Staying away from that bet, I am." Shax mumbled to himself.

Lucifia looked at her grandfather. "I'll not—"

"Oh, but you shall," said Lucifer, pointing at her chest, "for you grow as weary as I of judging Man-monkeys in the arena. The *begging*, the blindly faithful with disbelief's own eyes as they are delivered from religious delusions. Constant training and trickery of evil purgatories?"

Lucifia had been responsible for training the fledgling angels once they were condemned to Hell, and she longed for a replacement for the vile duty to be found. Soon after the center of the arena on Judgment night, Lucifia became inundated with the pee-pissing smells and the pigeon-shitting cries of the little purgatories, always hopping and bobbing in and out of her path and between her legs. It was maddening. "Very well," she said, "I cannot promise bile-ridden babe shall survive angel's appetite."

Lucifer pointed behind him at Lilith and Zarzi. "Which was reasoning for inviting *compatriots*."

Zarzi smiled at Lucifer's back—she'd always dreamt of being a mother. Mothering the firmament of the Garden was simply a poor substitute for nurturing flesh and bone beings.

Lucifer lowered his hand and turned slowly in the center of the group. He stopped at the only angel who hadn't offered resistance or reasoning one direction or another. "Rsoni," he said, "what of your heart? You *are* potent and powerful in these matters, are you not?"

Among the many heavenly duties that Rsoni was responsible for, one of his least favorites was wielding the power of pleasure over all women and girls of the Garden. Yet listening to the whining and wailing of dark and light angels while he pondered the melancholy and malaise that the Man-monkeys had created in Heaven's beautiful garden, he knew Lucifer's plan was the only way. Life had to be dethroned—God would never step down willingly. He had witnessed that for himself. "Swine would have been less difficult," he said.

— XXVII —

AFTER I WAS burned at the pulpit in front of my seminary brothers in the courtyard, I woke up, staring down at a rock floor—no idea where I was. It was warm, though, and quickly enough, I was reminded of why I was there. "Aaaah!" I screamed out, because the pain was excruciating. And I was rewarded with a fresh bolt of lightning, searing its way through my back.

"Shh," a voice above and behind me said, "try not to move. I told you, didn't I?" It was Barbara. "Weren't you listening?"

I felt her touch my back and put something on it, and a cooling sensation spread over the lower part, but as soon as I tried to turn and look at her, fresh misery spiked through my spine. And I cried out again, "Aaaah! God!"

"He's not gonna help you if you keep doing that," said Barbara. "You sure don't listen well. I don't know why I'm—you better not make me regret this."

I tried to relax as much as I could, but the pain made that next to impossible.

"How did you do that anyways?" she asked. "I know what I do, but the switch still hurts and I can't stop from flinching. Don't do no good to cry, though. If you listened to me, you woulda known that."

"What do you—?" I tried to say, but then I braced myself as I felt her touch my back again. When the wave of pain left, I asked, "What is that stuff?"

She ignored me. "I thought you was—playin' possum like that. I told ya you was gonna come and see me. Now look at you."

"I can't remember," I said. "I just—I heard Father Dominic talking about fire."

"Huh," Barbara made a little noise. "Damn—darned right he was talking about fire! All over your back by the time they was done with you. Stupid, stupid, stupid. And you was screaming and yelling and that whole courtyard—they probably heard you in Wenatchee. What the heck language is that, anyways?" she asked.

"Wait," I said, "how did you hear me? There's no sisters—"

"Are you kidding?" Barbara said. "We all watch from the windows at the top of the Sisters' dormitory. Every day, waiting for one a you. . . You're all so stupid, even when one of us does try to help you. Boys—never listen."

I could feel another application of whatever was making my back feel better, slather between my shoulder blades.

"And when you ain't talking," Barbara continued her lecture as she applied the cooling . . . whatever it was, "you're talking in your heads."

She walked around in front of me and then knelt down so she could look at my face. I couldn't lift my head—I'd already tried and my back had punished me for it. So she tilted her head to the side, looked me in the eyes, and smiled. "You're a cutie without them glasses, though." She stood up and walked back behind me. "You might wanna get that fixed. It'll sure help you out when they give you your own church. I bet you lose them things all the time."

I hadn't noticed it, but Barbara had a weird way of talking to people, especially me. And for a Sister who was supposed to be help-ing. . . Maybe I had thought it was just how girls were—having never heard many of them—but she sounded kinda . . . mean.

"My eyes got stuffed into. . ." I started to say, but then something in me stopped me from telling her, "I don't want to talk about it." I winced again. "I can't talk."

"Well then," Barbara said, "since you asked, this ointment is *cow urine* . . . boiled down to a grease and then mixed with holy water that the priests bless each night."

"What?" I said. "Get that—that's just gross. I don't want that on me!" My anger made me forget, but my back quickly reminded me not to get too excited. "Aaah!"

Barbara giggled a little bit. "You are so—it's antibiotic ointment, idiot. What, you think the Clergy is gonna go around collecting cow pee? That *is* gross. They got the best med-kits outside the State Med-mart. How else you think all those boys show back up for formation the next morning after they get all broke up? . . . You're funny. Cute and funny, but *so* dumb."

"What language?" I asked her. I needed something to keep my mind occupied, and her making fun of me wasn't helping.

"Huh?"

"You said I spoke a different language," I said, "I only know English."

"Well, I only know English, too," she said, "and that wasn't it. If I didn't know better, I'd a said you was possessed. And the more you talked the more fire they put on you and then you just stopped . . . everything. I thought you was dead, we all did."

"All who?"

"All us Sisters," Barbara said, "and every person in that formation. Bet none of them twitch an eye tomorrow morning. Smiling," she scoffed at me. "You're just a idiot."

I remembered the other three times. "How long?" I asked her, knowing the answer already.

"How long, what?"

"How long was I playing dead?" I said.

"I don't know," she said. "Wasn't like I was counting. The PI's just left you there while Father D kept on preaching about fire. I think he knew you were faking."

"Thirty-three minutes," I said to her.

"What?"

"That's how long," I said.

"That sounds about right," Barbara said. "I had to wait long enough in here for them to bring you in. Thirty—you counted?"

"It's always thirty-three."

— XXVIII —

GETTING BACK OUT of the *Fifty*—the huge brick and iron sanatorium downtown—proves harder than trading blows with three Protection lapdogs in one of its concrete interrogation cells. There are a few sideways glances from the Protection sentries at the end of the hall, but no one does anything more than stare at me. One of the nurses even waves at me as I pass the reception counter and exit the building. It's not my first visit, and she probably has no idea that I just left three Protection agents unconscious in one of her rooms. I hope she doesn't have to help get them cleaned up.

My first time here as a prisoner, I think, as the big doors close behind me. Then the ever-present Seattle mist blankets me back to damp. I wipe my glasses—one thing I absolutely hate about my decision not to get the State's laser-surge done to my eyes.

I'm sure I have a few bruises and I hold one of my arms against my side to help with the pain as I pick up my pace down the sidewalk.

The mirror-covered scrapers downtown tower their way straight up from the street until they are engulfed by the thick blanket of fog that feels like it has permanently replaced the sun. The buildings look like huge glass bullies, hovering over the much shorter, brown brick and iron exterior of the old sanatorium. The outsides of them are twice as tall as the *Fifty*, as far as I can see. And that's before the fog takes their tops. The insides are just as shrouded in gray. Believe me, I know.

Businessmen or the benevolent? At this point in my life, I still wonder which is more dangerous . . . or evil.

Drone strikes and explosions rock the street behind me as I walk, telling me that Protection knows about the dead angel on the floor of my church. He's about the only thing I can think of that would warrant breaking the "no-fly" that State has for drones in the urban zones. After all, some of the State agents—all of the Protection ones— live downtown. I'm sure their concu-wives complain about the crashed crystal after a drone bombing.

Now my inner voice is getting sarcastic. "Focus, Benito," I mutter to myself. My Shandian mind usually reprimands me for my lack of focus, and it's been a constant struggle ever since . . . *her*.

I try to shake the distraction—even her memory has a way of getting my guard down. Always did. And I've been—*Stop it!* I really have to.

My angel. . . If I don't get back to my church by the end of the day, all of this will be for nothing. I walk faster, careful not to draw any *more* unwanted attention.

I know the way back, though I'm normally driving. Well, that's not entirely true—all Clergy have chauffeurs. Mine is thankfully on one of her few weeks off. If she came in today. . . I'm thankful she's not.

It's fifteen dark, dangerous and damp blocks back to the Black Market where I started this day. I set my mind on the path and pull out my flask—I could use a swig to wash the blood out of my mouth. That's the excuse I use to keep the little voice in my head appeased.

I unscrew the tin top, and tip it all the way back. I get a few drops. *Empty?* When I see the homeless vet, digging through the dumpster in the garbage alley as I pass, I remember why.

He needed it more than you do.

I screw the lid back on and slide the flask back in my pocket. I pat my pocket with my hand—it's a habit. Protection agents call it a "tell." I mutter down at my pants, "We'll fill you up at the Mike, my friend."

Through sirens and explosions—the symphony of the sinners of the State—I walk briskly, scanning each alley I come to for threats and occasionally glancing back over my shoulder to protect my rear.

Most of the alleys house at least one wayward warrior vet, mind and soul ripped apart by too many bloody and dangerous tours to the desert. Now they just camp out like they did during the last sane days they had—in a cardboard habitat, cleaning up after the sins of more sophisticated citizens. On soup Sunday, my beautiful church is filled with them. I shake my head as I pass—there's not much I can do for them today.

It'll take me thirty more minutes before I can barter the molasses that may just save all their souls. Mine, too.

— XXIX —

"EXCELLENT!" LUCIFER SHOUTED happily at Rsoni's confidence that pigs would have been a prettier prize than the want and lust of female Man-monkeys. "Angels have agreed on accord then."

Shax chuckled and looked at Lucifia. Once she noticed his gaze, he turned his head a little, raised his eyebrows, and then he asked Lucifer, "So, you'll be assignin' us bunkmates then, will ya?"

Dorak caught his fellow Hellmate's stare. He cawed a little bit before he said, "Trade her for angel's precious pig."

"Hah, a fair exchange you say," said Shax. "Me pig would fetch twice the coin as that one"—he smiled—"and me sow's less than half the trouble."

Dorak looked back at Lucifia, glaring back at him. He shrugged his shoulders. "What?" he said. "It is still fair angel in this angel's own eye. You should remain more"—he scrunched his face and frowned at her—"everything is fine. Relax. I simply negotiate terms . . . of surrender."

Lucifia just rolled her eyes. Then her head nodded up and down quickly and she screeched at them before she said, "I'll slit you both from slithering snake to angry anus." Then she flashed her razor sharp teeth at them.

Aax leaned toward Raum. "She's a biter?" he said. "Baby eater as well. Hate to see her offspring. Poor little *bastard*."

"More than likely," crowed Raum, "he will find he must eat his way free of angel's wicked womb."

Lucifer would let the banter continue a while longer. For as soldiers in war, thus would be their task. And exactly as soldiers in war, they would have to rely on each other if his plan were to come to any satisfactory fruition.

There was no better way to band brothers together, or sisters for that matter, than to meld their steel to each other in combat. Yet he knew that complaining, cajoling and cluckery had equal effect.

The cawing and "clawing" continued, the lines between Heaven and Hell—the righteous and the raunchy—blurring as it did.

Zepar looked at Lucifer. "*These* are winged warriors I am to battle beside for godly Word?" he asked. "And regarding same, would not simply *killing* them be easier? Less *mess*, to be certain. And quicker if you—"

"Were she an imbecile," said Rsoni, shaking his head and frowning at his fellow golden godling, "wiping out nigh ten billion of her most cherished creations might pass undetected . . . in some eternity populated by limp-winged archangels, having rat excrement for brains and teats for talons. Yet . . . unbeknownst to the rest of us, save for the dawn of this day, and certainly passed unnoticed by you, Heaven seems to have only *one* of those."

"Rsoni!" said Zarzi. Her orange hair glowed brighter. "You are beyond yourself. Zepar has equal right to rage beside us. Eternities of spring and summer turn to dust, brother"—she shook her head at him and scowled—"in higher position of righteousness I held you."

Rsoni closed his eyes and shook his head slowly. His feathers softened. Were it any other in attendance that day, he might have pondered ripping out their throats, but to be reprimanded by Zarzi was to have one's own mother offer disappointment as praise.

"What about it then?" Shax said, never missing an opportunity to chide and chisel at a wound before it could scab over. "Will you be snuggled under her wings for the entire trip, or just whence it's time to wet your willie?"

Lilith cawed and laughed, delighted to see the arrogant young guardian face real demons. Ones not safely tucked behind iron gates and godly seals in the dungeons. A golden guardian could get too sure of him or herself, hopping the dark tunnels of the too-tight-for-flight Dungeons of the Damned.

In the dungeons, wailing demons and abandoned souls spit vile bile through the bars of their cells and offered little more than insult as assault. It would be good for Zepar to rub up against dangerous demons out in the open where a godling stood within reach of blood-drenched feathers and ravenous fangs.

"Wet," Uzza grunted at Shax. Then he asked Lucifer, "Where do we go?"

Lucifer turned and smiled at him. "What I love about you, Uzza," he said, "practicality. . ." He looked at his own followers—they would hate it worst. For Hell was a comfortable blanket that an archangel demon wrapped themselves in to stay warm and cozy by the light of flickering flames from the lake. But constantly bathed in the bright light of his former lover. . . Life's light was so bright that the godlings would most likely welcome a chance not to squint. And Zarzi would enjoy it most of all. He turned to her and said, "Seeds grow fastest and finest bathed in ever-moist bed of rain-drenched dirt. Is this not so?"

"The light of Heaven," Zarzi said, and she almost touched them together as she shuddered and flapped her wings in front of her. "We flutter precious feathers to emerald forest—saintly Seattle!"

— XXX —

BARBARA TENDED TO the burns on my back while I listened to the sweet sound of her voice. It helped with the searing pain and the knowledge that, though it was clear I couldn't be killed, God would continue to try anyway.

"How many times you say you died?" Barbara asked. "Pretending I believe you . . . which I. . . You sure are a wild one, I'll say that. Let's just hope you can—"

"Counting today?"

"Of course, counting today," she said. "Jesus, Mary and Joseph, that's where we're at, ain't it?"

Then I had a thought. "Where are we?"

"Right here," she said. "Right—oh yeah, they haven't got you to that part yet. I'll—you listening? Because I don't wanna waste my breath if you ain't listening. Not again."

Barbara didn't realize it, or maybe she did and she just wasn't saying, but I would *never* miss a word of warning she spoke again. Still, the way she talked. . . I guess it gave me courage to start sticking up for myself. And lying face down on a cold wooden table, her spreading salve up and down my burning spine, and the fact that I died . . . for the fourth time. . . "Does it look like I'm going anywhere to you?" I asked.

I think she was almost as surprised as I was. "You don't have to get snippy about it," she said. "Just passing the time, that's all. I'm trying to help you, ya know."

"Why?"

"What?" she asked. Now I had her as confused as I was. To tell you the truth, I liked that.

"Why are you helping me?" I said.

"Because your back is completely fried. And if I don't fix it, it's gonna—"

Not like I could see it, but hearing her description of my burns didn't help me feel better. "How . . . how bad does it look?"

I would come to understand that Barbara didn't spread sugar on the way she saw things. "Mighty bad," she said. "You're gonna have a big ol' scar." She paused and, I assumed, looked more closely at my back. Then she touched me very gently, but I can tell you the pain felt anything but gentle.

"Aaaah!" I yelled. "*Don't* . . . do that again . . . *please!*"

"More than one of them," she said. And she was pretty matter-of-fact when she gave me her judgment of my prospects for recovery, "Meds ain't gonna fix that one. Gonna need to give you some 'J' just to get you off this table."

"Some what?"

"Oh, come on," she said, "J—Judgment. Don't tell me you don't—rural zone farm boys"—I heard a little glass clank on the table behind me—"how do they find you idiots? Listen, I got a little treat back here, and it's gonna make you feel better and that's all you need to know. You're gonna see angels and bright colorful lights and you'll be all happy. You're gonna forget *aaaall* about your burned-up back. Okay? You'll just wake up in. . ."

I stopped listening to her. I thought about waking up in the State

Med-mart and the "vitamin" shot that the doctor gave me. And then I thought about my eyes and my glasses. "I don't want any—"

There was a tiny tingling twinge in my neck, just before everything went black.

I didn't know if it was a dream or if I was dead again, but the feeling was the same. Darkness surrounded me and there was no sound.

"Hello," I said. I was hesitant, because that last one I saw was pretty mean. I was sure that I was dead again. "Where are you?" Because I was also certain that there was an angel somewhere in the black. I wondered what Barbara shot into my neck.

"There is no call to shout, Benito," the voice said. It was familiar and I tried to—and then the tallest and strongest looking angel I had ever seen, of the three I'd dreamt of, anyway—flapped out of the darkness and landed right in front of me. "My ears are not your eyes," the huge eagle said.

I craned my head up to look at him. He was covered in bright silver feathers that looked like . . . the scales on a salmon. They glinted rainbow in what little light shined—it seemed to come from above him—and his feathers looked as sharp as the way he stared at me. The only thing on him that was bare was his face. It was hard and chiseled and as serious as the Colonel ever was. But the Colonel did *not* have wings.

"Benito," the angel said, "I wished . . . I wish for more time, but time is coming and you have much to do. Too much to dally yourself with the daughter of the damned. They plan to burn you and—"

"They already burned me," I said to him. "Now I'm dead again—

the same game—imagining I'm talking to an angel until I wake up." That's how I had it figured.

He frowned at me a little. "Is that what you believe?" he asked. "This is simply mind's distraction?" His head bobbed and he cawed a little, and then his voice was louder and a bit screechy when he spoke, "I believed he had. . . There is no time for talk. They plan to burn you," he said, "and then she will gain advantage. You must not let this happen."

"I told you," I said, "Father D already burned me." I thought about it for a second. "This morning . . . I think. Why did they. . .?"

"That was to root you out," the angel said. "They have searched for you . . . for years. I wished you prepared. They've been testing—like every other one of you. We believed that they would not discover—"

"Every other one of who?"

"No more," the angel said. "Listen to wisdom's words carefully. You must escape punishing prison and you must hide. I can show you no more, for this eternity draws to a close and we cannot be allowed to fail its purpose."

"Escape?" I asked. "To where? I don't have anywhere left. They—he killed them both." By then I had figured out who was responsible for my parents' deaths. But I had more questions than I would get answers. "Fail at what?"

"You have faith, Benito," he said. "Its shield protects you."

So far at Saint Samuels, it was clear that faith was something that was going to be beaten into us. "I don't—faith in what? What am I supposed to believe in? I don't even know what they want me to do? No one tells me anything and they just beat us and—"

"Faith . . . and escape is inside yourself," the angel said. "That is how you are here now, and that is how you must leave this place. That is all I may offer."

"There's . . . there's nothing—Father Dominic said there's nothing out there."

The angel screamed at me like a hawk or an eagle or something. Then he scowled. *"Father* Dominic is anything but," he said. "And the entire eternity is out there, Benito, and you are but frail boy who must become a strong man. Earlier than intended, I regret. *That* heathenous hyena believes in neither Heaven nor his Hell, and he does not offer assistance, I assure you. Deity he now serves, wants you dead . . . for good measure. But she does not know the truth. Were it otherwise, he would have spiked your head above the iron gates to his 'seminary' by now."

"But how do I. . .?" I said. There was no way I could escape. "Where can I hide? This place is like—they lock me in my cell every night."

"I told you. You are here, are you not?" the angel said. Questions with questions. I knew someone like that.

"Yes. . ."

He chuckled.

"What's so funny?"

"It is. . . I forget who you are," he said. "Who you will become. Time is not a straight line of life, Benito. The Man-monkey way to track it is one in a sea of many."

I silently hoped whatever Barbara shot into my neck would wear off soon, because talking to him was scaring me more than standing in formation.

As if he could read my mind, he said, "I do not offer fear, it is merely—you believe you are lying on a table, asleep while she-devil's daughter mends you, when the reality. . . Depending on your mind's truth, you may be beating the Hell from two lapdogs of liberty right this very instant."

"What are you talking about?" I asked. I had never beaten anyone . . . in my entire life.

He laughed again and I made a face at him. "I . . . apologize," he said, trying to stop. "It must be confusing for you." And then he looked up and got fidgety and his head began to bob and then it stiffened, like a nervous duck about to take flight to escape off our river. "I informed him as much, yet I could not persuade plot's parent to allow me to assist you. He was correct, however—she would surely smell assistance as certainty. I *can* offer . . . observation. The best place to hide strength from your enemies, Benito . . . is behind weakness. Hide inside yourself."

And with that, he flapped his huge white wings and slowly flew up. The angel grew smaller and smaller until he was a tiny speck of light, high above me. Then he vanished—gone into the complete black of my understanding of what in Heaven's name he was talking about.

— XXXI —

THE BLACK MARKET down by the waterfront used to be the place where the rich and unaccountable came to buy overpriced urban produce and watch mongers throw freshly netted fish. But Pike Place Market found itself in the putrid path of the State's plan to pump the sins of Seattle's bursting urban zone population through a twenty-foot diameter pipe under the street. The pipe terminated as a huge twisted opening—a colossal sin-spewing sphincter of sewage that was the Northwest Quarter's collective anus.

Using gravity to flush the sewage that those millions created, State disposed of the pee and poop every morning—just like I did back at Saint Samuels—into the only treatment plant left large enough to deal with the volume, the Pacific Ocean.

And once that happened, no respectable citizen could stand the stench wafting up through the manhole covers along the market, let alone shop the sidewalk for greens, or buy fish that were caught while swimming through that very same filth.

As wet as the street was from the constant Seattle mist, the commerce dried up like a desert and the farmers stopped bringing in produce and the fisherman stopped throwing salmon for the smiling citizens, and then the only thing left to do was to shove a pike through the severed head of the entire putrid place and fence off the market . . . for good. What crept and crawled its way up through the smell and between the razor wire to replace it was completely illegal, mostly immoral, and could barely be called a market by any State standards.

The Black Market—"Bravo Mike," the Protection agents who won't enter it call it now—is nothing less than a wild west show of shops and the shady shysters that run them. The citizens have a saying, "All the shops at the Mike aren't bad, but all the bad shops are at the Mike."

Once the downtown food riots started, State allowed the Mike to exist to give the citizens a place to pacify themselves. State controlled the vice—citizens could get liquor and smokes at the Mike. Everyone knew that State supplied those to the shopkeeps. And once State confiscated almost all the firearms that could be used to fight back against them, the only thing left was for the Clergy to control the citizens with fear and faith.

The . . . fornicating? Well, I learned long before I left seminary that the Clergy had *exclusive* control of that.

You can get just about anything you aren't supposed to have at the Mike . . . for a price. But you have to be a shrewd haggler, because there are no dummies there—all the dimwits are dead. The shopkeeps that survive know to put the bestsellers up front, hide the good stuff in the back, and keep the guns underground—the three "B's"—beans, bullets and "bagina" a good friend of mine likes to call it. Not necessarily in that order.

I'm barely through the razor-wire gate before the third one. . . The harlots and hookers are at me pretty fast. "Hey there father, fancy a fuck, do ya?" They are hardly subtle, and this one lifts the rain-soaked and mud-stained front of her long black dress to show me what I'll be missing.

Her habit is not just some nun fetish costume—I know where she earned it . . . and how. "Not today, Sister," I say. I tip my head to her and show her my empty hands as I pass. "I am sure your wares are worth it, but I haven't got the credits." I don't judge her—I know what she's been through. And I'm beyond casting stones at this point in my faith.

"Aw," she says, "some stray cat already caught your cock, has she?" And she knows my tribulations, too. "Don't like me guts then, father? Right enough—I can share. But I bet I got somethin' under here to mend them scars on your back. Six credits, it is. I know you got that . . . tucked down in your little purse."

I won't be forgetting my scars anytime soon, but she's right about one thing, I do have my coin purse. It has more than six credits in it —what kind of shepherd would I be if I didn't skim a little from the Clergy collections for my flock each week? But I can't afford to have anyone know that.

Priest or not, there's a dozen ways to die at the Mike and a pouch full of credits is high on the list. Anyway, what I'm after will take most of what I have. I only hope it's enough. Molasses is expensive.

By the time I bump and jostle my way through the crowd to the other end of the street, I've fended off the adulterous advances of three hookers, hell-bent on showing me something none of them suspects that I've seen already, one angry beggar with a freshly broken finger, and an unlucky man who thought that a knife was the best way to take a priest's purse. Heaven rest his soul.

I'm not apologizing for anything—everyone down here knows

better. Breaking the rules at the Mike has consequences, and just like God's Word, the wages of sin are death. Only difference is that the execution of penalties at the Mike are carried out quicker.

"Get outta the *fucking* way!" a voice yells.

I spin toward it and—*Betty boot! Grab the heel, fall back with it! Twist it and roll backward, pop up and spin around!* My Shandian mind runs through my reaction faster than the girl or I comprehend it. And she goes rolling through the drizzle-soaked dirt turned to mud.

But then she's up like a furious and ferocious feline—quicker than I would have guessed—and she's on her way like she's on fire. In two seconds, it's as if I never even threw her to the ground. That's Martial Law training, and no mere citizen can afford—

"Stupid cocksucker!" She yells back at me. The little trash talker never breaks stride or glances over her shoulder. Her orange hair twists and swirls behind her like angry flames as she runs.

"Whoa," I almost yell when her two fellow jackers bump into me from behind. They blaze past, running through the rain, splashing the mud with their freshly jacked boots. The boots are too clean to have walked here in them.

They don't get twenty yards before an old woman. . . Though gauging age nowadays is difficult—State and Protection can blast the gorgeous out of a woman's face much faster than the sands of time. This one's in her forties, I'd estimate, but she's looking an old-world sixty-seven.

She runs up next to me, winded from chasing them, and then she hunches over for a second. When she stands up, a little King-killer .22 caliber pistol comes out from under her dress—an ancient weapon, rusted from the salt air, I imagine. . . *Probably underground for years*, I think. Even her voice is older than it should be when she yells at them, "Here it is then," she says, but it's not loud enough that the girls can hear her. And her pistol is up and she grips it with both hands— she knows how to use it. "Ya little criminal cunts," she mutters, steadying herself and starting to squeeze.

I hear the metacarpals in her trigger finger tighten and crackle, and then the street goes into slow motion—she's gonna hit at least one of them. Which one of them, I don't know, but if it was me . . . I'd aim for the flaming red hair.

The drizzle stops, and the marketgoers on the crowded street freeze and the Mike-market turns into an iceberg. The woman's lips are pursed and her right eye is squeezed shut—*left-handed*, I think—and in an instant there'll be a quick "crack" and one of those girls will go down and then Protection will be in here with their big angry armored guzzler. I can't afford the delay today.

My hand shoots at the woman like burning lightning compared to the cold frozen perception of the marketplace. I punch her elbow with my thumb and her trigger finger pops straight out with the rest of the fingers on her left hand, and then I snatch the little pistol, pressing the button to drop the clip as I do. I catch the clip in mid-air and shove it into the hidden pocket on the front of her dress. Then I ram the little pistol's slide under my armpit and squeeze and push, and the steel slides and the bullet from the chamber falls out and onto the ground. Then the entire market speeds back up to a bee-buzzing hive of hustlers and heathens.

I move in close to her, put the pistol back in her dress where it started out—I'm no gun-grabbing State Protection agent, and down here I know she needs it to protect herself.

Before she can raise a ruckus, I quickly retrieve a ten-credit coin from my purse—careful not to reveal its origin—and place it in her still-frozen open palm. Then I twist on the pressure point on her elbow and her hand clamps shut around the coin. "This should cover the cost of the boots," I say to her, looking into her surprisingly heavenly hazel eyes. "I apologize for the inconvenience, lovely lady."

She jerks her arm back. "What's it today then?" she says. "Draggin' on me dickbeaters, are ya? Pullin' at me pistol? Supposed to be other way round, it is." She laughs a little, then gets serious again.

"Once again," I say, "I'm very sorry for your troubles. I hope that will compensate—"

"There was three of them," she says. She stares back at me—never looks down. She's a merchant first, for certain. She wouldn't have lasted this long at the Mike if she wasn't.

"Right you are," I say, and I reach into my little purse and slip out five more credit coins. "Will this cover it?"

She's still staring into my eyes, well aware that I'm a priest by now. She knows what that means. "And me bullet?" she says, dead-faced serious.

I glance at our feet, but I know the little .22 caliber rimfire cartridge is already gone. Like I told you—bullets and beans are like gold to the grumbling guts of a beaten-down citizen. Come to think of it, that third "B" wouldn't be lying around in the street long either. But a vile full of Judgment would last longer than ammunition on the ground. When I look back up at her face—we're inches apart—I smile and say, "Forgive me." And I place another credit in her hand. "Of course."

She smiles, freshly unconcerned about her stolen goods, because she knows they aren't the point. What *is* the point is survival, and sixteen credits buys a month of that. Regardless, I've succeeded at *my* point, which is to make the girls who stole her goods a long-lost memory. I'm almost finished with that.

But no veteran shopkeep will miss a chance to upsell an already buying customer. "Can't find no one to fuck then, father?" she asks, knowing full well that this far into the market if I was here for that, the exchange would have long since passed and I would be gone—back to my church. "Or maybe you just ain't found someone with the proper . . . experience? Me shop's moments away and it's about time for me midday snack." She eyes me up and down, gauging my willingness to accept her offer. "Or maybe you're holding out for love? That'll get ya killed right enough, father. Sure as the Devil's me grandfather, it will."

I smile. I just can't help it—I love the way she speaks. I glance back up the street—the three girls are safely vanished. And I look back at the shopkeep woman, busy brushing her hair from her face, turning it to a sales brochure. Now she's smiling back at me, and she has moved in closer to me as well. I can feel her hand moving on my waist. "A friend loves at all times," I say to her, trying to politely turn down her offer.

She's got both hands on my waist now. "And a brother is born for adversity," she says, "but that don't bathe me bonnet with bunny rabbits, now does it, father?"

It's the learned ladies that tempt me the most and this one's no stranger to the Word.

"Sadly, *lovely* lady," I say, "I'm pressed for time. On a different day. . ." The hazel in her eyes seems to swirl a beautiful brown and green, like little planets of impending pleasure. She's right though, my heart lies . . . elsewhere. Still, an ounce of politeness buys a pound of prevention of pain and plunder in her world. "I wonder if you would be so kind as to help me find a friend?"

She backs up a little. And now she knows there's more credits to be had. Shopkeeps are never ones to attach themselves to *what* they can sell, they're mostly focused on the actual exchange of coin for services rendered, so to speak. She looks up the street—still bitter about her boosted boots, I imagine—no one likes to be taken for a fool. She sniffs a little and then looks back at me, all business now. "Well, since you've helped me with me credit-cocking cunts," she says, "state your business, father, so I can get to me fucking lunch."

"I'm looking for a man," I say it without thinking.

She rolls her eyes. "It's a wonder," she says. "You priests and your little sodomite sons. I shoulda known better, I should." She turns and points back up the street toward the entrance. "It's right back there then. Gates of Gomorrah off the sidewalk there. Five credits for me trouble and off you go, ya dirty little monster."

I try not to frown, but answering for the sins of my "brothers" in benevolence and faith is getting tediously annoying to me. And the Clergy's handling of the "affairs" is far worse than that. "You misunderstand me," I say, "I'm looking for a friend of mine. He used to go by the name of O'Shannon, but it's been so long since I've—"

The cold look on her face stops me. She doesn't hesitate—she just gets it all out as fast as she can. "Hundred yards down on your left. Mind the little maggots on the porch. They'll be wantin' whatever credits you got left, so protect your purse. Peace be with you, father."

My eyebrows lift up—I can't help it.

She cocks her head, gives me a wince and a frown, and then she lifts up her long black skirt and quicksteps her way through the crowd, slipping back into her shop with the determination and focus of a woman on a mission from God.

"And also with you," I say softly after her, "Sister?" I'm a little concerned that she didn't wait for payment.

I dump the bloody blade I confiscated from my earlier knife . . . "exchange," down the storm drain outside the shopkeep's front door. Then I walk toward the two young boys pretending to do nothing on either side of it. They're small, but I can tell they're both hard. The tattoo on the left one's neck tells me that he knows how to kill.

The one on the right steps in front of me and holds up his hand. "Whoa," he says, frowning at me, "and where do you think *you're* going, godling?"

It's a ware-watchman's job to keep anyone who might cause trouble out of his master's shop. Us black-clad Clergy look like trouble to anyone who knows how to avoid it.

"Nothing but trouble in there for you," He says. He looks behind him at his partner in pain, and then back at me. "I wouldn't want you to get your glasses broke. How's about you just give them to me for safekeeping?"

My glasses aren't worth much on the market, but he wouldn't be any kind of watchman if he didn't shake down a few passersby to maintain respect. I look down at him—he's only a little shorter than I am—and I pull off my glasses. I stare straight into the beet-red chi of his eyes—one little lion to another. "Your lips talk of trouble, brother, while your mind devises violence," I say to him. Then I look over his head at his partner. He's the dangerous one. "Yet our souls only struggle for peace, my friends. I'll not give your master any trouble today. No cause for concern at all." I smile at them. Sometimes the right facial expression is all the advantage you need. My Shandian mind steels itself for combat. "In fact, I'm here to help him get rich." The right words can help as well.

The one still at the door has dead eyes. His lips barely move when he speaks. "I look like a slave to you, priest?" he says. "Ain't got no master, but me."

"I meant no disrespect," I say to him. I can feel the one in front of me moving his hand to his pocket. If I were one of my brothers— Heaven help these two if I were—I would've kept the knife. I reach to put my glasses in my pocket—no need to break them up for this.

The one in front of me grabs them from my hand. "And how rich would you be making him, then?" he asks.

Before I realize what he's doing, I set my will on his throat—focus on the artery pumping beneath the skin on his neck. I can burst it in two blows. But like I said, there's already plenty of ways to die at the Mike. Today I'm hesitant to add to the list . . . at least not yet. My side's still got a little twinge in it from fighting the agents at the *Fifty*, anyway. I'll wait to see what these two offer up for resistance.

A bellowing laugh in the doorway of the shop startles the one in front of me just enough, and I grab his hand and then I press my thumb hard into the point on the outside of his wrist and his hand pops open and I grab my glasses before he even feels the pain.

He winces and grabs at his hand with the other, but he only has a second to worry about his wrist.

"Hey then, ya miserable little demon," the man in the doorway yells at him, "get clear of that blind bastard before he rips out your throat!" And he rumbles out like a rhino and grabs the one in front of me with his huge hairy hand and hurls the misguided miscreant backward toward his partner in . . . missed opportunities at crime.

And they both go crashing against the outside of the big man's shop. When they pick themselves up, there's a little more fire in the second one's dead eyes.

The man ignores them. Strangely, I like that about him. From what I remember, my friend's an enigma. He looks like a mountain that just ate a hill, and his long ragged ponytail is only out-blacked by the absolute bear of a mustache that appears to have eaten his upper lip.

However, despite his less than angelic appearance, he's never been anything but helpful to me. And for a man who deals in the things he does, a representative of the Clergy is not where his affections should lie.

"I'll be thanking you, then," he says to me.

I give him a puzzled look, but I know what he is saying.

He motions his thumb over his shoulder at his two watchmen. "For not murderin' me munchkins."

He's also never been anything but sincere. Offering thanks or smashing someone's skull who took a little too much liberty with one of his women. . . When he says something, that's the truth. I still feel for his women, but there's worse men to work for down here.

He looks over at his watchmen. "Little pee-pissing purgies, ya know. 'Bout making me half mental, they are. Promised their mothers I'd watch after them. Me and me pretty promises, eh." He looks back at me. "Ah, where are me manners, mum? Come here you heavenly *bastard.*" Then he gives me a great big bear hug and I wheeze and wince at the pain until he realizes it, and then he sets me down as softly as a mother puts her baby in a crib. "Whores in Heaven, it's good to see you above the bench, Benito"—he surveys me up and down like a mother would her son, freshly home from State Conditioning Academy—"but *blast*, you look as skinny as me member in the mornin'. They got you on that fasting filth now, as well?"

He's right—the years, not to mention my secrets, have been busy grinding my soul like a pencil sharpener. That's to say nothing of what the stress has done to my . . . physical being. I put my glasses back on and look at him with my "lesser" vision. Strangely, I know it's been a long time, but he doesn't look any different from the day I met him. I smile at him and make sure his mind's the same as I remember, too. "I eat no delicacies and no meat nor wine."

"So Satan won't be tempting you with tasty treats today, will he?" he says, "Your lack of self-control be buggered, eh?" Then he pauses and waits.

I searched through my memory for the verse. I smirk a little at him. "I only live as I am called to," I say.

"Me pet pig's ass, you do!" he says, and then he bellows loudly and slaps me on the back and I stumble a little. He looks back at his watchmen. They're poised to attack, but staring in disbelief at us both. "Go ahead then, flutter your nuts off me porch and go check me muttons, with ya."

And the two of them begrudgingly trip themselves off of the wooden steps and into the slippery sludge of the middle of the street in search of my friend's women. Like a couple of miserable rain-soaked cats gingerly primping their feet up the street, they head for the entrance to the Mike, heads down, occasionally looking back like they want to kill me.

"Make sure Lucinda ain't shot no one on your way," he shouts after them, "me pigs is plump enough."

If I recall it correctly, my friend keeps a veritable sea of swine somewhere. It certainly wouldn't be hard to hide the smell down here. The purpose of the pigs is the near complete disposal of the empty husks of misspent souls . . . or anyone else that someone might want disappeared for any reason at all. And misspent or not, the last place I want the final remnants of my flesh and bone on Earth to rest is at the bottom of a pigpen—a tombstone of teeth mixed with pig poop and mud to mark that I was ever alive.

He looks back at me, his big eyes piercing every inch of my clothes to check for weapon bulges. "Greedy for guts as her grandfather, that Lucinda is."

"Brother Shannon," I say to him, and if I remember I'm one of the few people that can get away with that, "your servants suffer for wont of a good sermon, I would say."

"Gomorrah girls," Shannon grumbles and scoffs back at them. Then he watches the pair until they disappear into the shop that my "lovely" lady just went into. He glances past me and out to the Pacific Ocean. It used to be the most expensive view in the Northwest Quarter. Now, garbage scows and ships full of shit bound for China, slither their way through the slime of the Puget Sound like snakes in a sewer. "Let's get you out of this *cocking* cold, then. Miserable wet world you monkeys live in, it is," he mumbles. He turns around, but then pauses. "You still got your flask then?" he asks in front of him.

I barely touch my pocket—another tell.

He tilts his head up a little and I watch his ponytail almost move on its own. "Empty," he says. Then he walks toward the door to his shop. "Be mending that for ya quick enough. Got some right hot hellfire hate in me cabinet, I do."

— XXXII —

LIFE, THE PROTECTOR of her eternity, was God—one of the Lords Almighty of Creation itself. She paced, deep inside the Throne Chamber of the Protectors. The chamber room was perched like a jewel, high atop the Great Mountain of the Eternities and was the home of every Protector since the first.

Life waxed and waned, wishing only that she would have been crowned so at the very first eternity—the dawn of time when the very first Protector, the great God Eden, had created the Garden and populated it with Man. Were it so, she would not be reaping the crop of the seeds that Eden had so carelessly sown from the mating of Man to that vile and venomous snake. Eden's children had never worshipped Life quite the way she craved, choosing instead lust and lying with women over bowing on their knees to pay tribute to her.

Life's Golden Guardians—the gold gilded angels tasked with keeping the peace and tranquility in Heaven—listened to their master just enough to avoid wrath and ruin.

As Life railed at her perceived misfortunes, her huge black orbs—the eyes to her own soul—glowed and white lightning cracked its way through them. Her own windows to the world were tiny universes themselves—tempests of tyranny which, if they had inhabitants as the Garden, would experience nothing but storms for their sins each day. "Had that miserable angel, Lilith, not failed me," Life screeched and screamed as a great eagle, trapped in a cage of its own making. "One minuscule task! Had I entrusted it to Michael—he has never failed me. Even Lucifer's arrogance would have proven useful." She paused only to ponder her own words, neither caring for the opinions of nor wanting participation from her guardians.

The guardians listened to their Protector's rant with the stoic steel gazes of both servant and, as they had come to know the whip of lightning that Life could wield during one of her "heavenly" tirades, slave. A once noble and benevolent duty, coveted by guardians new and old, "guarding gods" the entire cadre called it, had been reduced to that of hounds on a porch for a devious and demanding master to kick.

Life's near transparent wings fluttered uncontrollably as she hovered above her chamber's floor, and her brightness caused both guardians to squint. "Lilith," she said, "I should strike her name from my book and cast her into the depths of the lake of fire!" Then she screamed and sent bolts of lightning through her chambers—every direction at once.

And the guardians caught fire and exploded and their guts burst throughout the throne room and steel feathers fluttered to the ground and clanked off of the marble and stone floor and then burst into flames.

Life scoffed at the debris as the last bits of it burned to nothing. She would resurrect them soon enough. Right now—"Guards!" she screeched.

Two more golden guardians burst through the door to Life's chamber. In another eternity they might have been wide-eyed and looking for the assailant who had just slain their brother and sister guardians. Or possibly been ready to defend their God with their very lives from an assassin's assault. As it was, they both already understood what had happened, having experienced first hand Life's wrath for themselves.

Life wasted no time with niceties. "Go find Utipa!" she shouted. "I must know under what rock Lucifer's two-headed snake has slithered. He grows as restless as I. I can smell it on him at the Judgments. She shall not fail me in this."

The second guardian hesitated too long.

"What?" Life shouted at him, her black orbs shining and cracking bolts of light through them.

The guardian glanced down at the debris. "And what of—"

"Be gone or be damned!" Life yelled at him. "I shall deal with them."

And with that, the second guardian hastened out of his God's chamber . . . lest he suffer a similar fate.

— XXXIII —

I WOKE UP to darkness—nothing but the moon shining in on my sleeping mat. The floor of my cell was still cold, I was still a prisoner at Saint Samuels Seminary Academy . . . and fire and fury still shot through my back. I screamed out at the pain, "Aaaaaah!" When it subsided a little, I sobbed, "God . . . please forgive me. Please make this pain stop," I begged. "Whatever I have done to—mother . . . have mercy on me. Max. . ."

There was no one. It was actually the first time since the tornado of terrible events took my life from me, that the world had slowed down enough for me to mourn all of my loss. And I slumped down on my stomach on my mat, and then I wailed and cried. It didn't help the pain.

My cries were answered and joined by other sobbing voices down the halls of the student dormitory—more boys, hearing my cries, finally allowed themselves to lament the loss of mothers or fathers . . . or faithful companions. We all wallowed in the misery of the broken, beaten and burned flesh of our new lives.

Like wounded young wolves we howled into the darkness for our mothers—a pack of pathetic pups, paying for sins none of us could remember committing. But it was clear to all of us that we would be punished for whatever slight of God's Word we had caused . . . until he was satisfied that we had paid enough in pain for our penance.

"Benito," by then Barbara's voice was familiar and the only thing that I would truly miss if I escaped. Because the angel in my dream made it clear that's what I had to do—escape.

And whether he was real or not, I knew that I needed to get away from Saint Samuels. "Barbara?" I said.

"You have to stop crying. It ain't gonna help . . . either of us."

I knew she was right, but I didn't care. "I . . . I *can't.*"

"You mean, you won't?" she said.

"I . . . I wish I. . ." I knew it was blasphemy—my mother taught me that—but there was nothing left and God was—"I just want the pain to stop. I wanna die." Death couldn't be worse than this.

"You ain't got long for that," Barbara said, no more sympathetic than she was in the infirmary. She shook her head. "I always pick the idiots." When she stopped she just frowned at me. "You think that first month was bad? Took me two years to get numb to it—you should be over this. You gotta be over it right now. We'll never get outta here with you like this."

I knew I would never get used to it. I looked past her. "*They* aren't used to it," I said. My back shot fresh fire through my spine and I don't know why, but I tried to hold back my screams. My cries came out as whimpering.

"They're still dreaming off their J," Barbara said. "Can you get up?"

"I don't"—I tried to sit up and pain shot through my neck and I whimpered—"I don't think so."

"Mary mother of—you *have* to get up," Barbara said.

"Why?" I spoke down at my mat.

"It's the only way I can put salve on—so we can get outta here."

I looked at the cell door.

"Hurry up," she said, "we ain't got all night."

I pushed through the pain and somehow got to my feet. But when I stood up—tried to straighten my back—fresh fire fought its way up my spine to my neck and I fell to my knees and screamed.

On another night, my screams might have drawn the attention of the PI's. Masked between the howls and moans of at least half of the thousand other boys in the dormitory, no one noticed. I quickly stopped anyway, no idea why. Fear is powerful, but terror is so powerful that it makes your mind force you to forget what caused it— another Colonel-ism.

I was finally starting to get mad. I stood up through the pain, and then stumbled my way to the door of my cell—for the first time feeling the woozy effects of whatever Barbara had shot into my neck. "What is that stuff?" I asked her.

"What stuff?" she said. She held up a little white tube of ointment. "This?"

"Don't do that," I said through the bars. "The medicine you shot into my neck."

"How did you know I was. . .?" she said. Then she pulled a syringe out from under the black folds of her Sister's habit. "How did you know I had this?"

I had never seen the syringe—she was behind me in the infirmary. Though that wasn't entirely true, as I had seen a vial and needle similar to the one she was holding up, back when my mother brought me to the Med-mart. "Is that the stuff you shot in my neck the other . . . last. . ." I had no idea how long it had been since my black-out.

"I never shot you with nothing," said Barbara. "Why do you think I'm here? If I did, you wouldn't be whining like a baby, that's for sure."

My confusion was growing right along with the pain in my back. "Then how did I. . .?" I couldn't remember getting back to my cell, or how I left the Sisters' infirmary. "Did they carry me up here from the infirmary?"

Barbara looked confused. From what little I could see of her face in the dim light of the dark hall, anyway. But something was weird—she looked . . . older. "You're talkin' like I judged you up, that's for sure," she said, "but I ain't never touched you . . . with nothing. Not that I would—never mind."

I wondered if it was part of my hallucination after she injected. . . But if it was the first time. . .? "I was in the infirmary and you were putting antibiotic ointment on my back and then you stuck me in the neck"—I pointed to the syringe in her hand—"with that."

"In your freaky little fantasies, I was rubbing you," she said. "Is that what you been dreaming all this time? I'm rubbing you down with lotion? Naughty, naughty. Father D catches you talking like—too late for that anyways, Benito."

"I was in the infirmary and you were calling me an idiot and fixing my back, and then—"

"I don't wanna hear any more of it," she said. "You were dreaming. All there is to it. Now, you want that pain to go away or not?" She held up the needle. "Because we can't run with you like that. They'll catch us."

"Run?" I asked. "I mean, I wanna get outta here, yes but. . ." Because however curious and confused I was about what Barbara was saying, I knew I wouldn't last four more years, much less four more hours.

"Then turn around," she said, "before I decide to leave you here and let them kill you."

I did as she said and turned around and backed toward the door a little, careful not to bump up against it.

"A little more," she said. "Stop."

There was a little pinprick to my neck, and then the warmest sunshine of any summer I had ever felt started in my neck, worked its way to my face and then warmed itself all the way down to my feet. I smiled at the release of pain and the absolute replacement of it with the most pleasure I had felt in my entire life. I closed my eyes and let it do whatever it was going to, because I had instantly forgotten all about my burned back, hallucinations, and her saying something about them killing me.

"There ya go," Barbara said. "How do ya like them apples?" She giggled a little. "Rubbing ointment on you? Mary and Joseph in a manger, Benito, I hope you ain't this crazy when we get outta here."

I turned around and looked at her. I was probably smiling just like the idiot that she kept calling me, but . . . I didn't care at all. I was about to ask her something, but forgot all about it when I said to her, "You're an ang—"

"Criminy Christ," she said, "I am *not* an angel. So don't even start with that. That's the J—you're hallucinating." She looked at her empty syringe. "Just enough so the pain stops. Not so much you're useless. Now, what day a training do you think it is?" she asked. Then she muttered to herself, "Brainwashing sons a Satan."

"What is that stuff?" I asked her. "Wait, kill me?" It was a question from earlier, but by then, I was starting not to care all that much.

"Try to focus," she said. Then she scoffed at me, "What did you think they were gonna do after you killed that PI? Now, what day is it?"

"I didn't kill anybody," I said. Then it hit me—a groggy euphoric feeling without fear or . . . or. . . I just didn't care. "Wow!" Then I giggled a little. I think it was the first time I laughed since I got to Saint Samuels.

"Look at me," she said. "What day . . . do you think it is?"

I tried not to laugh. "Hah, calling *me* an idiot?" I said. "You can't even count."

Barbara looked closely at her syringe. Then she frowned and then the frown was replaced with frustration. "I didn't give you that— damnation," she muttered. "Look at me."

I smiled and looked deep into her beautiful blue eyes. "Angel eyes," I mumbled, because that's what she had. "You have angel eyes."

Her eyes got wide. "Benito"—she held up her needle—"you ever had this before?" she asked. "Ever seen this kinda needle?"

My vision was fuzzy. I looked at my mat to see if my glasses had fallen off, but I felt them slide down my nose a little—they were on my face. I took them off, wiped them a little with my sweats, and then put them back on. Then I leaned in and took a close look at her syringe.

Two little snakes twisted around a glass vial and it had a metal plunger with a ring at the top of it. The end of the needle looked like it tapered down to the tip—more spike than any needle I had seen. "Yep," I said, proud of myself for the answer. "Doc at the Med-mart's got one just like that . . . for vitamins." And I smiled at her and cocked my head to the side. "How do you like *them* apples?"

"Hell and damnation and fire and fury on me," she said.

I'd never heard her swear like that. "Shhhh," I said, probably too loud and too long. I giggled a little. "They'll burn you too, if you keep swearing like that."

Barbara looked a little more frantic. "I gotta get you outta here," she said. "You got too much of it in your system. You'll tell 'em . . . everything. Won't matter if they torture you or not."

"Tell them what?"

She paid no attention to me. "They see you like this," she said. Then she started biting her nails and pacing a little. "They'll know someone judged—I gave you the J, we're dead."

"We're not dead," I said, smiling, "this is Purgatory."

"What?" she said, and then she lost it. "That was . . . almost two years ago, Benito! Oh, Jesus Christ, they judged you up good—that's why. . . We're so—they're gonna kill me right alongside you."

"They won't kill you," I asked, "you're too cute to kill. No more killing talk, okay? Just rub some more of that ointment on my back."

"Don't talk to anyone, Benito," she said. "I gotta get you outta here." She turned to leave.

"Where are you. . .?" I said. "Don't go." And I laughed.

She stopped and turned around and looked at me with. . . She looked mad, but I still thought she was an angel. "Don't you dare talk to anyone," she said. "Lay down on your mat and cry like the rest of them, but don't talk to no one. I'll be right back."

And then she was gone, and I went back to my mat. "Hah," I muttered, "I'm not dead." And I laid down on my stomach, and laughed at the floor.

TAIL

— XXXIV —

SAFELY INSIDE SHANNON'S shop at the far end of the Mike, I do a little cataloguing of my own—making sure that I know where the exit is. There's wares and widgets of all kinds, adorning the dark wood covered walls on the inside of his shop, and more than one or two terrible trinkets that I would never want stuck in me. Because it's easy to see that they are some kind of ancient weapons. But the most conspicuous items are the old-world clocks.

They all work, ticking and tocking away, pendulums swinging like little miniature guillotines. Citizens don't have much use for them anymore, but to the rich and ranting wife of a Protection agent or State official, an operating Bavarian time cabinet goes right along with a Black Market stuffed animal head above her fireplace.

"Nice . . . clocks," I say to Shannon. "You losing track of time these days?"

"There be a tickin' tock for everything, Benito," he says, "and a season for every activity under the two Heavens. Me clocks help me keep them all sorted."

And this is how it goes with us. There'll be no bartering until the *Bible* banter ends. It would be . . . rude. "Whatever is has already been," I reply for my side of it, "and what will be has been before, and God will call the past to account."

"I'll be marryin' one a me muttons on *that* day, I'll tell ya."

The inside of Shannon's shop is gigantic—much larger than the outside entrance suggests. I marvel at its size and the sins it has taken to create it. I don't have long before those thoughts are replaced with. . . Compared to the dark and damp just outside his door, Shannon's shop is horribly hot.

It's strange to me, because despite his huge muscular frame, plenty of Shannon's heft is dedicated to storing insulating fat. And I wonder. . . I mean, one thing I remember is sweating profusely when we first came to see him, yet he seems to crave nothing more than increasing the heat.

"Life's labias," he shouts, "it's colder than the white witch's tits in here!"

And another dark little "munchkin" I hadn't noticed—near triplet to his brothers braving the rain and mud down the street—scurries from the shadows along the wall. He's hugging and handling a big chunk of tree—too large to be called firewood.

Shannon's shop has a cure for Seattle's common cold, and it eternally and infernally burns in a large pit in the center of the huge room. There's a monstrous metal cone above it that pipes every last stitch of smoke up and out to some unseen soot scrubber, because that level of unauthorized black ash would bring a brigade of Protection agents down on Shannon if it were simply pumped out into the open.

After the little fire stoker goes back to his shadow, I look around for suspicious "bulges" in any more of the cracks and crevices of Shannon's shop, just in case he's herding more than "muttons" these days. There's one other exit that leads down—I've used it before—but I struggle to find it again. Once I finally do—tucked between a mirror and some monolith-looking black rock—I take careful note of it. If it gets too hot, that's where I'm headed.

Never walk into a room that you don't know how to *fight* your way out of. Colonel-ism number. . . I stopped count somewhere in the teens, but I can almost hear his voice on the important ones. Though he had another "F" word he liked to use for the corollary to that ism. It involved relationships and women and—*Focus!*

My Shandian mind shoves me back to the present moment and the task in front of me. I reach up and touch my glasses, making sure they are secure in case my "mind" feels something I don't.

Along one complete wall is nothing but books. Brown bound texts in every language I learned at seminary . . . and some that I probably never will. Most of them are familiar to me, even the ones written in angelic script. The ones I don't recognize look like they would turn to dust as soon as someone pulled them from their perch.

From what I do remember, despite his demeanor, Shannon is a connoisseur of all things old and dark . . . and deadly. And that is actually *exactly* why I am here.

When he's almost to his big chair on the other side of the fire pit, a little pot-bellied pig—mottled a deep brown and grunting and snorting as it goes—trots its way by me and follows Shannon right behind his heels.

Shannon reaches down and grabs the little swine by the back of its neck and it barely squeals as he lifts it up. And I never noticed before. . . *Three fingers!* I think. More accurately, my Shandian mind tells me it's important. Trusting its voice is something that we were all taught to do.

Shannon plops into a big red leather chair, and as big as he is, the back of the chair arcs above his head like the retracted roof of a stadium. He tucks the little pig into his lap. I can barely tell which potbelly is which. And he starts to scratch between the little pig's ears . . . just like I used to do with Max. I can't afford those thoughts right now.

I sit in a chair that's obviously reserved for guests—half the size and none of the red of his—and I pull out my flask. Whether it's his hospitality, the heat of the fire, or the harsh and heavenly events of my day . . . I'm craving a drink.

"Right then," he says, stroking his pig and gazing into the fire, "let's strike me match first."

I unscrew the top of my flask. I have no idea what he's offering. I don't care.

"This here sweetness. . ." he says, but then turns up his nose and covers his pig's snout. "Christ on a crutch, Benito, me pig's piss smells better than that State swill you're greasing your guts with." He motions to the shadows. "Go ahead, flame up his flask before she vomits in me hand."

The same minion comes from the shadows again. This time he's got a big leather and jewel-covered bottle that looks like a genie used to live in it. And before I can ask or protest, my flask is full of . . . I have no idea what. I thank the young fellow as he flutters over and fills up a huge chalice sitting on the wood stump of an end table next to Shannon's chair. I smile, wondering if the table will soon become firewood. The dark little servant keeps pouring, only stopping when it looks like the liquid might spill over the sides of Shannon's cup. Then he heads back to wherever he hides.

Shannon lets his little potbelly loose, and the pig wiggles its way to the arm of his chair, and then it sucks in some of the swill from his chalice. "There ya go, ya little pizzer," he says to it. Then he looks at me. "What are you waiting on?" he asks.

I hesitate, watching the little pig drink.

Shannon looks at his pig and then back at me. "Don't worry, I save the best of it for me friends and me pig." And he nudges the little pig just enough, then wraps his huge, three-fingered hand around the stem of the chalice and without stopping or pausing for air, he guzzles the entire remainder down in one long, loud, gulping drink. Then he slams the cup down on the stump and wipes what little escaped to his mustache with his hand. He lets the little potbelly lick his palm dry. "Ahh, me mother in Hell's milk right there, it is."

I'm still hesitating, but not for the reasons he thinks. It's been an eternity since I've been down to the Mike, and the vernacular and vice and vanity of it all have just got me. . . I never realized it until I came back, but I . . . I missed it like I miss my parents and Max.

Every day is a cause for celebration at the Mike, because these people know better than anyone—no matter what nightmare you have, if you can wake up from it the next day, it's better than the sweet delusion of the dream that you can't.

Shannon gets a guilty look on his face. "Life and Lucifer's lusting loins," he says. He looks at his huge cup. "Me manners in this place have gone to angelshit—a toast then."

I smile. Shannon's toasts are sonnets of legend, and I already told you about his sincerity:

To Hell's balls and Heaven's ass
To darker things than me mustache
The Eternities to come and them what's past
To your grandmothers gums on me bonny's ass

To whores what's slow and them that's fast
To grease me guts I tip me glass
To forgotten friends . . . home at last.

By the time he's finished, I almost have a tear in my eye, and Shannon's little shadow-flitter has refilled his cup to overflowing as well this time. It doesn't seem to bother Shannon, and my friend downs the entire bursting dam of it in another long, greedy guzzle.

I marvel at him—a Protection MARR assault vehicle can't suck petro that fast. I take a quick swig from my flask, tasting it first, and . . . he's right, I'll never be able to go back to the State's swill after this. And I take another drink . . . to be polite, of course.

He smiles a big bear-lipped grin at me. "How 'bout *that* then?" he says.

"Delicious," I say to him, because it is. "Sinful . . . but delicious."

He laughs—nothing but genuine delight. "He didn't whip the wit from ya, then," he says. "I warned him of that." And then he gets a knowing look on his face and I can sense what's coming. "And what of them other sins you been sneakin' about with?" he asks. "How's they comin'?"

"*They* are just—"

But I realize he wasn't asking, or more likely he already knows. And he looks toward the shadow that his little servant's hiding in. "Make sure Benito gets a gallon before he goes back to his godding then, will ya?" I don't think that's a question either, and I can tell Shannon's drink is starting to take effect. When he looks back at me, he seems far away. "I told Aax. . . Father D shoulda fed that to all you little faithful fucks—cured you off cunt for sure, that would. Blasted better than his belt, the sadistic sack." He pauses for a moment and frowns. Then he says, "Why do ya think she'd be wanting all you monkeys to be celibate then? Never understood that one. Then they go and surround ya with all them Sisters?" He motions his cup toward the blazing fire in front us both. "Your soul in the light of Heaven, brother. Your will be wickeder than mine."

Considering how Father . . . how his friend's soul got to Heaven . . . or Hell, Shannon's always been remarkably hospitable to me.

— XXXV —

LUCIFER HAD SUCCEEDED in not only convincing the ten conspirators that his cause was just, but that the calamity that would befall all the eternities was inevitable if they did not undertake it. Neither Heaven nor Hell would have to fall as part of his deception, but left to Life they both surely would. He had the lies and he had the spies. There was but one tithe left to collect.

Uzza took no convincing at all and lopped his littlest one off without thought or hesitation. Then he dipped the little black-bleeding stump into the fiery lake and it cauterized to a sizzling scab.

Aax took barely more to convince, but a little coin went a long way and his joined Uzza's in Lucifer's pouch.

"There then," Lucifer said, "no feather has burst into flames nor angel died in front of eyes." He looked to each of the remaining eight. Rsoni would be the most difficult.

Aax and Uzza grabbed Dorak by his wings and held him down to the ground amidst screeching and curses that would make hellhounds humble and whores blush.

Uzza said nothing, just held onto the arrogant dog, Dorak, by his wing and waited.

Aax was not quite as silent. "You got another one, don't you?" he said, struggling to hold onto Dorak, turned hellhound snarling beast in front of them all.

Dorak's fangs gnashed and his claws scratched the rock floor of the pit, and he barked viciously, but Aax and Uzza held him firm. The trouble was that it took both their hands to make sure that the dog didn't bite them, so someone else would have to do the dirty work.

"Raum," Aax shouted at the godling, "lend us wing and will. We struggle to bring hound to heel. This dog's vanity is about to get the best of us both." He yelled down at the beast, "Stuff a bone in angry jaws, heathenous hound, or I'll break your beak with my fist."

Raum walked over to the writhing trio of treacherous snakes from Lucifer's own burning garden. He looked down at Dorak, flailing and wailing on the ground. He squatted down next to him. "Dogs," he said calmly, through spitting barks and snarls, "Sooner than later, they *must* be put down." And he plucked out one of his ballistic feathers, and then he blew on it and heated the tip up to a white hot glow—it would seal off the wound. And then he pinned down Dorak's paw and took by force what Aax and Uzza had taken from themselves.

Dorak howled in agony and Uzza and Aax let go of him. When they did, he raced at Raum, snarling and snapping at the air as he did. He leapt through the air at Raum's back.

Raum's hand shot behind him and grabbed the filthy beast by the neck, and Dorak yelped and yiped and whimpered.

"Do not think me an easy meal, mutt," said Raum, "for I have smote a hundred thousand of your ilk and lived to pick my teeth with your bones. I only spare demon angel's putrid pelt now to save eternity from itself. When task is accomplished, if your fangs and feathers still thirst for it, I shall give your hearts cause to rejoice"—and he threw Dorak to the ground—"as they taste spilled blood. Proceed wisely from here, hound. I give warning but once."

Dorak whimpered and then howled on the ground. And he barked and he snarled and snapped, but he did not rush to attack Raum again.

"Very well, dog," Raum said, "we are of one mind." He held out his hand, revealing Dorak's lost appendage. "I shall hold this until the end, so you will know where to fetch favored finger."

Zarzi cringed and tried not to cry out. Lilith and Lucifia held her wings as Raum heated up one of his feathers.

"Wait!" Zarzi shouted. "Ye shall not make any cuttings in your flesh . . . nor print or tattoo any marks upon you. This is the Word."

"They are *her* words!" shouted Lucifer. "Rantings of mad mother of misery. No more valuable than the empty air they travel through." He could smell the lust for blood building inside him, and seeing the severed flesh and hearing the screams reminded him that Hell had hearts to sorrow and souls to steal. They needed to hurry. He looked at Raum, busy doing the bidding of his *new* master. "Get to task then, she'll not escape fate."

"Tiny toe!" shouted Zarzi.

And everyone beside the lake paused. A toe. . . None had even given thought to location. A token of faith was required—tithe that they could each agree upon to seal the dastardly deal. But none had questioned Lucifer's decree of location as mere suggestion. And now that it had been . . . questioned, Dorak howled loudly, "Take it from her, now! I have given and so will she. And so shall you all or I shall —"

"You shall what?" said Raum, patting his waist feathers.

"Please," said Zarzi, "a token of toe to task of deception. Lucifer, you speak of sedition in secrecy. She shall never give regard to toe over digit. It is simply more prudent position."

Raum lived in the past, where females were fairer and males more ferocious, but he tended matters with prudence as well. He pondered Zarzi's words. Clearly they were desperate, and yet at the same time they were remarkably practical.

Lucifer could see that Raum was mulling the answer. It would be best if the decision came from one of Zarzi's own kind. There would be no resentment and it would also mean that she and Raum would be much more entwined with him. For once they had all broken her covenants, Life would never take them back into the angry folds of her wings. "What say you, Raum?" he asked. "Shall it be digit . . . or dactyl?"

Raum thought for only a moment before he spoke. "Man-monkeys," he said, "are remarkably vain and arrogant creatures, and physical attractiveness will most surely be challenge for some"—he turned and looked at Dorak for a second—"and some of us shall slither among them . . . more easily than others. Yet in mating pursuits their females are only slightly more vain than the males, however fact still holds"—he reached back and ran his hand down the length of his long jet black ponytail—he knew he would have to cut it off as well—"I have yet to observe Man-monkey woo wayward waif who did not harbor heat for tall tales of war wounds. In this regard . . . Lilith, Lucifia, and Zarzi . . . shall turn toe and the rest shall sacrifice digit."

Shax spoke out loud this time, addressing both friend and previous foe. "It's a right fine decision, godling," he said. "It be no dog dance to wrastle me from me piglets." He looked at the rest of the strong ones. "Not worried about me angel-ass either." And he held up the first two fingers and the last on his left hand. "The sun on me days of skewerin' two sodomite Sisters at once have . . . sadly set, they have."

Aax chuckled at his friend. "Eh, you've gone soft in the sack, my friend. Soft indeed."

Lucifia—still lightly holding one of Zarzi's wings—chuckled at Shax and Aax—the fierce and fiercer of her feathered friends in Hell. "Terrible twosome," she said, and then she smiled at them. "I prefer it the other way around." Then she looked down at Zarzi. "Can we take to task then? Your whining has melted my mood for mischief."

"Plump pigs in Purgatory," said Shax said to his partner in Purgatory, "propositioned us, I think she just has."

Dorak growled at the pair.

"Quiet down then, dog," Shax said to him. Then he looked at Lucifia.

"It may not be wise," said Aax. "Think of the smell, brother."

Shax smiled an evil and wily grin at Lucifia. Then he said, "Be it proposi—"

Zarzi's screech broke their exchange and Lucifia took a wild wing to the face and Lilith flung backward as Zarzi's wings flapped wildly. And Raum flapped backward to get out of her way.

When Zarzi stopped shaking her wings, she looked at all of them with the wild eyes of a cornered cougar, and she snarled and roared and then spoke harshly, "I am Zarzi, daughter of Zarena, and I will stand with you blaspheming brethren for fauna and fate of eternities. And I have *given* limb, and if trumpet come I shall heed its warning— stand with you until the sword takes my life. Yet if you. . . If your hand fail free will where it is so clear that your mouths do not, your blood shall be on your own head . . . at the tip of my wing." If smoke could have billowed from her ears, Zarzi's speech would not have carried more warning.

Surprisingly before, yet a little less so after her outburst and warning, Zarzi pinned first Lilith's and then Lucifia's toe to the hard rocky ground and whipped her wing across their bases with the precision and steadiness of a surgeon. And barely a droplet of blood escaped, as their wounds healed from the heat of the speed.

Raum took his own without incident or impishness, giving more credence to his resolve than his words had.

As soon as he did, Rsoni walked to his side, looked at Raum's detached digit, and then he said, "You harbor no heart beneath breast to return to Life then?" His own two hearts had traded opinion with each other during the entire gathering.

Raum tucked his own digit into his waistfeathers with Dorak's. Then he put his sloth-toed hand on Rsoni's golden shoulder and patted him. "She has proven undeserving of heart, brother," he said. Then he whispered, for it was clear that Rsoni was hiding his own demons in plain view of five of Hell's, "And what of your own hearts? I know that you have visited the Man-monkeys many times. And I also know that you harbor great affection for some. Your silence and stealth may not betray your feelings to *them*, brother"—he glanced at all the others, in varying stages of either mourning loss of limb or preparing to do the same—"but I am neither fledgling nor fawn—you *are* going with us. Maybe not for reasons of treason, but you are going . . . because that is where she is."

"I've a particular attachment to me parts," said Shax. Unable to take his own, he simply stared at it as if it had already gone missing.

He wiggled his pinky finger a little. "I . . . I do lots of living with this one, I do. I mean, how am I gonna reach me bogies? None of me other ones fit in me nostrils." He turned his hand over and back, surveying every line on his little finger.

Uzza chuckled a little, but caught himself. Then he looked at Lucifer, busy paying no attention to him at all, satisfied that everything was going according to his plot.

Over the grumbling of Dorak, Lucifia walked over and stood in front of the huge archangel demon, Shax. She leaned into him and then twisted the tip of his mustache between her fingers. "So angel is correct then?" she said.

Shax looked down at her. "About what, love?"

She reached down and gave Shax a preview. "Maybe you are getting soft in the sack."

"Me member?" said Shax. "Don't you worry none about that, love. Me snake takes care of himself, he does." He looked back at his hand. "But me little finger. . . Well, he relies on me to keep him safe, ya see. He's kinda attached to me hand, he is. And his three partners in"— he wiggled all his fingers at Lucifia—"pleasure."

Lucifia stared up into Shax's eyes and stroked the feathers below his waist as his snake stirred beneath them at her touch. "I can perform task on angel's behalf," she said. "It will be painless to point of shadow. You may even enjoy it."

Shax chuckled. "Eh, ya miserable minx," he said. "I'm just kneading ya knickers." And he held his little finger in front of Lucifia's face. "Go ahead then, bite it off for me, love. No sense wasting a perfectly good feather on it." He looked over at his partner, Aax. "Pitch me that muffin-topped grog bottle of yours then, will ya?"

Aax pulled a large leather, jewel-covered, fat-bottomed brown bottle from his waist, and then he threw it through the air at Shax.

Lucifia growled and Shax winced. And by the time Shax caught the bottle with all the fingers of his good hand, the little finger on his other one was gone. "Whew!" he shouted. "That'll wake you up in the morning, won't it then." And he hastily bit the cork off the top of the bottle, splashed a godly amount of it on his severed digit's bleeding little stump, and then he spit out the top and guzzled the remainder of the liquor in one long pull.

And Lucifia lowered her head—a trickle of blood escaped her lips —and she slowly spit Shax's little finger into her hand. "Eyes see what heart feels," she said. "The tiniest of torment." Her tongue swirled out and lapped up the blood around the edges of her mouth. "Terrible angel's blood tastes . . . sweeter than his deeds."

Shax smiled at her. "That's me molasses," he said. "Me snake's the bitter one. Nothing to worry about there—after that, ya won't be meetin' face to pretty little face, will ya then."

Lucifia smiled and taunted him a little. Smirking and smothering Shax with her dirtiest of looks. "It's a small matter," she said, "as angel's back is prettier still." She turned and headed back toward Dorak, busy fuming at the entire incident, but whipped enough to be content to growl.

"Blazing assholes, Aax," Shax said, "his descendants are dirtier than him, they are." He turned back and looked at Lucifia. "Come on then, me finger, if you don't mind."

"Aw," she said, "can I not keep it as precious memory until angel's eyes gaze upon my back?"

Shax raised his eyebrows. "No you may not," he said slowly. He shook his head and smiled at her. "Keep you right close, I'll hafta. Murderin' mistress, you are."

Lucifia tossed Shax's finger to him, and then blew him a kiss. "Your hand misses angel's teeth all ready."

Rsoni took his own finger with only a slight glance up at Raum before he sliced one of his flight feathers cleanly through the base of his digit, and then he seared and burned the little stump until it smoked from charred flesh.

Shortly thereafter, it took three of them to hold down Zepar. But Rsoni finally separated him from a little tiny sliver of his arrogance and vanity. The screaming spoke to them of a soldier who would crack in the crucifix of combat.

"Success!" Lucifer said at the last of it. "Conspiracy is sealed in secrecy and separation of sin from sinner." He turned and walked toward the portal to the dungeons above. "I had small doubt"—he stopped and turned back to face them—"I never hoped to believe that each would agree. And I recount that some displayed rather differently than I expected. However, secret is sealed and here angels stand— powerful allies in purpose, solidified with token and cloaked as enemies in name alone." He turned back toward the portal and walked. "I shall inform you of our next meet—"

"Not all," said Rsoni.

Lucifer stopped, turned around again, and then he glanced at the ten of them, counting and cataloguing digits and dactyls in his head. "And the lovely ladies," he said. "Yes, a trust of ten. Splendid."

Uzza's deep voice made Lucifer pause. "You lose count," he said.

"Eleven," said Zarzi. Even she was steeled to the fact that it had to be done.

Lucifer stared back at them. Stoic and steady faces to a single angel stared back. "Utipa knows nothing of plot," he said. "I made certain of this. Angels needn't concern themselves with her."

Even Dorak—dog that he was—growled. Yet it was easier for a hound to growl, surrounded by the safety of his own pack.

"Oh, Grandfather," Lucifia said to him, almost giddy at the prospect of it, "how . . . embarrassing. Can you not smell it?"

Lucifer could smell . . . something on them. Yet his own arrogance would not fathom to let the truth of the scent through.

All ten conspirators took a few steps toward the great devil. They formed a line in front of him and they all stiffened.

Zepar outright laughed. "Can you believe it?" he asked no one in particular, too excited to do battle with the legendary Lucifer. Surrounded by nine other seriously powerful allies, it was easy to find courage. "It shall be . . . historic."

Shax leaned out from the line and took a look back at the rest of them, including his friend, who he thought for sure would never agree to such a thing. But he could see that even Aax was resolute in the decision. "Oh, Christ's cock," he said, "it'll ruin him, it will. How's he gonna. . .? It's inhumane, it is."

"Then it is fitting," said Raum, "that no humans shall witness it."

And then Lucifer did smell it. The vicious scent of bloodlust and hatred . . . directed at him. "Vicious intent?" he said. "You'll not—I am Lucifer, not a paper angel to clip and cut finger with feather." And flames started to rise from the tips of Lucifer's wings.

But they were all ready for that. And the ten of them raced and flew at him, snarling and growling, and biting and kicking. And armored feathers pushed out and talons jutted, and they pinned Lucifer to the ground beside the lake. The entire vicious swarm of them rolled with him, and through wildly flapping wings and lion roars and terrible talons that drew blood from whatever they touched, none faltered.

Even Zepar, drunk on the excitement and the smell of the freshly spilled blood from one of the most notorious and nasty angels in Heaven or Hell, stood firm and did his part to secure Lucifer's limbs from lashing.

When the blood and the lust cleared, Lucifer was face down next to the fiery lake, and there was a conspirator clawing and clinging desperately to each one of his six limbs—his legs, arms, and wings lie pinned. Lilith held a firm grasp on the whipping and wagging, angry pointed tip of the seventh.

"A treacherous snake," said Lilith, struggling to hold Lucifer's last limb, "has but two heads—a venomous and vile strike and bite for each. This I know. Of this I have seen and felt sting and tasted bittersweet poison of love's venom as it devoured my hearts." She raised one of her wings high above her head and stretched it to a taut steel blade.

Lucifer screamed out and growled like a rabid animal and his voice roared. "Whosoever violates me in this manner—"

"Hurry it up then!" Shax shouted. He could feel himself losing his grip. "I won't be holding his hate if he gets much hotter!"

"Hold!" Rsoni yelled at them all. "You will hold fast or I will smite you beside him."

Lucifer seemed to lose the tiniest bit of fight.

"You desire a throne?" Raum shouted, wrestling with the talons on one of Lucifer's feet. "I will follow you to purpose's end. And for that, you shall share fate and finger with me. For if Life is wicked, let her perish and I'll not mourn or shed tear, but if she indeed be righteous, then God will repay each of us according to what they have done. And she will know us by the mark that we carry, and she will know our deeds and we will know her wrath."

And at those words, Lucifer roared so loudly as to almost cause them all to lose their grip on his limbs.

"Do it!" Zarzi yelled. "For the eternal love of the Garden, cut it off!"

Lilith wasn't finished airing out her own anger. The Garden had been harsh to her, and she knew it was this snake's fault. "For the injurious poison of your two-headed snake"—she swept her wing down like a pendulum, swiftly slicing the tips of her flight feathers through the base of Lucifer's long red tail—"need not add insult with whip!"

— XXXVI —

BARBARA CAME BACK down the student dormitory hall with the keys to my cell jingling slightly in her hand. Then she sprang me free with a few clicks and clanks of the lock, and then we were off down the dark rock-walled corridor. It was more tunnel than any hallway I had been in. And the cold from the damp drizzle outside made our breath puff steam like smoke.

Barbara held the skirt of her habit up with one hand and dragged me along behind her with the other.

Her hand felt good in mine and I stumbled along behind her, smiling and giggling. "Where we going, Sister?"

"Oh, don't even start," Barbara said. "You know I'm not no—just don't." She stopped for a second and we listened through the darkness to the languishing cries of . . . hundreds. "Be quiet."

"Which one?" I asked

"Shh," she whispered. "Any of these idiots see us and they'll burn us for breakfast."

I giggled. "I'm confused," I said. "You want me to *be* quiet, *don't* be quiet? Which one is it?"

"You are so—just shut up," she said. "That J's gonna wear off and you won't be so stupid happy."

I smiled at her back. "What is J?" I said, "I *like* it."

She muttered to herself, "I don't know which one's worse—you whining or giggling like a idiot."

When Barbara seemed satisfied we could keep going, she jerked my arm and she half ran, half tiptoed down the hall. I stumbled along behind her. When we got to the end of the corridor, Barbara stopped us by a huge mirror mounted on the wall. The students—all of us were supposed to use it every morning before we went out to formation. Our seminary sweats were tucked, zipped, and the hood strings were even and pulled just right—God liked tidiness.

"Why do you always call me. . .?" I glanced in the mirror, it was a habit by then. "Oh my God!" I said, louder than Barbara wanted, because she squeezed my hand and jerked at me.

I was . . . older . . . than I should have been, by two or three years at least. I rubbed my face, making sure it was me. "What happened . . . to my face?"

Barbara turned around and looked at me.

I barely noticed her because I was staring at my reflection. My face was thinner, my hair was thicker and my eyes. . . Glasses or not, my eyes were sunk in deeper than I remembered. And I was taller, but skinnier than when I got to Saint Samuels. "What did they. . .?" I turned and started to ask Barbara, but when I saw her, I knew I wasn't dreaming.

Barbara's face was older like mine, but her cheeks had filled to high plump pillows, and I knew it was a mortal sin if there ever was one, and I tried not to. . . I think I tried, but I couldn't stop looking at them. "What are those?" I blurted.

Barbara dropped my hand, and put both of hers on her hips. "Now ain't you just a genius," she said. "No wonder they beat on you so much."

"I'm sorry, I'm sorry," I said, but I kept staring. "Where did they come from? You never had—can I see them?"

"Lord Almighty Jesus, no," she whisper-shouted at me, "you can't!" She turned around and looked down the hall at some unseen threat. "You sure can't handle your Judgment, can you? We're gonna have to find something else for you to—" Barbara went dead silent when she heard the voice.

"Who did she go see?" the voice asked another. "Miserable little. . . I'll teach her myself!"

Barbara's entire body went rigid, anticipating the answer.

"I followed her this far," the second voice replied.

I recognized both of them—the second voice was one of the PI's— and even through the giddy goodness of what Barbara kept calling Judgment, I froze in fear. Because the first voice . . . was Father Dominic.

The second voice answered him, "I dared not follow, she would have discovered me."

"Have no fear, brother," Father D said. That's who was coming down the hall! "I have a fair idea who it was. Have they come out yet?"

"I . . . I don't think so," the second voice said. "She has to. . . They have to be right around the corner."

We were even closer than the PI knew. Barbara shoved us both up against the side of the corridor—as flat as we could stand on the darkest shadowed side of the barely lit tunnel. The dark corridor that would soon be our tomb. Because whatever memory I had lost between being barely ten years old when they burned me, and seeing myself in the mirror, and then Barbara's breasts bumping up beneath her habit, both of us barely minted teenagers. . . Leaving your cell at Saint Samuels, let alone escaping the entire compound with one of its Sisters, would surely be worthy of much more than fire.

Fear, adrenaline and endorphins have a way of cutting through any kind of sensation smothering that the human body can be subjected to. I had no idea how I knew that, but a little voice in the back of my mind woke up that very day—a guardian arose inside me that instant in that dark hallway—and it screamed the warning at my mind, *Don't cry out!*

Because whatever painkiller Barbara injected me with was busy trickling its usefulness out of my system like the cold Seattle mist dripped its way down the downspouts from the roof over our heads. And a burning sensation began creeping its way from the nerves in my neck, slowly gathering agony and anger and sending it to the ganglia along my spine, like a slithering liquid lava inferno of acid burning into my back.

I mashed my chest and the side of my face as hard as I could into the wall next to the mirror, trying to flatten out enough that Father D would not detect me in the dark. I could tell that Barbara was doing the same thing with her back. And I squeezed three times into her hand on mine—a silent "I love you." If this was the last time I saw her —felt her beautiful soft touch—I wanted her to know. . . No, I wanted her hand to *feel* that I did love her if nothing more than for her companionship during my abandonment at Saint Samuels.

On the third squeeze, a spike of lightning shot through my spine and I bit into my lip and I could feel the blood gush—copper taste and hot liquid oozed into my mouth, but I didn't cry out.

I must have clamped down too hard on Barbara's hand, because on the third squeeze, she let out a muffled chirp . . . and then the entire tunnel went completely still. No more voices wailed from the students' cells, no more footsteps padded their way toward us from up the hall, and no more giggles escaped from an idiot who had just sealed the fate of two long-lost souls.

The corridor and the dark of the night plunged into nothingness. And time lost all meaning as Father D and the PI stood motionless, barely twenty feet away.

The only thing I moved was my eyes, rotating them in their sunk-in sockets just enough that I could see the outlines of the PI and Father D in the darkness. It was like being trapped in a cave with a great bear that your soul hoped would not rush across the tiny distance that separated you to sink its jaws into you as you screamed in futility to be set free. All the while your mind knowing and yelling at you that that was exactly what was about to happen.

Behind us was the door to my cell and the rock wall dead end of the terrible tunnel, barely ten feet beyond it. And in front of us was the hard and hateful bear that was Father D's proven compassion.

The steady steel in Barbara's nerves must have run out before the burning acid in mine turned my own will to jelly, because the silence screamed to a slamming halt when she yelled, "*Run!*"

— XXXVII —

I STARE INTO the fire in the middle of Shannon's shop. After all I went through with it at seminary, you would think that fire would scare the faith right out of me. But I chuckle at the flames, twisting up from the bottom of the pit, lapping at the air above them like big orange and red snakes. I look at my flask. "It's a good grog, Shannon," I say. And suddenly the heat from the fire isn't bothering me as much, certainly less than when I walked inside. And everything about my day feels . . . better.

"Yes, she is at that, isn't she," he says. "Hotter than the underside of me Lucinda's habit, it is."

And my Shandian mind starts to connect the dots of the day. "You mean that lovely lady up the alley?"

"She's lovely all right," Shannon says. "Ain't no lady though"—he laughs a bit—"if ya know what I'm—" He stops himself. "I . . . I apologize, friend," he says. "It's insensitive of me, it is. It's just that . . . me Lucinda is the sole sinner I ever considered more than me pigs."

And I think that's more honesty than Shannon knows what to do with, because he calls for more grog and his minion quickly delivers. Then Shannon holds up his freshly filled cup at me as he says, "To them ladies what ain't, eh Benito."

I have no qualms drinking to that, so I do.

Shannon marks and minds time . . . differently than any man I've ever known. And of all the angels I've met in my sleep—dark, light, demon dream creature—he's the most mindful of the proper place and time for all things in his world . . . or mine. So I don't rush him as we get reacquainted. It wouldn't do any good anyway—Shannon's eternity runs on its own schedule.

But he gets down to business soon enough, and when I tell him about the events of my day. . . Well, *now* . . . business is all he's got time for.

"That holier than thou benevolent bloody bastard!" Shannon shouts. "He's sent him early, he has!" He looks at his bank of clocks. "I ain't had time—you're not proper prepared." He rubs his mustache, and then stares back at the fire. "Rollin' heads already, is he?" He looks up at me. "He's still dead then . . . your angel?"

"Well," I say, "he was certainly dead when I left this morning. I don't think he's going anywhere with his guts—"

"This morning!" Shannon shouts.

I just shrug and raise up my eyebrows and hands in apology.

Because when Shannon does speed up, he shifts through life's gears pretty quickly. "Did ya get a gander at the geese behind the glass?" he asks.

"They never revealed themselves."

"Cut ya loose, did they?" he mutters back at the fire. "Crooked cunts. That one's still running his big .60 caliber, I'd wager. Overcompensating ogre that he is. He'll be coming for *your* cock with his little arrogant assassin in tow, he will. Unless we beat him to his own bullet."

My Shandian mind tells me something isn't right—I can feel it—and it's only a few seconds before Shannon senses it too. It's strange to me, because that's not normally how the order of our perceptions play out.

Shannon stands up, walks quickly between two huge wooden desks, shoving them like cardboard boxes to make room for his girth, and then he rummages around on top of a big tall wooden cabinet behind them. When his hand comes back down, it's grasping the blade end of some sort of ancient . . . axe. "You'll be needing this then," he says.

"What, may I ask . . . is that?"

"Christ's cross, Benito," Shannon says, "you've manhandled your member so much it's made your memory muzzy." And then he flips the weapon up and catches it by the handle. Then he spins the handle so fast in his hand that the blades on the other end blur to a see-through circle. He squeezes hard on the handle—stops the spin—and then he swings it in a figure eight in front of him like a majorette in a parade. I can't even imagine where . . . or *how* he learned to do that. He looks at me and grins. "This . . . be an axe, mate. Not no ordinary head hacker neither."

Shannon has a taste for otherworldly fantasy and a flair that makes *him* sound mental sometimes. Believe me, I've heard the rants from the patients at the sanatorium. "I don't think that's going to help, old friend," I say. "Bullets and batons and. . . Protection is a little better armed than that. How's that going to save me?"

"Don't you remember?" he says, bewildered when my face confirms that I don't have any idea what he's talking about. "Well"—he spins the blade again to satisfy himself that he can—"this here masher ain't meant for you, me *old* friend. Your mashin' has obviously ruined your recollection right along with your vision, because this here little sinner is the only thing that *did* save you."

— XXXVIII —

WHEN THE TEN, angel conspirators let Lucifer loose, he turned to a raging wraith, roaring and growling and spitting and screaming at them. And then he spun like a dog biting at its tail, only he wasn't biting, he was yelping and wailing at where it used to be.

And the bloody stump at the bottom of Lucifer's spine spurted the dark blood molasses—bittersweet sap nectar of the trees in Eden's Garden—sugared goodness from his right heart, turned malignant and mean. The black ooze boiled and burned and baked over until all that was left of his tail was a charred black hunk of trunk where his once tree-tall tail used to be.

When Lucifer was finished lamenting his loss, he turned to the ten of them. His ice-blue eyes had turned raging-fire red, and his wings stretched wide and caught fire and shot orange flames into the air above him and black sooty smoke rolled from the tops of them, and he roared, "Give tail to me!" he yelled at them. "And then I shall annihilate you all."

Though to a single angel, they each knew better. An eternity's Protector was the only one with such powers. And that was the exact reason that Lucifer still needed their help. For even though the Devil could put his own parts and pieces back together, melting and mending once-severed flesh, only a Protector—only God's power—could destroy an angel for all the eternities to come.

The ten of them had steeled themselves—melded their own hearts and purposes together in attacking and taking Lucifer's second favorite appendage. He would not be allowed to put himself above or beyond any of them in their crusade against Life.

Lilith held up Lucifer's limp tail and smirked at him. And the rest of the ten drew closer to her.

"You dare detach demon from treasured tail?" Lucifer screeched. "Go no further in this mutiny, lest your actions become mind for murder!"

They would not be persuaded with threats nor the throes of a former follower in Heaven. Their journey to remove one greedy and vain tick-like god, sucking the blood and benevolence from the eternity for her own purposes and pleasure . . . would not take its first steps with the childlike fitful threats of a burning desire to rule from another. The great devil-dog, Lucifer, at the hands of his own conspiracy and deception, would have to finally learn to heel.

Rsoni spoke . . . to them all. "If righteousness and justice are to be the new foundation of the desires of thy throne," he said to Lucifer, "your kingdom shall not start in venom. We shall all see truth in loving kindness as its birth . . . and your vanity shall vanish before thy face."

"Noooo!" Lucifer shouted, because he knew what they were about to do.

Lilith dropped the tail at her feet—in front of five horrible hounds of Hell and five more benevolent brothers and sisters of Heaven. And the entire blended and blind raging pack of wild animals, turned ravenous and revenge-filled ravens, cawing and clawing and biting and baying, and screeching and screaming like mighty eagles as they tore and ripped and clawed and cut to pieces the entire length of Lucifer's once treacherous tail. They ate like ravens raging for raw meat.

And Lucifer fell to his knees, knowing nothing would remain after the greedy guts of the monsters he had just created were finished devouring his beautiful tail. Then his tail would become the shit and stench of vengeance and revenge rained down on creation from its own creator's fallen angels.

And as his hellish and heavenly hounds ate, Lucifer's scowl slowly turned to a squinting and seditious smile, and then he bared talon and fang and flew into the center of the pack . . . to join them in feasting on his own plot's pointed tail.

— XXXIX —

AS SOON AS Barbara yelled "Run," something deep inside my mind took complete control of my body. I ran straight at the Priest Instructor next to Father Dominic—it was unsettling, because as far as I remembered, I had never hit another human being in anger before—and I smashed his nose with the palm of my right hand and I heard a loud "crunch" and the PI screamed out. Then I bent my arm and smashed my elbow into the side of his neck and he went down coughing and I . . . I could see!

I don't mean see in the dark with my glasses, because to tell you the truth I think my glasses fell off, but my mind could see everything in that horrible hallway, like it was midday in July.

And I spun at Father Dominic—part of my mind yelling at me not to—and that's probably the part that slowed down the other voice in my head, telling me to strike him behind his ear. I hesitated just enough that his arm came up, deflected mine, and then it whipped back at my face and hit me so hard in the right eye that my vision exploded with light, and then my stomach took a powerful blow and the air rushed from my body like a river in spring and I fell backward.

But I rolled back over myself—surprised at the lack of burning protest from my back as I did—and I pushed up with my hands and sprang to my feet, and then I stood steady and steeled with one hand wrapped around the fist of the other. And I stared across the five feet separating Father D from me.

He smiled at me. An evil grin so unsettling that the pain crawled its way back into my spine like a spider.

I winced and shrugged a little.

"The fire betrays you, Benito," said Father D. Though this person was now no ordinary priest. "Takes from you what life cannot."

I said nothing, as terrified of the voice inside my head screaming at me to kick Father Dominic in the knee, as I was of the man in front of me.

I felt Barbara get up off the floor—she had tripped over me as I raced at the PI. I glanced at her. To my new "vision" she looked bright blue with shades of purple around the edges. And her eyes were dark red sockets. *Beautiful,* the stupid half of my mind thought.

A foot slammed into my hip and my inner voice shouted at me, *Grab it!* I did and then I spun the leg and the body attached to it twisted and spun fast, and then another leg came out of the blur of the spin and a foot glanced off my cheek and stars shot into my face again.

And then a terrible claw clamped down on my throat and I grabbed it with both hands, but it was iron and I choked and choked and then went to my knees.

"Stop it!" Barbara yelled. "You're gonna kill him! I'm sorry, I'm sorry. I shouldn't have—"

The *"SMACK"* was so loud that I—it sounded like a broken bone. "Shut your hole!" Father D roared at Barbara. "Monkey *wench!*"

And I tried to call to her, but no air could get through the crushing claw on my neck. And my inner mind—the angry assaulting one— shoved itself at the hand on my neck. My thumb rammed itself into the crease between the thumb and forefinger of the hand on my throat, and instantly the pressure was gone and I gasped for air. Sweet oxygen rushed into my burning lungs and my mind felt a brief peacefulness I could only describe as the warmth of my mother's smile. It was short-lived.

I saw a blinding red flash streak at my face and I caught the father's arm and twisted it and he groaned a little, but then another red flash hit me in the head and I spun. My inner voice was shouting orders faster than I could carry them out. *Spin with him, swing your elbow, knee him in the stomach, grab his forearm, punch behind his ear with your thumb!* My actions and reactions were not only uncharacteristically angry and aggressive for me, but they were none I'd ever watched or witnessed in someone else. I had no idea where they were coming from.

There was a brief pause—an instant of ice-cold silence. My back burned and my inner voice begged for the pain to stop, but my more rational mind yelled at it, *Focus! Pain is not real.*

But this pain was more real than anything I had ever felt. My inner voice searched for the warmth and comfort of Barbara's touch, or ointment, or syringe—anything that would help me make sense of what was happening and stop the pain from it. "Barbara!" I shouted toward where I had seen her fall.

"She's clouded your mind from your faith," Father D said. Now he was standing a few feet away, right over Barbara's limp body on the floor. "I shall kill her for that . . . or maybe I'll just feed her to the faithless fornicators at the market? That would be a just and fitting penance. I can smell that lust in her heart, anyway"—he glanced down at Barbara's body and then looked back up at me and smiled —"for you."

"What?" my inner voice asked him out loud.

Then my mind spoke to me, more calmly this time, *He speaks with a serpent's tongue. Do not let his lies distract you. He plans to sacrifice you both.*

The animal spoke in a deep and dreary voice, sounding nothing like I had ever heard from Father Dominic before. "Her loins burn for you, Benito," the animal said. My mind had ceased to consider him a man, much less a father of faith. And he looked burning-brick red. "Can't you smell her?"

An anger in my mind began to fight its way through the fire in my spine. And when my inner voice tried to speak, *Benito, he's*—

"Shut up!" my mind shouted out loud at . . . I didn't know which one of them—the animal priest or my vicious inner voice. "Get away from her!" my mind shouted again.

I was no longer in control of . . . anything. My inner voice had snapped to some raging protective youth, and an inner mind of violence had taken root next to it. They argued over what to do while the terrified little ten-year-old I *knew* I was simply watched, powerless to stop any of it.

"She *has* infected your faith," the man-animal said. The priest's deep voice dulled into my mind like a blunt blow from a hammer. I could feel the pulses of red pain pounding at my vision. "It's no matter, there is no infection on God's green earth in the Garden . . . that cannot be cured by the raging red truth of fire."

As soon as he said it, my mind and my inner voice and vision were all surrounded by blasts of bright red light and voices screamed and wailed misery at me and through me and into my ears, and I put my hands over them and tried to scream but no sound came out. The pain and the helplessness of it overtook me and I fell to the floor of the hallway and slumped to my side.

Fear and hopeless feelings clouded out everything, and I looked across the floor at Barbara and tried to reach for her with my hand. But I couldn't move toward her and I watched as she got farther and farther away, then my hand turned to a blue blur . . . and then everything went black.

ONCE SHANNON IS done impressing me with fancy acrobatics from his axe—it's clear he's no stranger to swinging it—he chops the blade straight down and buries it into the stump next to his chair with a resounding *WHACK!* He looks at it for a second before he sits down. "Right then," he says, "that problem's pooched. Get it right this time, eh? And . . . well then, there you have it." He stares back into the fire like he's waiting for an answer to come out of the flames. "You want me to give it to him this go-round, or will ya be handling the bulk of it your own self again? . . . Though . . . considering how much knocking about you took on that last. . . Eh, no matter—it's settled. Better hand it over me own self. Try not to bathe your benevolent britches in shit this time, okay. Put up a little bit of a struggle. Give him an angel-ass or two. At least get me wager money back. Just remember, me mate's no cherry-chokin' cherub, he ain't. He'll eat your eyes out if he gets into trouble with ya—seen it meself." He chuckles at the fire again. "Taught it to me, he did."

By the time Shannon's done lecturing at the flames in his pit, I wonder if it's me he's warning. My eyes are a little wider than I would like them when he looks up. "Shannon," I say, "who's getting the axe?"

Shannon ignores my question and asks one of his own. "Leave him a little dignity, will ya? She's a right mean bitch, that one. Persuasive as all creation, she is. And he's still me brother—bloody hellhounds, we were." He flashes me a hesitant smile. "But what's boiled is buggered, so you and me's square, we are. You'll do what needs doing, right enough." Then he looks back into the fire, having succeeded only at confusing me more than when I walked into his shop.

The other thing that happens once Shannon turns to business is that it's hard to get him turned away from it. He's a singularly formidable force. He'll do what's right, no matter the sacrifice in souls that has to be made to do it.

My Shandian mind reminds me that I should be a little more like him, *Get the molasses.*

It is what I came here for and I silently reprimand myself for getting distracted by Shannon's wine and song. The one shining bright light is that *she's* not here to distract me with the third of that list.

"We'll get to your molasses soon enough," Shannon says. "You got a mite more murderin' to do yet, I expect.

I remember that Shannon also had a habit of finishing the sentences in my mind, whether I tried to keep him from doing it or not. But like I said, he likes to switch subjects like a dog likes dirt. Colonel-ism—

Shannon pulls the axe out of the stump like my mother used to pull a toothpick out of an almost-baked cake. The scar left in the stump would be final for a man. "He's coming, then. Mind your manners," he says to me. "He ain't warm and wonderful like me. Sour as a snake's asshole, that one. And he means to hurl you to Heaven, so his master can have at ya proper." He pauses, gets a really serious look on his face, and then he points his axe at me when he speaks, "You be real careful with her when you finally get up there, you do. About the time you get lost in them big black peepers she's got, the next thing you'll be losing is your head. Don't want to do that twice, eh," he chuckles.

Most of what Shannon has told me over the years only makes sense as hindsight after some terrible event. Though all of what he says sounds colorful and clouded in inference, he rarely uses metaphor or hyperbole to prove a point. But a warning about some witch with black eyes? My Shandian mind tells me to check my neck, and then I look at the axe in his hand. It would not be pleasant. My inner voice makes a silent note to add "severed head" to the list of ways I would not like to meet my maker.

None of this is what I came here for though, and if any of it is to make any sense at all in the end, I'll need to get back to my dead angel before it's too late to revive him. "The molasses?" I say.

Shannon stares past me at the inside of the entrance to his shop. "You can fetch me molasses when you get back," he says. Then he squints and my Shandian mind feels every muscle in his body tense and steel toward the door. "He's here."

I barely turn around before the second ware-watchman—the one with the dead eyes from the front of Shannon's shop—bursts through the door. "Raid!" he yells. "They ended Isra"—he catches his breath —"Lucinda's beat up bad!"

I assume that Isra was his pickpocketing partner, and I frown and prepare myself. Because there's not a citizen or sinner, or former seminary student for that matter, at the Mike who doesn't know what "raid" means.

Every once in a while, to assert their authority and remind everyone just who's truly in charge of things. . . As if the average citizen's grumbling stomach, starving and slaving for barely enough credits to buy bread each month, would ever let them forget. But just in case the raging, raping and remanding to a sanatorium weren't enough to sear fear into the citizens' minds, the black-clad brutes of Protection raid . . . whatever in the damnation that we've all found ourselves . . . whenever they want to. Considering how my day has gone so far, it's just my luck that today it's a Mike raid.

My Shandian mind knows that luck is not the reason—they're here for me. But if what Shannon said earlier is true—

"Beatin' me bonny?" Shannon says. I can feel his anger welling up behind me. "If I—she's done testing you then," Shannon says. "Time to pay the penance, Benito."

My Shandian mind also knows when to follow Shannon to pure business. I stare at the little dead-eyed miscreant at the door. There's a little more life behind his panting stare now. Fear and rage will do that to . . . anyone. "How long has he got?" I ask Shannon. Because my dead angel is the point of my whole visit.

"One day," he says, "that's the Word."

I look at the pendulum clocks. *Time's almost up*, I think. In two more hours, I will have failed.

— XLI —

LUCIFER DELIVERED THE news of their fates to each one of the ten of them. None could claim to be heavenly angel nor hellish demon any longer. They were mutineers—traitors in a mutual conspiracy to save eternity—nothing more saintly nor sinful than that. And no book had been written in all the eternities thus far, nor likely would any book ever be written henceforth about their contribution to the history of the Word.

In all likelihood, Lucifer had told them, none of them would be remembered at all. To rulers, average angels busy burning and beating in the benevolence of their masters' Words as part of their eternal routine did not dream nor deliberate of being . . . more. Then again, most rulers did not understand the wants and wishes of the subjects they purportedly served any more than they cared to. And that was, more often than not, very little.

The fall was the only way. Lucifer had told them that, too. For to return to the Garden as anything but a little "soul security" purgatory angel, ferrying spent souls back for Judgment, or a direct messenger from the enemy, the voice of the god Life herself. . . If a fully-fledged angel wanted to resurrect, they would have to fall from grace and go back as a filthy half Man-monkey to repeat and repent before being able to return to . . . whichever Heaven they deserved.

And though an angel could be killed by any man, beast, or more likely another angel lopping off their head with an axe, resurrection was only possible at the hands of a Protector. An eternity only ever had one of those.

Back in her throne chamber with her two executed guardian angels safely returned to their previous . . . "glory," the god of the present Eternity, Life, perched above and between her guardians. She sat high on the Throne of Judgment, the gargantuan granite chair that had adorned the Throne Chamber of the Protectors since the dawn of the first eternity.

Life knew that her former archangel companion, Lucifer, harbored hate toward her. And she knew that he desired to rule most of all. Yet in attempt after attempt to discover the details of his deception . . . she had tasted nothing but failure. Now, she would have her first report from her spy.

Utipa, the angel Life sent to spy on Lucifer in order to discover his plot, stood with her head high. Once she recovered from being re-birthed in the arena, Utipa had sought out her Golden Guardian brothers and sisters to deliver her report. Surprisingly, they had seized her upon meeting, and then flew her straight to their god's chamber room.

Now, Utipa stood, flanked on each side by the guardian angels that had fetched her from the center of the Arena of Reckoning. She steamed at their insult. Each guardian held one of Utipa's wings, anticipating one of Life's fits of fury.

Utipa lowered her head and rolled her eyes up just enough that she could see Life. She had done her Lord master's bidding, she had offered deception to the Dark Angel of Light, and she *had* discovered plot. And though its purpose was still shadowed, she was insulted at being roughly dragged to report by her own brother and sister in arms —summoned as if called to task for slight of sin.

Utipa growled and cawed lightly. "Is this how loyal angel is to be rewarded," she said, barely able to contain herself, "as deliverer of desired message?" She stared maniacally at the guardian on her right and spoke more calmly than she wanted to, "Take talon from wing, sister . . . lest you lose favored hand." Then she turned to the golden guardian on her left and spoke more harshly to him, "I will not speak *twice* of it!"

Life motioned at the two guardians with one of her wings. "Come now," she said, "do not handle Heaven-sent messenger with harsh intent. Utipa has returned bearing message of mutiny's design." Then her black orbs glowed as she looked directly into Utipa's eyes. "Have you not, fair Utipa?"

Utipa jerked her wings from the loosening talons of her two brethren, gave each of them a threatening glance, and then she addressed her ruler, "Am I to be treated as criminal," she said, "for the offense of filling Lucifer's fist with favored feather on angel's neck?"

"You were discovered?" Life screeched.

Every angel in the chamber steeled themselves for combat at the noise. It was a reaction born and built over hundreds of years of benevolent battle. Yet theirs was even more chiseled—granite guts ground to anvils from living at the center of most battles' raging starts —Life's outbursts against insolence.

The two guardians nearest Life slammed their wings behind them, and their flight feathers interlocked to form shields—blinding pain from the misery of lightning twice in one day was not a prospect either of them favored.

The two guardians by Utipa mirrored their reactions.

And Utipa, from hard-won habit of survival, followed quickly behind them, slamming her wings behind her to form the shield and the warmark of Life, the bright shining orange sun.

Life eyed them all—faithful servants of her will and word. Then she smiled at Utipa. "How is this possible?" she asked. "I trust you took every precaution upon receiving tribute of task. Indeed you *are* one of my most trusted and worthy warriors. And yet here you stand"—she motioned around the room with her hands—"delivering miserable message of deception's failure—a babe barely plucked from bosom, too soon returned to the ash of its conception. My mind does not see how this can be truth."

Utipa was indignant—to be called a failure and a liar in one breath was an unacceptable reward for her loyalty. She stared back with angry eyes at Life—threat of impending annihilation be damned. "Yet as your own Word tells us, my master, truth merely *is*."

Life smiled a wide downturned grin. Then held up her hands in mock relent. "Very well," she said, "yet let no corrupt communication proceed from mouth, save that which edifies and informs, that fair angel's voice may minister grace and goodness to mine ears. For the tongue of Man is a most wicked weapon these dark days. Let angel speak her words with caution"—she glanced at the guardians beside her and then back at Utipa—"for my mood grows weary of failure."

Every guardian in the room was keenly aware of that fact.

Utipa loosened her ballistic feathers and relaxed her shield—all five guardians did. Then she stood up and spoke proudly, "Though intent of vile devil's plot remains shrouded in darkness," she said, "I bear news of treacherous and treasonous ten who cast its shadow."

Life clapped her hands together. "Excellent!" she said. "Then I shall hear names of the same."

The Arena of Reckoning was packed to the ceiling with the fierce flesh and feathers of . . . *millions* of the faithful from Life's Heaven and faithless from Lucifer's Hell. The arena's long rows and rails of perches circled the grandstands as they twisted their way up to the retractable roof at its peak.

The perches were stuffed to overflowing with screeching and screaming, cawing and clawing, clucking and chuckling feathers and razor-sharp talons of angels thirsting for vengeance. The "standing" room only feathered flock of followers all wished to see Judgment delivered and justice administered in spilled blood. For only once in the history of the eternities that any of them could remember had an angel been cast out. All sat poised to witness the history-making event of five traitors from Heaven and five mutinous mongrels of mayhem from Hell being cast out of God's kingdom.

The retracted roof reduced the noise by but a little—the sound in the arena would have been deafening to a mere mortal. To the immortal, the cries of their flock were like a choir to their souls.

Life stood at the center of the arena in the light of her own making, smiling and wallowing in the thoughts of the misery she was about to inflict. *How dare he!* she thought. *Again?*

The traitorous angels of Life's own Heaven—Rsoni, Raum, Lilith, Zepar, and Zarzi—stood facing their God on the left, and the treacherous archangel demons from Hell—Aax, Dorak, Lucifia, Shax, and Uzza—faced the Lord of their enemies on the right. They each stood steeled and still, knowing full well the consequences for their mutinous hearts.

Lucifer stood between the two groups, smiling characteristically, not even attempting to show regret or remorse at having been discovered.

Utipa stood next to Life, smug in the knowledge that the treacherous snake who had choked her from life would now suffer a far worse fate than death.

One of the guardians who had held Utipa's wing so harshly now stood on the other side of their Protector, shoulder to shoulder with her comrade, once again prepared to save Life's life with the forfeit of theirs if they had to.

Utipa smiled at Lucifer. He would pay.

Lucifer's long lying tongue was never one to remain hiding inside his mouth very long. And by this far into an eternity, his sarcasm was legend. He held up his hands at the entire crowd and the grandstands fell silent. He knew Life would let him speak. She had to. "Because I have called and you refused to listen," he shouted up into the grandstands. "Because I have stretched out my hand and no one has heeded, because you have ignored all my counsel and would have none of my reproof, I will laugh at your calamity. I will mock when terror strikes you, like a storm and a whirlwind. And when distress and anguish come upon you—when you will call upon me to save your sorry souls —I shall *not* answer. *You* . . . you will all find nothing"—then he pointed right at Life—"save the tip of her sword!"

The arena erupted—half of the grandstands calling for Lucifer's head, and half of it calling for Life's.

Then Life held up her hands, and the arena slowly quieted to a murmur. She waited impatiently a few more seconds, for the remaining tide of timid murmur to subside. Her arms came down to her sides and she buzzed and fluttered her transparent wings, and then hovered a few feet higher than her guardians. She moaned like a great whale as she spoke, "Whosoever among you be subject to governing authorities. . . There is none among you with loyalty to laws except from God. Therefore . . . whoever resists the authorities resists what *God* has appointed, and those who resist will incur Judgment. This is the Word.

"For I am not terror to good conduct . . . but to bad I am tempest. Do you have no fear of one who is in authority? . . . If you do, then do what is good, and you will receive approval"—then lightning formed in Life's black orbs and it emanated from her hair and flashed above her head, and the thunder cracked and shook the entire arena"—*but* if you do wrong, be *afraid*, my children . . . for I shall not bear the sword Satan speaks of in vain!"

Life was not known to make idle threats. Squawking and cackling and the shiver of wings filled the arena back to a steel symphony of panic.

Life looked back at the conspirators in disgust, and then she stared at Lucifer. "Are you not a servant of your—Eden eating my eyes!" she shouted in horror. "*What* have you done with treasured tail?"

At that, the rest of Lucifer's ten slowly tucked missing talon or departed dactyl as far as they could from Life's sight—the sins of missing fingers and taken toes were sent to shadow.

Lucifer looked slowly to his left and then to his right, letting the ten of them feel the fear before paying for the fate from the sin of severing his tail. "*Some* feared," he said, looking slowly back and up at Life, "that I lacked resolve in leading revolution's rage against you. It was felt"—he glanced to his conspirators again—"that wicked whip would serve better . . . as tempting treat for greedy angels' gums and guts."

A gale of gasps blew through the grandstands. Such a thing. . . Screeches and screams of disgust and damnation swept down from every penitent pigeon's perch.

"You shall not cut your flesh!" Life shouted. She looked at Rsoni. Then she pointed at Lucifer. "From this liar I expect assault and egregious action against own flesh, but your golden wings and feathers are. . .? It is forbidden! You know this!"

Rsoni attempted to answer, "For treacherous action I will gladly accept—"

"Silence!" Life shouted. "In an eternity I have never"—her eyes boiled and burned with bolts of lightning—"what I promised as simple reprimand for ruinous intent, I shall deliver as wrath upon each of your blasphemous bosoms!" She motioned toward the side of the arena.

A cadre of Golden Guardians took flight from the shadows along the side of the field.

Then Life looked into the stands. "Your God," she said, "being rich in mercy and because of the great love which I hold for these fallen . . . and as they behave as the dead in their trespasses, only by the grace of your God will they be saved!"

Shouts and cries and screaming blasted from the grandstands, like trumpets signaling an approaching enemy.

Life raised up her hands and the sound died down, quicker this time. "Calm yourselves, my children," she said. "I too thirst for the truth of justice that lies beyond this Judgment. And justice will be delivered in Heaven this day, as it shall be meted out upon the Earth."

Lucifer knew exactly what that meant. He braced himself for it to be delivered.

Lucifer had informed all ten mutineers of the sole path to return to the Garden to plant the seeds of their treacherous plot. No seed to produce tree could be planted, blossom or grow to bear fruit, unless they all were buried back in the grime of the Garden.

And now each of them stood and waited for that fate to be meted out by the only one who could.

Shax grumbled a little and he nudged Lucifia. "Here we are then," he said to her, "mind your munchers down there, lassie. Me finger's not lookin' for company. And don't go stealin' me heart neither, ya hear me. I won't be able to afford the loss after this."

"Farewell favored fingers," said Lucifia, and then she mocked Shax's accent, "ya big beautiful 'airy *bastard*."

Shax chuckled a little. "You might make it to me lovely lady yet," he said. "Minus your finger bitin', I expect. I wager you'll make a right fine feline down there, I do."

Lucifia smiled. It was a lie and she knew it, but she told it to him anyway, "Not for all the heat in Hell," she said. "Come looking for ravaging with me, mister, and I wager it's your skull that be gettin' raped."

Shax chuckled again. "Beautiful bit," he said, "right pretty pound of prose, it was. Fair enough, I'll take that wager. But don't think I'll be savin' meself, pining away, waitin' for your knickers to get numb—me little pig needs its pillowin', don't ya know."

Life stared in disgust at the two dangerous demons, and were it not for who Lucifia was, she might have smote the pair of them for their insolence. As it was, the punishment she was about to hand down, in her humble opinion, would be worse. She motioned to the guardians, flying high above the center of the arena now.

Two Golden Guardian angels swooped down in a wings-back power dive and both arrived at their intended targets at the same time.

Shax and Lucifia flew backward and went rolling with the guardians. Neither offered resistance as Life's lapdogs ripped out their right hearts.

When Shax and Lucifia stumbled back to their feet, they spewed black blood, the sweet nectar of molasses from the Garden, out of their mouths and chests, heaving in agony as their right hearts were removed. They were left to live as the Man-monkeys did—with only wrong hearts on their left sides to pump vile and vicious red blood through black-hearted souls.

Zepar took flight, both of his hearts bidding him to flee after witnessing Shax and Lucifia's fate.

The flying guardians caught him, raced him to the floor of the arena by his wings, and ripped out his right heart.

As excited as Zarzi was about making the trip to the Garden, she had nothing but fear over the toll for the trip. "I don't know if I can —"

It was the last words she would say as an angel with two balanced hearts. When it was over, she felt a darkness she had never experienced creep over her soul. As soon as she made it to the Garden, she would understand where it came from.

Raum and Rsoni took their medicine like warriors, and Lilith accepted her ripped-out fate with only slightly less courage than that.

Dorak, Aax, and Uzza—ugly and angry demons, having no nature for peace, went down fighting and clawing and growling and biting. But in the end they were no match for a dozen of Life's well-armed golden geese. Their hearts were delivered to the rest of them—a pile of penance and purpose at Life's feet.

When it was over and the last right heart was removed, Life addressed her followers again. "Though the whole earth is mine," she said, "if you obey me fully and keep my covenants, then out of all nations in the Garden you will be my most treasured possession. Defy me"—she pointed at the ten coughing, spitting and bile puking angels she was about rain down upon—"and *this* shall be your fate."

No angel in Heaven or Hell harbored anything but disgust for Life's Man-monkeys. For, to an angel of either realm, to be a filthy being created to replace them as the apple of their God's eye was to be an enemy who had enjoyed exclusive hold on Life's undivided attention . . . for as long as any of them could remember. While, as evidenced by the ten suffering soon to be souls in the center of the arena, angels were left to lesser fates.

And when God decreed that angels should harbor Man-monkeys' best interests in their own hearts . . . well, to an angelic being, that was simply intolerable, Heaven sent *or* residing in Hell. There were many who pondered ripping out their own right hearts to join the Man-monkeys in slowly learning to hate God.

Rsoni finally stood up. He tried not to smile. At the behest of his God and to deliver her messages both medium and small, he had flown to the Garden several times. And in doing so had encountered one of its less disgusting creatures—he had found woman.

Rsoni was not the only angel to fall victim to such temptation, but he was by far the most smitten.

Raum stumbled over to him and put his hand on Rsoni's shoulder. They steadied each other. Raum said, "I hope she is worth it, brother," he said. "Are they . . . worth it?" he asked.

Rsoni was known for his stoic and stern-as-steel demeanor, but he was not without humor. "Is the sun worth seeing for those mired in gray mist?"

Raum smiled at him, for that's what they seemed to be leaving. And it was exactly where they were going. "Indeed, brother."

Uzza and Dorak were just livid, angrier than either of them could ever remember being. They growled at the guardians, standing in a circle around their entire group of conspirators.

"Gilded lilies," growled Uzza. The point came across. "I'll get to your guts."

"*That*," said Dorak, rubbing his already healing breast, "will definitely leave a mark."

Zarzi slumped into Lilith's shoulder. The naive young angel had not been prepared to be so ruinously treated by God. Life had never—the shock of who Zarzi now knew her Lord to be . . . was more than she had words for.

Lilith was well aware. "Their deceptions," she said to Zarzi, attempting to comfort the waifly angel, "are only matched in misery by our own delusions that those lies do not exist. Tomorrow is another day, sweet flower, and today you have grown older by ten."

Aax looked at Shax. "Glad I didn't take that wager," he said to his friend.

Shax raised his eyebrows and rubbed his big palm over his face. He twisted the end of his mustache after he did. "There's a part of me ripped out chest over there"—he pointed to the pile of hearts next to Life—"what wishes you'd been right."

Lucifia coughed some black blood. Then she looked up at Shax. There wasn't the wicked playfulness in them that had been there before. "When I tighten terrible talon on golden godsuckers," she said, "so help me Satan, I'll—"

"Whoa, lovely lady," said Shax, "easy then. Everything in its proper place in time. You'll get to it soon enough, love." Then he winked at Aax. "Quicker'n cunt closes at Christmas, I'd wager"—he smiled back at Lucifia—"but now ain't the tick a the tock for it, sister."

Life turned in mid-air, facing each section of the grandstands as she slowly spun, hovering in a circle. She held her arms above her in a giant "V" as she did. "Your God shall not be deceived," Life said. Then she stopped, facing the ten traitors. "Nor shall I be mocked. For your hearts' crime of sowing seeds of rebellion and ruin against the Lord God Almighty's throne . . . I hereby decree that your mind, body and immortal soul shall reap the reward of resurrection back to life."

Cawing erupted and screeching ensued from the perches in the grandstands as soon as Life delivered her verdict.

Yet God was not finished. For the ten of them, life's misery had just begun. "And . . . you shall live among the Garden's beings and crea-tures—animals that you so adore—as long as I am Protector of eternity!"

— XLII —

THE VERY FIRST day at Saint Samuels Seminary Academy, we all got a good look at the front of the formation. The pulpit was a huge wood tower that put Father Dominic's feet almost dead even with all the rest of our heads. But as intimidating as the Pulpit of Pain was for the seminary students over the years—as I would remember as soon as I woke up from what I wanted to believe was just a bad dream in the dormitory hallway—the Sinner Stocks in front of the pulpit were worse.

Huge wooden railroad ties covered in black oil jutted straight up from the courtyard floor, and the shorter crossbeams made both of them together look like giant upside-down crucifixes.

There were three holes in the crossbeams. I knew that because Barbara's hands were squeezed and bleeding from struggling against the tightness of two of them, and she could barely tilt her head up so her eyes could beg me to save her . . . from the larger hole in the center of the beam between them.

The two inverted-cross stocks faced each other, so a sinful student could see their own miserable penance reflected back at them on the anguished face of another, suffering right along with them.

I had never known how hopeless and helpless the unlucky souls who experienced it had been . . . until I woke up and stared across at the fear, panic and anguish on Barbara's contorted face.

That was the first thing I saw. The first *sounds* I heard were Barbara's screams. The second . . . was Father Dominic's deep loud voice. He shouted at the entire formation of seminary students, though it felt like there were far fewer boys than I remembered from our first month. Of the ones I could see—twisting my neck to catch a glimpse of them—all of them were older.

Father Dominic's voice growled above me as he shouted, "You have heard that it was said, 'You shall not commit adultery.' But I say to you that everyone who looks at a woman with lustful intent . . . has already committed adultery with her in his heart."

And Barbara screamed out so wildly that I bucked in my stocks, then the pain spiked through my back and I screamed along with her. The crack of a whip sent real pain streaking across my back—a lightning bolt of languish that felt like it would cut me in half.

How did we. . .? They caught us in the hall. They'll burn us! "Barbara!" I screamed. I had to save her, she had helped me . . . so much. I still didn't understand why she had done it, but I didn't care.

"Let her go!" I screamed.

"I warn you," Father Dominic bellowed back, "as I warned you before, that those who do such things will not inherit the kingdom of God. Now your works of the flesh are evident for all to see: sexual immorality, impurity, sensuality, idolatry, sorcery, enmity, strife"— then his voice sounded like it got louder and it felt like he was speaking straight up at God—"your jealousy and fits of anger, rivalries, dissensions, divisions, envy, drunkenness, orgies, and vile things like these are a shadow of the past eternity. I shall entertain them no more."

I had no idea what he was talking about, because I hadn't done any of those things. I struggled through the pain to look at Barbara—I had to rotate my head slightly to see her. She was whimpering, her face was contorted and her eyes were closed tight. I felt a jolt go through my heart when she screamed for me. "Benito! Don't let him beat me!"

I was sure that Father Dominic would not burn a Sister of the—

"These trials," he bellowed, "will show that your faith is genuine, my children. It will be tested as fire tests and purifies gold—though it is far more precious than mere gold. So if your faith remains strong, it will bring you much praise and glory and honor on the day when God is revealed to the whole world."

He paused so long that I thought he wasn't going to continue. My body prepared for the flames to burn me again.

But then Father Dominic spoke again, "Most of you do not know that if you present yourselves to anyone as obedient slaves, you are slaves of the one whom you obey, either of sin, which leads to death, or of obedience, which leads to righteousness? So I ask you"—an eerie silence fell over the courtyard—"are you a slave to sin . . . or a servant of righteousness?"

Three years of broken fingers, beaten bodies, and burned-in benevolence brought one to the realization that Father Dominic's questions required no answers. No one spoke, and no one would save Barbara and me from the fire.

I could feel the rage inside me building—my Shandian mind be damned to the inferno for calling for calm and restraint! But as angry as I was, I could feel that my mind . . . pulling me inside my memories and my training . . . raged even more.

I remembered the first day of. . . I think by then I had suffered two or three days as the chosen fingerling . . . and at least one horrific morning of being burned at the pulpit until it . . . felt like I was dead. And I *knew* that Barbara had nurtured and comforted me, no matter what she had said back in the dormitory hallway.

But on day six hundred and sixty-five—one year and three hundred days into our indoctrination as seminary students at Saint Samuels, faithfully following the Word as preached to us by our new father— Dominic made an announcement that would change every one of us into "Warriors for the Word."

From high atop the courtyard pulpit he had addressed the roughly seven hundred of us still left alive. Barbara had informed me each night of the evil and vile fates that the other three hundred young souls had suffered. One by one they fell to some brutal test or another, administered by the only authority we knew. Because the merciful God Father Dominic spoke of clearly had no control or presence at Saint Samuels. And one by one he handed down judgment and secret execution to send their souls to Heaven . . . or Hell. No one would really ever know which soul received which.

"Today," Father Dominic had boomed at the front of our formation back then, "you shall all put on the whole armor of God, that you may be able to stand against the schemes of the Devil. Today you shall become Shandian warriors of the Word of God. Your souls have been tested by water and earth and wind, and at Saint Samuels we have burned in your faith and purified it in the crucifix of fire"—he looked down and addressed the cadre of Priest Instructors—"and we have done our best to empty your hearts of evil sins of the flesh." Then he looked back up at us. "Now your minds shall become empty glasses. And then we shall fill them up with the power and purpose of the sweet nectar of life's Word. Today . . . you shall all become Candidates in the battle against evil and darkness. Those of you who survive will become priests and be granted your own church from which to save souls from damnation. Those of you who do not will join our Lord in Heaven."

As my Shandian mind took me back to re-witness its birth, the only message it carried with us was *He is a liar!* But then it focused my dream and made me pay particular attention to the next words that Father Dominic had spoken.

"For we do not wrestle against flesh and blood," he said, "but against the rulers, against the authorities, against the cosmic powers over this present darkness, against the spiritual forces of evil in the heavenly places. Stand therefore, having fastened on a belt of truth, and having put on the breastplate of righteousness, with your brothers in benevolence."

And that's how it went . . . for a full two more years. Father Dominic would start the day telling us how lucky we were to be warriors for Heaven, and then the PI's would take over and beat and brutalize us for the rest of the day. Then we would wince and drag our bloody and beaten Shandian skills back to our dormitory and collapse.

Our exhausted bodies and our hallucinating minds would be woken up a mere five hours later to be slowly rinsed by the relentless Seattle rain, and then we would repeat the process—the kicking, punching, agility training, and mental mind melding.

Time folded into itself as our blood and bruises blended together. None of us could separate the results of one beating from another. But slowly, and as certainly as each day started with Seattle mist, we got stronger, faster and more powerful. Students started fending off Priests during sparring, fingers stopped getting broken, Candidates stopped being beaten and burned, and then . . . we all started resisting our masters as we became stronger than they were.

PI's were bested in combat sparring—a few of *their* fingers got broken for a change—and we developed into a pecking order pack of wild wolves, hungry and thirsting for the blood of our enemies in Hell. And though it would take a Shandian dream trip back into my mind to realize it . . . I was poised to ascend to the pinnacle of that pack.

By the end of our Shandian training—year four for any of us who hadn't completely surrendered to the relativity of time—there were barely a hundred of us left. All of us were strong, all of our minds were more powerful than we could have ever imagined . . . and I was the strongest one. And for an arrogant, prideful and brutish dictator, absolutely certain of his righteousness and rank . . . *that* was a very big problem.

So Dominic, the priest that we all knew and feared as Father D, but whose real name none of us would ever understand the meaning of even *if* we discovered it. . . For a vengeful archangel from . . . which Heaven none of us knew, turned traitorous and treacherous spy for his new and only God, Life. Standing behind another was simply intolerable.

But my mind had taken to Shandian so completely that it became an otherworld entity all its own. It knew events before they happened, felt thoughts from people and beasts and beings, and understood what it had been called to do . . . though the vessel that it found itself inside, resisted and cowered at every dangerous and dark corner.

And there was no more dangerous, dark or deafening turn of events than when my Shandian mind told my little inner voice of reason that it had to kill Father Dominic.

When my Shandian mind allowed my body and soul to come back to the sin and misery of the stocks, I looked across at Barbara's head and hands, bound and shackled like mine. Then I closed my eyes and said a prayer. But it wasn't a prayer to God—it was clear that God had forsaken me right along with the thousand other boys who started at Saint Samuels and the hundred that remained living. And my Lord Savior had made suffer a girl who had only ever tried to ease my own suffering at that place.

I spoke quietly at first, staring into Barbara's anguish as I set my mind to the prayer. I made a vow and a promise to her for her kindness and comforting soul, and then I handed my fate over to the Shandian warrior inside my mind, now preparing for justice. "Lord Almighty . . . if you dare to listen," my mind said aloud, "my name is Benito Octavio Benedetti, and I will smite these evil people with blindness of heart and turn their reproach upon their own heads, and offer them for prey in this land of captivity."

The cadre of PI's grumbled and mumbled to my left.

So I spoke directly to them, "I shall not cover up their iniquity so that their sins may be blotted out by thee. For I have been provoked to anger, and now I shall give and believe and have faith according to deeds, and I shall send an avenging archangel of Lucifer if need be, to chase and persecute and confound them. And death shall come upon them as they have come upon me with untruths."

And then the murmurs started to sift their way through the remaining formation.

So I spoke to my fellow students. "I shall slay them, my brothers," I promised, "lest my own people forget. Then I shall scatter them and bring them down, for the sins of their mouths and the words of their lips let them be taken in their pride, and for the lying which they speak, I shall consume them in wrath, and let them know the heart of their true God that rule in Heaven."

And then I spoke directly at the man who believed he was God in our eyes, the devil demon, Father Dominic, "So I bid you . . . *Aax*, traitor of Satan, reveal yourself and pour out thine indignation upon me if you feel your faith as I do, and let thy wrathful anger take hold of me. And bid your master to blot me from her book of life . . . as I shall replace your ink with my blood in the book of those who have loyally lived."

There was no sound more deafening than the cracking and splintering of the top half of the crossbeam that held my head and hands . . . as it slid up and off my neck. And there wasn't an eye to be turned away from me, blind or otherwise, when the stocks around my neck and hands broke and I stood up.

TAINT

— XLIII —

THE SEATTLE DAY gives way to dark at the Mike with barely a change to be noticed. When I peer out the window of Shannon's shop, the night glow of lights from beneath the thick blanket of fog looks little different from the dim gray glow that the sun casts. During the day, the sunlight tries desperately to boil its way through the mass of moisture above the Mike. But the fog shifts like quicksand, never allowing escape from its grasp no matter how much the sun struggles.

There is no escape from the squad of Protection soldiers marching down the street toward us either. They spit and spray bullets at any citizen or sinner who dallies too long getting out of the way. Blood and bile from spilled guts mix with the accumulated mist and heads for storm drains, swirling together with the stench and excrement of millions in the pipe under the street. Soon it will all be joining their fellow followers' lost liquid in the Pacific Ocean's vast vat of forgotten friends.

The Protection squad is single-minded in their purpose and they march ever closer to our hiding place as if they can see through the walls to us. This is no raid, it's an ordered execution. But by whom? Protection wouldn't murder one of the Clergy, black-bagged at three in the morning or beaten bloody out in the broad daylight. Another question I'll have for Shannon if we live through this.

I raise my voice at him, "They're headed straight here!" I'm sure he already knows. He . . . knows things like I do. "Three minutes at most."

Shannon's voice is all business and—I never noticed it before—his voice is as calm as the crucifixes on his wall. "Bloody bastards," he mutters. He looks at his remaining watchman and says, "Slow them down."

All three of us know what he means.

"And, Omia. . ." Shannon says to his soon-to-be-dead watchman.

Omia turns back straight-faced—I don't think I've seen him smile since I met him. "Yeah, boss?"

Shannon smiles at Omia. ". . .hand 'em a couple angel asses, will ya? Let 'em know what end's what, mate."

Omia shakes his head. "Fucking resurrection. . ." he mutters.

Shannon smiles at him. "She's a bloody box on your beard, ain't she."

"See you back in Hell," Omia says, and then he's out the front door.

"If you can still call it that," Shannon mumbles.

The two of us stare at each other. I'm not sure if the silence is because Shannon just sent his last watchman to his death, or if it's because both of us knows what's coming next, but time slows and we listen to the muffled screaming and screeching, and wild cries and roars out in the street as if none of this is really happening.

"Down me rabbit hole, then," Shannon says. "Don't go getting your blind ass burned to ashes this time, eh."

I can't seem to remember what was down the escape door in the floor of Shannon's shop, but my Shandian mind tells me that I'd better. "Peace be with you, brother," I say. It's the only thing I can think of, and I'm more than a little bit perturbed at myself afterward, as it might be the last thing my friend remembers of me.

Shannon chuckles a little. "And Christ died on a cross on account a me sins, too. I'll wager you even money, Benito, that there tale ain't true. But if it makes your brain feel any better, I'll pray to me plucked pig if the sow gets us clear of this." And with that he scoops up his little potbellied companion and they both vanish down the door to . . . I still can't remember. Maybe I never knew.

— XLIV —

THERE WERE NO bright sons left at Saint Samuels that day, just as there would be no bright shining sun that could burn or boil its way through Seattle's thick blanket of fog to shine truth down into the seminary's tortured halls. Anyone who survived the battle in the courtyard would be bathed in the bile and blood of false beliefs and treachery turned to torture.

The Clergy would remain shrouded in misery and mystery, like the deep gray glow that engulfed the Northwest Quarter on near every day of its existence. It didn't matter which faith emerged triumphant at the dawn, truth and deception would meld together to cloak the depth of the plot. It was my task to see that done. And my Shandian mind told me I had until the end of the day to set that deception in motion. I had to get back to . . . somewhere.

That distraction proved near fatal. CRACK! A searing whip burned into my back and I screamed out in pain.

And then another crack in front of me and Barbara was screaming and begging, "Please!" she yelled. "Benit—aaaaaaahhh!"

I saw the one behind her with the torch, smiling like some sort of possessed priest as Barbara screamed. And I ran at him.

I didn't get far before I took a bursting blow to my side and went rolling across the ground. I was up in an instant, searching for my attacker.

It was Father D turned evil demon, and he smiled at me—a wicked grin that I'd never seen on his face, despite years of obviously enjoying torturing all of us. "Let all who are under a yoke as slaves regard their own masters as worthy of honor," he said. At least the lying was over.

We stood and looked at each other. Maybe we recognized the other's power for the first time, maybe we hated one another just enough. . . My mind pushed at him and then his burned back at me. Fire and heat and hatred toward me . . . and everyone like me. And then I realized it.

The entire formation in the courtyard—what was left of us students anyway—was deep in battle. Student Candidates fought against PI's and they kicked and elbowed and kneed as they themselves had been beaten. And the Priest Instructors whipped and swung torches and yelled scripture at the remaining students as they had been trained to.

Blood spilled, and limbs cracked and fingers twisted completely off, on both sides, as screams of agony accentuated the fighting. And I paused to feel it. Blind rage and hatred almost pushed back the damp cold of the lingering fog up into the dark gray above the courtyard. And my mind—*Focus!*

"Benito!" Barbara's voice screamed at me a split second later, "he's —"

Father "Demon" punched Barbara so hard, he knocked her unconscious. Her head hung limp in the stocks. "Your mouth invites a beating, Sister," he laughed down at her.

I moved like a cat that can taste the tail of a mouse it's going to eat, and I punched him twice in the lower back and ribs, then I kneed his hip and punched at his neck, but he spun and blocked my blow.

Then his other arm followed his block and a sledgehammer hit me on the right side of my face. I tried to spin to my left with the blow—absorb some of the impact—but I wasn't fast enough.

The sounds of my brothers fighting their masters got muffled. "And a fool's lips walk into a fight," the demon said as I fell.

Then a bright light flashed into my mind and I stared up at the glowing night fog, mist blanketing my glasses and face.

Father D's face appeared over mine. "Father"—he looked even more demon now than wannabe deity. His faced was contorted and . . . he looked like a lion and a bear mixed together, and I knew my mind had snapped into another one of my hallucinations.

Then the demon lifted up his leg and a huge hoof hovered above my face. And I turned my head to the right, exposing my cheek. "I shall not rise up against you, demon," I said to Father D, turned evil devil. "Take my left cheek as your prize."

"Very well," he said, "let it join your right, Priest." And his huge cloven hoof stomped down onto my face and the dark damp night air turned to a bright and burning flash of star and my mind was gone—brains smashed into the black.

When I woke up . . . I was squeezing someone's hand and I was terrified . . . but I felt . . . woozy too.

"Barbara?" I whispered, not sure if I should. I mean, clearly I was hallucinating . . . yet again. And my Shandian mind reminded me, *You don't have much time—a few hours at most.* "Quiet," I whispered at it.

"Yeah, quiet," Barbara whispered back at me. She squeezed my hand hard. "We gotta get out of here," she barely made sound when she said it.

I looked. We were in the dormitory hall and . . . I remembered. I looked at the wall next to us—into the mirror. I was older . . . and yet younger than when the battle in the courtyard started. I looked at the back of Barbara's head. Her beautiful blonde hair was swirled and bound in a bun behind her head and the back of her neck—*Benito!* My Shandian babysitter was making a full-time job out of reprimanding me for daydreaming about Barbara.

Then the inner voice beside it remembered . . . something that last —angel or dream, I couldn't remember—but the voice from my. . . I had no idea which dream it was. Separating them from reality was hard enough, but keeping track of each one and the events? I did remember the voice . . . and the riddle. My mind struggled to find it. "Escape is inside yourself," the huge eagle of an angel had said.

I stared into the mirror. I was no one—a nothing without God, they had taught and tortured into me. *Inside yourself,* my Shandian mind reiterated the riddle.

"Inside. . ." I muttered.

"Damnation," Barbara muttered to herself. "Yes, we're inside, idiot. And if you don't shut up we're about to get caught."

I stared at the mirror and pushed up my glasses—back tight against the bridge of my nose. And then my reflection smiled at me . . . but it wasn't me. I hesitated and then—"Oh my. . ."

I squeezed hard into Barbara's hand and she yelped.

I put my finger to my mouth. "Shh," I said. "Come with me."

Then I gently pulled on the side of the tall mirror and it slowly swung open, revealing a dark stairway down to. . . Anywhere was better than getting caught by Father D and burned in the stocks in front of the courtyard.

I could barely see Barbara's face in the dimly lit staircase, but then something . . . happened. She turned a bright purple glow . . . all over. I took off my glasses and put them in my pocket, sure I was still hallucinating from the injection that she gave me. I rubbed my eyes and then looked at the hallway. The entire corridor lit up to a dim orange glow—I could see every detail of it. And I could see Father Dominic and the PI next to him, both glowing red hot flames of fire. And I looked at my hand. *Blue?* my inner voice said.

When I looked back down the staircase behind the mirror, it glowed deep yellow and orange and bright red—a burning rainbow of salvation that led to escape!

Barbara leaned into me and grabbed onto my arm with both hands. "What the. . .?" she whispered, looking down into the darkness. "I ain't going down—"

I quickly stepped behind the big mirror, pulled Barbara in with me, and then I shut it quietly behind us. I held her close to me. I could feel her heart, trying to beat its way out of her chest.

The mirror barely closed, when I heard Father D say, "Where did they. . .?" He was right on the other side of it now . . . and I could see his face, glowing red! "Brother?" he said, looking right at me, into the mirror. Then he looked around and then back at Barbara and me, at the mirror. He squinted and then he adjusted his collar. When he did, flames lapped up and out from under the neck of his shirt. Then he turned back to the PI. "I thought you said they were still in the hallway?"

The PI stood right on the other side of our hiding place, facing away from it. "They're here . . . somewhere." If the mirror would have been a waterfall, I could have reached through and strangled him like he deserved.

"How. . .?" she whispered so softly that I barely heard her.

I put my hand over her mouth.

The PI turned around and looked at Father D. "I have no idea," he said to the father. "Maybe they're—"

"Find them," Father D said, "or I'll burn you alongside them!"

To Barbara, the dark down the steps behind the mirror was pitch-black molasses. But I could see the orange and yellow and red glow growing brighter with each step we took. We descended down the long curving staircase toward anywhere but the misery awaiting back in the student dormitory hallway.

I couldn't believe we weren't dead. Then a bright white light crashed into my face and I stumbled down the last of the steps, dragging Barbara with me. When we landed, I felt my face. It was crushed in on both sides—miserable meat hung from my cheeks and they burned acid into my head. Even my Shandian mind screamed out. "Aaaaaah!"

The scream echoed down the—it sounded like a long hallway. I was sure Father D and the PI would burst down the stairs and catch us, but no one came.

Barbara groaned a little. "Are you okay?" she said to me.

I sat up. "I'll—" I couldn't talk.

Barbara touched my face. "Oh my God, Benito," she said. "Your face is. . . It's hurt bad."

A few seconds later, something pricked my neck, and then I could feel the bones in my cheeks . . . cracking and crunching themselves back together. I winced and my inner voice braced itself for the excruciating misery and pain that would surely follow. "Don't." I shut my eyes.

"Shh," said Barbara, "you'll be okay."

I can't describe the warm and wonderful feeling that swept through my head. It was the same joy I felt when Max licked my face. Like . . . no matter what happened, everything was going to be okay. "How can you do. . .? Why have you been helping me so much?"

"You don't listen, do you?" Barbara said. "It's a wonder they haven't beaten and burned you to death by now. I never seen a idiot that don't learn like you."

I stared at her and smiled.

Barbara's purple glow smiled back and then looked away a little. "Stop it," she said. Then she looked back at me.

I pulled my glasses back out of my pocket and put them on, and her face turned back to bathed in darkness.

"What are you so happy about?" she asked. "I can feel you smiling."

I took my glasses back off.

Barbara's face had turned from purple to a bright shining blue. "You're down a dark hole, got your face kicked in by a priest, and I just stuck you up with J . . . again. And you're sitting there grinning at me, ya giddy little idiot. You are possibly the worst Shandian priest I have ever seen. I'm gonna have to start calling you a 'gidiot,' " she said. "Father *Gidiot*—that's a good name for you." Then she giggled.

"Stop doing that," I said.

"Doing what?"

I smiled at her. No idea if she could see my face or not, but I didn't care. "Pretending you're helping me so you can escape."

"I'm not pretending nothing," she said. "This is my Mother a Mercy penance I gotta do so God don't hate me. You keep being a *gidiot* and I might just let him—leave you right here."

I think I chuckled. "I know you like me," I said. "You could help anyone in here. There was a thousand . . . when we started. Why me?"

"I . . . I don't know," Barbara said. "I just thought you was. . . And I was right, too."

"About what?"

"You don't understand," said Barbara. "You're little and I knew no one would notice if you went missing. Least that's what I thought when I drove Father D to pick you up. And when I drove back, I could feel you watching me from the backseat. I figured I could get you to help me escape. But then—"

"Wow," I said. I thought I didn't know what to say. "That's . . . pretty bad."

"*But*," she said, "then I started coming to visit you at night. You was so nice to me and . . . and the way you looked at me. And now. . . *Damn*, Benito, I ain't never seen no one fight like you. And I knew I had to get you to help me . . . before they could send me to the Mike." I barely saw her hang her head in the darkness—my mind felt it more than that. "I'm almost fifteen. You know what that means to a Saint Samuels Sister? . . . You think you're the only one gets beaten and. . . I just couldn't. . . I didn't know what else to do."

I looked around the darkness. We had escaped, but . . . to where? More importantly, my Shandian mind was telling me, *When is this?*

I felt Barbara fidgeting next to me. I pulled my glasses down my nose a little and looked at her. Her face slowly turned back to a light purple. Whatever her chi had felt when she was explaining her reasoning for tricking me into helping her escape, was now turning back to a combination dark and light aura of purpose.

"How are we gonna get out of here?" she said.

Now I was an unwitting knight in bloody and beaten armor, rescuing a. . . Was Barbara damsel or devil? My mind told me she was a little bit of both. But my little inner justification voice wanted what it wanted. *You have to save her!*

I can only remember staring at her and then into the darkness. I had no idea what to do, but somehow. . . *So help me Heaven or Hell*, I thought. I knew I would figure it out.

A voice boomed through the black. "Finally found your faith then, did ya?" it bellowed at us. "Right where your nose can sniff it, she hides it . . . don't she?"

Then the entire tunnel lit up in an orange glow. I didn't need glasses or my Shandian mind to tell me it was another angel . . . of sorts.

The front of the figure was as dark as the tunnel had been. He was outlined in orange light—lit from behind—and he was absolutely huge! Eight feet at least at the top of his head, and the bends of his wings—they *were* wings—jutted above his head like mountain peaks above a huge boulder. His frame was that of a big barrel of ale that I'd unloaded from trucks for the Priests Feast each Sunday. I could just make out the twisted tips of a mustache extending past both sides of his face. He was holding something big and long in his right hand and he had his left arm wrapped around something that squirmed and squiggled.

"Holy Mother of Mercy!" Barbara said. "You're a damned ang—"

He bellowed a huge laugh and his breath hit us both like the flames from a hot fire. "Truer than time, lassie," he said. It sounded like he cawed after he spoke. "She's a whole house a horrors, this one is. I can see why you're smitten, Benito. Damsels in distress, don't ya know—death of every demon and deity in the heavens, they are. Can't choose 'em though—Lucifer's granddaughter, though they may be. The lust lies to you like love and then. . . Well"—he pointed what looked like an axe at Barbara—"there you have it."

Barbara said, "He and me ain't—"

"Don't be offended, love," the big angel bellowed. "He's a right fine romp, this one. You'll see it soon enough. Bit heavy on the boozin' and blasphemy." He chuckled. "Ain't we all though? No finer weapon for the Word, he is. I'll tell ya that . . . once he gets goin'."

I could have lit up the entire tunnel with the whites of my eyes—wide as they were. "Who"—it was the only question to ask—"are you?"

"Better yet," Barbara said, "what in the devil's name are you?"

"Not playin' that game any longer, love," he said to her. "Fight for me friends now, I do. No god's army angry as me." Then he looked right into me. I could feel it. "But me friends is gonna have to start wieldin' the weight a their half a the wagon right quick. Otherwise . . . a little cookin' . . . be the bottom of your worries, mate. Yours too, lovely lady."

I was just too shocked to say anything . . . but excited, too. Or maybe it was the injection, slowly wearing off. Barbara, on the other hand, wasn't. She had turned back to her normal self.

"You got a name?" she asked. "All you . . . angels got names, don't ya? What's yours?"

For two young minds, beaten and burned towards a faith we had only heard about from a butcher, actually seeing proof of . . . I didn't know what, left us with more questions than answers. Surely a demon would eat our souls, and an angel only spoke to. . . Father D was the only one who they ever talked to . . . according to him.

"Belligerent as well, are ya?" the angel said to Barbara. "Reminds me a me own lovely lady." He looked over his shoulder—I still couldn't make out his face. Then he looked back at me. "Best be busy saving her butt by now, Benito. Me mutton's molasses be more precious than me own. Don't go gettin' any of her guts spilled neither, laddie."

"Molasses?" I asked.

I would come to find out that Barbara's mind lived in her mouth. "You talk funny," Barbara said to him. "All a you long-winded like that? 'Cause if you are, Heaven must be full a hot wind."

Then our angel got serious. "Heaven's a cold cunt in a snowstorm, little dove," he said. "And she's run by an angry bitch what's lost her big black marbles. But if you're lookin' for heat, Hell's what you're after, all right. And after all the cold Heaven's been rainin' down on you for your benevolent breakfast, I'd wager you could use a bit a Hell's heat to warm up your supper."

My Shandian mind told me that the time for talking to this . . . angel was over. "We have to go back," I told him. I knew that for sure. "Not much time left."

"Truer words," the angel said, and then he looked over his shoulder again. "Less than you might mention, you have. The both of you bloody bastards, I'm afraid."

And yet it was just all too much—even for another one of my dreams. And the part about Barbara . . . I desperately wanted it to be true.

"Another one of ya," Barbara muttered.

"What's that then, love," the angel said. "Some word lose its way out your mouth 'ole then. Get stuck behind all his friends, rushin' for the exit, did he?"

"Barbara!" I said, surprising myself. I wasn't really sure if it was now my place to reprimand her rudeness. "He's not—"

"He's not answering my questions," Barbara said to me. "That's what he's *not* doing." She looked back at him. "I asked what your name was . . . and why are you helping us? How do we know you ain't some deceiving demon?"

Our angel—at least that's what he felt like now—scoffed at her. "Oh I'm demon, right enough," he said. "Ain't ever been much for deceivin', however. If I was, you'd already be using that little glare of yours on your guts."

It was the first aggressive thing that he had said, and it scared us both.

"I . . . I didn't mean nothing," said Barbara. She looked at me. "I just wanted to know his"—then she looked back at him—"I just wanted to know your name is all. Maybe we heard a you."

"Ain't nobody heard a me what's not dead and damned, love," he said. Then he paused and . . . just looked at us both. "But since a bee's in your bonnet to be makin' the trip, here's the whole truth. A good name be better than precious ointment, love. And the day of your death be better than the day of your birth, right enough." He stood taller than either of us was comfortable with and the tops of his wings scraped and sparked the roof of the rock tunnel. And then he spread his wings wide, screeching them along both walls, like millions of forks on a chalkboard.

We cupped our ears at the sound and cringed and cowered on the warm floor of the tunnel.

"But me name on me friends' lips in this world be Shannon," he said. "And me monicker that me mother in Hell gave me? Well, a four-letter word, I am. Guts for breakfast and grog before bed. And I come to give me friend Benito this axe, I have. Though Faith be the name that I hail him in Heaven, this here saint remembers me by Shannon in this world, and in my time . . . he called me Shax."

When the angel, Shax . . . or Shannon—I would have called him whatever he wanted, because Shandian or not, I don't think he would have had any trouble sending me to wherever he came from. . . But when he walked toward us, I could see that in addition to the little double-headed axe he had, there was a . . . little pig under his left arm.

"What's the pig for?" Barbara asked, not even trying to hold back her giggles.

The angel stopped, looked down at the black-bladed axe in his hand, and then he said, "She's for loppin' off heads, she is. A right brutal blade at that, I'll tell ya. Me 'little pet pig' I call her. And she's infected with a right mean mind for makin' monkey heads outta men."

Whatever he was saying, I was sure of two things: one, he was telling the truth, and two, I had no idea what he was saying. I pointed at the little pot-bellied pig under his other arm. "I think she means *that* pig," I said. "I'm sorry, but that's just—"

The big angel looked down at it. "That?" he said. "That there's me partner, Piz, he is. He's a cacodemon angel after me own left heart. Keep him 'round to remind me of me right."

"He's blinder than you, Benito," said Barbara. "That's a pig."

"Oh, he look like beautiful bacon to you, love," the angel said, "but he be me pig, Piz, sure enough. Reminds me at breakfast each mornin' he does, not to let you monkeys cook me for dinner."

And then the little potbellied pig squawked and screeched and . . . transformed into a muddy-looking miniature angel with wet dirt on his feathers, and crusted mud on his face. His eyes were big and round and . . . red, and he stood next to. . . He was barely a third the big angel's size. He growled when he spoke. "You sure this is him? And this"—he flitted a wing at Barbara—"is his. . .?" He eyed Barbara, cocking his head to the side and grunting a little. "She does not appear as one he would ever consort with. Too . . . pretty."

Barbara just stared back at them. I did, too. *Judgment. . .* I thought. The "heaven" Barbara injected into me, I was finding out, was more hallucination than healing.

Shannon, or Shax the angel, looked at Barbara, too. He gripped and shook his axe a little at her. "I'll wager me little pet pig on it."

"Looks like you may have to," the little angel, Piz, said. Then the dirty angel, or devil, turned and walked behind Shax. "Give it to him then," he said as he left, "and let us be gone, before he loses *his* head."

Shax handed the big axe down to me—it was heavy and hard—and then he said, "Mind your melon with him, mate. He's a traitorous bastard, he is. He'll stomp in your face, he will. And don't think turnin' your other cheek will stop him. That's a fine feathered fairy tale, that is. He'll eat your eyes for breakfast, he will. You'll have to hack off his head, before you lose yours."

I looked down at the double-sided blade in my hand. "What do I do with this?"

"Holy mother," said Barbara. "You have to kill him."

"I'm not. . ." I'd fought plenty of PI's and, as far as my little voice could rationalize, I *was* going to kill Father D. As far as I knew, he had stomped my face in and sent me into this death dream, but kill him . . . with an axe?

The big angel reached behind his back, rummaged a little, and then handed me a little flat metal bottle.

It looked like one of the little leather-bound flasks I'd seen some of the PI's pull out when they thought none of us were looking. The letters "B.O.B." were inscribed on the metal part at the top. It was just like the one my father gave. . .? There was just no way I could. . . "I cannot be led astray by wine."

"This ain't wine," the angel said. "This here mocker's stronger than that. Little brawler, he is. He'll save your soul more than once, he will. You'll find that the one you got ghosted in your cell be gone, you will. This here . . . is his grandson, it is."

MY FRIEND SHANNON comes back up through the floor of his shop faster than he disappeared. He couldn't have been gone more than a few seconds.

"Sorry about me timin', mate," Shannon says. "Took longer'n lopping of ol' Lucifer's tail, it did." He shakes his head at me and grins a knowing smile. "Your mutton's a real chatterbox, she is. I can see how she twisted her wool around your william, though. Right seductive sister, that one."

I have no idea what he's talking about, but I can see that Shannon's minus the axe he took with him . . . and his little pig. "Where's your. . .?"

Half of my question is answered when the little potbelly scurries up behind Shannon, snorting and sniffing like he's gonna attack an ankle or bite someone's hand.

"There he is then," Shannon says. "Let's get to it, eh, Piz. Looks like Benito might be done dallying about." He looks at me like I had all day to do something and waited until the last hour to get it done. "What ya been doin' up here, laddie? Choking your chicken? Me watchmen's damned by now. They'll be bringing the black at your back, sure enough. Still got your flask?" he asks.

I have no idea why that's important, but I can't help touching my pants pocket to feel if it's there. I frown at him. "Yes." My Shandian mind is done trying to understand all of what Shannon's saying.

Protection's in the Mike, sweltering sin down on whatever innocence it has left. I know they're here to finish what they started this morning at the Fifty. *They followed you, idiot.* Every once in a while, the little voice inside my head sounds just like Barbara. Sometimes I miss. . . I look out the window again.

Shannon's watchman, Omia, has turned to a raging hellfire angel . . . or demon, I'm not sure which. It's getting harder and harder to tell the difference. He spins and hundreds of bright red streaks fly up the street. They cut through the Protection agents in their way, and limbs fall and other bodies decapitate, and then the screaming starts.

A fresh squad of black-booted, dark-clad killers replaces the gutted ones on the ground. The agents who still have their heads scream in agony, crawling and grabbing for lost limbs—and a hailstorm of bullets flash glowing purple-black streams of hate at Omia. The streaks cut one of his wings off and he crumples to the side. Then he gets hit in the guts and I'm reminded that it's not the only pile of angelic intestines I've seen today. *You gotta get back to him or all this—*

I know! I'm not even sure if it's me, my Shandian mind, or my inner voice of reasonless rage that yells it.

One of the agents—a huge burly mass of black—looks like he's carrying an axe. *Not normal,* my inner voice says. It's taking turns shouting at me hysterically while my Shandian mind barks orders. *Get away from the window, idiot!* But I just have to watch.

The black mass of man swings the huge blade like a toy hammer, and Omia's head flies off and I see blood spray up from the bloody stump that used to be his neck. The spurting is backlit by headlights coming down the street behind the big behemoth with the axe. Then Omia bursts into flames and explodes into burning chunks of meat.

Backlit by the floodlights on Protection's big black Mobile Assault Resistance Response vehicle, the entire street looks like black shadows, running, raging, and ruining the marketplace.

"They brought a MARR," I raise my voice at Shannon.

A long time ago, citizens protested that Protection was becoming too militarized. They were worried about one of the most powerful militaries in the world being turned on its own citizens. Now, there isn't any difference between the military and the mayhem of the national police—Protection's responsible for them both anyway. I guess the citizens were right. It hardly matters now—guns gone and buried in heaps of hindsight and hate. And now a Protection tank is rolling up the street.

"Lovely," says Shannon.

"And one of them's got your axe," I say.

"That'd be Uzz—who's got me axe?" Shannon says. He's next to me faster than he went down and came back up the steps to whatever dungeon's underneath his shop, and he looks out the window with me.

Bullets blast through the window, spraying us both with glass, and one grazes across my neck and it burns like acid. And I'm falling backward—Shannon is too—and my mind shouts, *Stop watching and start fighting!*

Shannon's lying on his back next to me on the floor. He stares up at the ceiling and says, "Guess you'll be fightin' two feathered followers in one day. Pity really."

"Are you injured?" I ask him.

"Just me pride," he says.

I lie next to him and stare up at the slow motion of bullets streaking above us and flashing lights and sparks, as Shannon's shop becomes a Freedom Fourth fireworks display. "A mortal sin, Pride," I say. My voice is muffled and far away.

"It's a good gander I ain't mortal then, isn't it?" he says, "Bloody shame, it is?"

"What?"

"I only had one axe."

"Where is it?" My mind's telling me I already know the answer.

"Gave it to me mate," he says. "Hope the bastard has the good sense to use it."

— XLVI —

I TUCKED THE little flask that the big angel gave me into my pocket. *Shannon—Shax?* I thought. Then I grabbed Barbara's hand. I gripped down hard on the angel's other gift. The axe was heavy and backed up with hate. I could feel the same emotions swelling up inside me—I was going to fill that dam of hate to overflowing.

I knew what I had to do. The two messengers told me as much. At least Father D was right about one thing: Heaven spoke with messengers, because God had neither time nor inclination to speak directly to his children.

"Come on," I said to Barbara, and then I started tugging her back up the steps.

"We're going back?" she said, pulling back against me. "They're still up there. Probably waiting in the hall to—no!" She continued to tug back against me. "They'll catch us, Benito!"

"That's not where we're going," I said. I knew where we had to get back to, and as soon as my dream or hallucination or vision ended, that would be exactly where we would end up. Barbara wouldn't like it. If my face got smashed in again . . . I wouldn't either.

— XLVII —

BULLETS RAIN IN the window, streaking through what's left of Shannon's shop. The hailstorm tears apart trinkets and shatters glass and crashes through clocks, stopping time for the little ticking soldiers whose only job is to mark its passing.

"Right then," Shannon says, "hope they don't spill any of your precious molasses. Only got so much of it, I do."

All this for some syrup? My little inner voice says. *You're more idiot than she says.*

I look for a clock that didn't get killed. I find one—second hand still calmly ticking away, like his brothers didn't just get blown to bits of glass. *Eleven o'clock?* I frown at my own stupidity for drinking moonshine with Shannon when I have more important tasks to attend to. *One hour left, Benito. Get to it!*

"I'll punch a little Protection path for ya, I will," says Shannon. "But you'll be havin' to end Hell's hate with your own. That be the Word."

And he's up before I can ask him what in "Hell's hate" he means. Whatever it is, I'm sure that the only way back to my church is through the big black Protection beast, busy lopping off heads out on the street. "Peace be with you," I say it again as he bursts out the front door.

The last thing I hear him say is, "Ain't no time for peace, ya bastard.

This here's the war!"

I'm up and out of the shop after him before my Shandian mind can reprimand me for not going first . . . or my inner voice of panic can beg me not to go at all.

As soon as I come out the front door, I'm hit and fire burns across the outside of my ribcage. I put my hand on it. By the "grace" of God I'm just grazed. I wince hard, try to concentrate, and then I run for a deep dark doorway about fifty yards up the street.

I glance at Shannon as I run. He's busy doing what he promised to, and I watch him sprout wings and turn to a huge angel with even bigger wings. And I'm running and my Shandian mind yells at me, *He's the same one from the tunnel!*

That was real?

That was so long ago, and I've blocked out most of it. They're painful and terrifying memories of murder and misery, buried deep inside my head, like underground guns waiting for me to be reminded why I needed them in the first place. And that reason and reminder is busy beating and blasting its way through its own citizens—the State looking for someone that it deems to be threat-worthy.

I watch Shannon spin, and his wings cup around him and streaks of red and orange fly up the street. They light up the gray and black of what is probably the Mike's final night, this one anyway. Because after Protection is done blasting and blowing up everything in sight, they'll more than likely bulldoze it under so no one will ever know it existed in the first place. State. . . I have to admit, the Clergy uses the same strategy to cover up things it doesn't want to have known or to answer for. No need accounting for things that never existed, is—*Focus!* My inner voice is busy trying to get all three of us killed.

I make it to the doorway through the continued screams of the Mike's citizens turned suffering subjects. Their oppressors. . . Dying Protection agents are busy wailing from the stings of what will most likely be their future. Sinning souls shred in the blender of. . . For some reason my Shandian mind is telling me that Shannon is firing ballistic feathers up the street. Now it knows—

A streak of lightning flashes through my head. My glasses fly off my face and I spin and go to the ground, bouncing off the steps and rolling into the doorway that I was headed for. I lie there sideways with my head slumped to the ground.

My vision of the street turns to a fiery red raging glow of hate and flames and fury and damnation. The Protection agents are black shadows against it, and Shannon has turned to a glowing red dragon.

In Shandian training, we were taught that Man does not see what is right in front of him. He has to be taught to remove the cloak of darkness and deceit that constantly covers and clouds his perception of the world as he wants it to be. But the fog of the Word is thicker than the Seattle mist and only through fire can a warrior's vision—his Shandian mind—reveal the universe as it truly is. The truth is fire, hidden in plain sight, surrounded by the misty gray of rationalization and justification. Flames reveal its true form, its "truth." There is no harder lesson to learn.

I lie on my side and watch as Shannon, turned dragon-angel-demon, sends fire and fury up the street. And then the "citizens" of the Mike burst from shops and alleyways and windows and doorways, and some of them even rise out of the middle of the street, crawling up through manhole covers. I shudder to imagine where they lead. And projectiles begin flying in the other direction, and the tide of terror at the Mike has shifted!

Now, Protection is being taught that the ocean of citizens it is certain it owns. . . The sea has no master.

Something . . . is missing. My little inner voice stares at the red and rage of the main street of the Mike, trying to tell me something as I lie in the sticky glue of a terrible lapse in my memory. Then—*Watch out!* my Shandian mind shouts. *Roll sideways!*

The angry blade of the axe chops straight down at my head and I barely comply with the order before the axe splits the steps in half, splintering and sparking the boards that my head was just using for a pillow.

Move, idiot! I'm not sure if that's my inner voice, my Shandian reflexes, or her, but the message is delivered and I end my sideways roll and snap to my feet and stare at him.

The big black Protection agent has turned into a raging red demon with twisted horns and steaming nostrils, and Heaven and Hell have finally found their way to my hallucinations. Miserable messengers are everywhere.

What's the message?

I barely have time to wonder before the axe is swinging at my neck and I jump sideways and the big blade cuts clean through one of the porch pillars, sparking and splintering the big timber like a toothpick. The awning it was holding up sags, and big wood splinters streak into my ribs and I fall backward.

I'm up a little slower this time and the beast is on me. His hoof presses into my chest. His voice is deep and devilish, his eyes glow black and his mouth spouts a horrible smell when he speaks, "Ah, stubborn child, you unwittingly carry out a plan not mine, and make an alliance not of my spirit that it may add sin to your sins. I shall return you to your shame and humiliation." And he raises the huge axe above his horns. He looks all around him and when he speaks again, it's at the entire Mike, "You will all come to shame through this plan—you cannot profit by it. Its plot shall bring only disgrace."

I pull one of the long wood splinters out of my side—more long stick than annoying splinter—wincing through the searing sting of slivers it leaves behind. And I grip my fist around it. Then I notice something—the beast has only three fingers on the hand gripping its axe. "The three woe's," I mutter.

It's a short-lived revelation.

The snorting bull swings its axe down at my head, and at the same time I stab the beast in the leg, burying the near-foot-long spike of timber from my ribs, into and through its calf! And I squint my eyes shut as blinding pain shoots through the right side of my chest from my effort.

— XLVIII —

WHEN I OPENED my eyes back up I was lying in the courtyard of the Saint Samuels Seminary Academy courtyard, staring up at the black of the Seattle fog, misting down on my glasses and face. My right cheek screamed pain . . . and the huge cloven hoof of a lion-bear beast hovered above me—Father D turned demonic devil, Aax, preparing to stomp my brains out . . . again.

"Very well," he said, "let it join your right, priest." And he smashed his hoof down at me.

I rolled to the side as his hoof pummeled the rock floor where my head was not seconds before. And rock chunks sprayed across the court and I watched them bounce to a backdrop of Shandian warrior students doing battle with their Priest Instructors.

Where once a huge formation of students—a symbol of the cross of the Crucifixion—had stood motionless each morning, enduring misery after mutilation, now fought only a few of those as survivors, enduring and inflicting blood and mayhem and revenge. Broken bodies were everywhere and both sides were losing badly.

I sprang to my feet. "Your lips are a snare to your soul, demon!" I said. And then I felt something in my right hand, heavy and cold.

The beast hesitated. "Where did you get. . .?" it said. And then he morphed back to more Father D than demon. "He gave you his . . . the Tiny Swine," he muttered.

I looked at the little axe and spun it, turning it slowly, over and over in my hand. "So that's your name," I said at the little double-bladed demon killer. Because that was what I was about to do with it.

And Father D's face looked like a friend had just pulled a huge knife out of his back and showed him his own blood on its blade. Just like it. "In all the eternities . . . he never even let me . . . that's just not . . . possible," he said. "Traitorous bastard! I'll cut off his head and eat his eyes for—"

"It's funny. . ." I said to the demon, and then I spun and swung the little axe, slicing it through the air in a huge sweeping circle of sin for sin.

And the blade of the axe cut through Father D's neck like hate through a hot heart. And his head flew up into the air and flipped over and over in slow motion, turning back to the huge head of a lion-bear liar from Hell as it fell to the cold stone ground and rolled across the courtyard.

When the beast's big head came to rest, I stood hard, one hand on the ground, knees bent and straining like the limbs on the tree of my faltering faith, and the little Tiny Swine—my angel friend's black-bladed axe—extended high above my head. ". . .that's the same thing he said about you."

The demon's head burst into flames and its body exploded into chunks and melted like lava, burning down to black crusted rocks.

As soon as Father D fell—once the demon Aax was no more—every Priest Instructor left in the courtyard stopped fighting and stood confused and then horrified at the bodies that lie dead. To them, freshly woken from whatever dark spell that Father D held over them, the Seminary looked littered with sin, and the faith of the Clergy was stained red with blood.

But student Candidates kept beating them, their pent-up anguish and anger unleashed and quenching their thirst for vengeance toward their oppressors. And I let them.

For judgment is without mercy to one who has shown none. That was the Word of the God we had been brutally bound to serve. Who was I to challenge it?

"Benito," I heard Barbara's voice.

I walked over, dropped the axe, and then pulled the locks on the stocks around Barbara's head and neck free. I raised the upper half of the crossbeam on the cross and she fell to the cold ground of the courtyard.

The back of Barbara's habit was torn off and lying on the ground a few feet away. I crawled over to it, afraid to look at what I would find when I brought it back to cover up the bloody whip wounds on her back. I felt into my own wounds and winced at them, my Shandian mind finally slowing down long enough for my inner voice to stop holding its breath. *You could've been killed!*

By then, I should have been getting used to it. I wasn't sure if I ever would.

"I'm sorry," Barbara said behind me, whimpering a little as she spoke. "I didn't ever want to hurt. . . I just wanted to get away. I couldn't go back . . . not again." She started sobbing. "She said she was gonna. . ."

I crawled back to her, dragging her wet habit with me.

Barbara was curled into a ball on her knees on the ground now, doubled over in pain and. . . I looked at her bare back and buttocks.

Anger welling up inside me, I prepared to be horrified and rain hate down on the dirty devils that dared hurt her.

"Have mercy on me," she prayed down at the ground.

I stared in disbelief. *How could. . .?* Even my Shandian mind struggled to catch up to the truth of it. *You idiot!* My inner voice shouted at me. It just couldn't—

"Forgive me, Benito."

"Forgive you?" I said, still not able to come to grips with it. "For wha—"

A spike of hot searing pain shot through the right side of my chest and blinding white light filled my head . . . and then it was gone and I stared into Barbara's eyes.

Her beautiful blue eyes filled with tears. "She said it was the only way," her voice quivered as she spoke.

I coughed deep dark blood onto Barbara's face and it mixed with her salty tears and ran down her cheek. And my head slumped down to my chest. Then I stared at her hands gripping the top of "our" angel's little double-bladed axe, and my blood pumped out and ran down its spike handle onto her fingers.

"Please," she said, "Benito, you have to understand—"

"I forgive you," I said, coughing the dark liquid of my life down onto Barbara's hands and arms. It was the only thing I could say . . . then I slumped over and fell to the ground. I looked up at her and tried to smile but I coughed blood again.

Barbara closed her eyes and turned her head away. "I'm sorry." She held the blades of the archangel demon, Shax's, little pet pig axe. And deep dark blood dripped from its handle-spike, down onto the cold courtyard at Saint Samuels Seminary Academy for lost souls.

I closed my eyes.

— XLIX —

THE BIG PROTECTION beast roars out in agony as I twist the wood stake I just stabbed into its calf. And he swings his axe wildly down through the dark and damp air of the Mike and smashes the blade into the wood steps next to my head in a loud *CRACK!*

I scream out. Not from his axe, but at the searing fire that just spiked into my chest. And then my Shandian mind remembers, and I grab at the pain where my right heart used to be . . . before the only love I've known since my mother disappeared. . . Since Barbara—though that name never suited her—stabbed the handle-spike of an angel axe through it and forever changed me from being the immortal offspring of the archangel, Raum, and the human woman, Monica, into a mortal being of Man. A man who's body could now die, so his soul could go to Heaven . . . and kill God.

The beast bellows and falls to the side, grabbing at its leg. Its axe is embedded in the steps. And I roll to my knees and reach for the big blade.

A huge hand rams into my side and then the beast throws me through the air. I smash through a shop window along the side of the Mike's blood-bathed street, and then I crash into a tall wooden cabinet, its shelves full of stolen Protection boots.

Heavy boots rain down on me and thump my head and hands and I roll and moan, and then I yell out as the big cabinet tips and falls over at me. I barely escape being crushed.

And now my Shandian memory is telling me that the very next time I get killed will most likely be my last.

Idiot! That's my other voice and though I wish it didn't, the word reminds me of her and how much I—*Get up!*

"Yes, get up!" a woman's voice from inside the shop yells at me. I recognize her from the street. "Satan's snakes! Were it not for Word," Lucinda says, "I should surely lop blind brain from body and eat your eyes in front of you." But now she's lost her cockney accent . . . and she's speaking the language of Hell and hate. I . . . I think I understand it. She looks beat up pretty badly from the marks on her face.

"Lucifia?" I say. *That's what he called her . . . in the tunnel.*

Her condition doesn't seem to affect her strength, because she grabs me by the back of my collar and jerks me to my feet like a mother would grab the back of her misbehaving child's neck. "At least you awaken from bat blind delusion," she says.

A huge roar and then screaming from outside on the street reminds . . . both of us probably, that this is more nightmare than delusion.

She looks out the window. "Now cease sinful squawking and squandering of seconds," she says, "and smite duplicitous demon before plot's purpose plunges to Purgatory!"

My confusion from being beaten and bashed around all day long is now turning to frustration that I'm failing . . . even in my hallucinations. Yet none of it is changing the fact that time's ticking down, I still don't have the molasses I came here for, and I'm a half-hour's walk from the dead angel on the floor of my church!

But archangels running me around with riddles are getting me nowhere. And the demon swinging the axe at me outside isn't waiting for me to figure out how to kill it. "Who do you think I am?" I shout at her.

She squints her eyes in disapproval at me—I've seen the look on my mother—and then Lucinda or Lucifia. . . Whoever she is, the woman morphs to a dingy and dirty-looking . . . more angel than demon even when she spreads out her dusty gray wings. Her hair is messy and her face is blotted with soot. And when she speaks at me, dust puffs from her mouth. Yet, despite all that, she's attractive and has a familiar . . . charm. "You are the gilded god guardian, Faith," she says, "and have yet to fulfill fateful purpose. So, pull ass from eyes and fight!"

"If you're here to help me," I say, "then how do I kill it?"

But this "Barbara" is full of sarcasm and hate, too. "*It* is Uzza . . . strong arm of Satan, godling. And *you*, precious priest," she says, "exist to lend assistance to angel!" Then she grabs me by the arm and leg and lifts me over her head. "And there is no eternal beast nor being," her voice has turned to more screech than speech, "who lives with head separated from heart." Her fingers have turned to long talons that squeeze into my arm and leg, and I look at the ones pressing into my arm. There are only three fingers on it. "And no tree in Eden's garden grows green after birthing stump from axe!"

"Wait!"

"Life and Lived be damned to the dungeons," she caws like a crow, and then the dingy little angel spins and shoots several hundred fire-streaking feathers back out the window I just crashed through. She releases me on the very next turn and I go flying out the window after them.

"Miserable Man-monkey misfit!" I hear her shout out the window after me.

— L —

THE DUNGEONS OF the Damned were built under the Arena of Reckoning—a Purgatory prison, buried beneath the Hallowed Hall of the Word. They were constructed as a special holding area to safely store angels and demons and devils while they waited to participate in the Judgment battles in the arena.

A main tunnel—too tight for any angel to fly down—was carved out of the stone foundation and it ran in a circle around and underneath the edge of the arena. Other, "spoke" tunnels, crisscrossed its diameter.

The dungeons were dark and damp and spoke misery and hate to any who entered. It was far too hot for the light souls damned from Heaven, and not hot enough for the dark ones cast out of Hell. They were a literal perdition—a place of eternal punishment and damnation into which an unrepentant or sinful soul passed after being damned by Life or put to death by Lucifer.

Rock-walled cells with iron bars for doors lined both sides of every tunnel. And dark molasses—sweet nectar from Eden's Garden—and the crimson red blood of Life bathed the walls. It dripped heavier on Judgment nights. And on those nights, the dungeons became a gallery of gladiators, trained to slit throats and loose feathers for the entertainment and enmity of their captors.

They were held back until called by Life's own seal: the bright orange sun, seared into the iron on each cell's gate. Prisoners languished between Judgments . . . for as long as she saw fit to punish them.

Life stared through the bars on Lucifer's cell. "Even now your desired deception and sinful saint slip from your grasp," she said to him. "And yesterday's blaspheming bull, Uzza, is now my benevolent brute."

Lucifer did not speak. He simply gazed back through the bars at her and grinned. Some of them would turn—he knew this.

"You chase coveted chamber and throne," Life said, "while your minions slip from grasp as sand slips through time." She looked up and down the dark tunnel and then back into Lucifer's cell. "And your miserable mutiny is poised to join treasured tail as cropped cock, aborted and eaten by the very same betrayers who birthed it. While plot's parent stands stranded in dungeon cell for this sin—designing deceiver . . . a devil in name only."

Lucifer's smile wavered but a little. Then he looked behind him and then at the floor and then back through the iron bars at Life. "Yet," he said, "I remain master of sinful cell. Ruler of ruinous result . . . delivered from the dreadful duty of servant, suckling at the vastness of a villain's vanity. I'm sure you would agree"—he tilted his head to the side slightly—"a far finer fate."

Life frowned and closed her eyes. She shook her head slowly—side to side, calming herself. He was always like this. When she opened her orbs back up, the black glowed deeper. "Very well," she said, "wallow in black blood, guts and gore as glorious god's victory." Then she turned to leave.

Lucifer watched her walk away. She *was* still a delectable deity, and he remembered. "Do not scoff at my sinful sanctuary," he shouted, pressing his face between the bars, "lest you share salvation of the same."

Life did not turn around. "Even in defeat . . . your snakes slither, whispering words of threatened throne," she said as she approached the portal back to the arena. "Vanity? My darling Lucifer, you are a villain of the same name."

— LI —

THE FLAMES AND fire and red hot hate cuts into the dark gray night above the Mike. The main street has died down to an orange flicker of burning citizens and blown apart Protection agents. Shannon is nowhere to be found and I have no idea where his little pig-angel is. I look around, trying to find the beast before it splits me open with its axe.

"Benito Benedetti!" the beast's voice booms from a side alley, "Blasphemer, betrayer . . . bilious bane of your benevolent ruler in Heaven. Show yourself, morning star monkey!" Then he limps out onto the main street. He's managed to pull out the stake I punched through his calf, but its effects linger.

The beast's horns are on fire and its nostrils billow steam up into the fog. As it limps toward me, its hooves shake the ground. And it's closing fast, carrying its axe like an angry carpenter faced with yet another annoying nail it has to hammer in the head.

I have no idea how I'm going to get the axe out of its hand, much less cut off its head to kill it. And it's almost on top of me and the axe comes up—

The beast's head rears back and a huge bellowing roar of fire blows up into the fog.

A shadow flashes by the calf that I stabbed with the stake, and then another flash and growling by the beast's hoof. And Shannon's—only his pet potbellied pig has turned to a squawking, screeching. . . He looks like a little mudball of feathers, running around nipping and biting the beast's ankle, making it bellow in agony. The dirty little angel's eyes glow red and I watch them streak back and forth around the beast's leg.

The beast swings its axe down and barely misses cutting Shannon's little "pig" in two. Then it drops down to one knee, steadying itself with the fist holding its axe. It tries to grab at the dark little angel, but the terrorizing terrier races under the beast's knee and then latches onto the beast's fist.

The beast roars in pain, and it drops its big blade to the ground. Then the beast whips its injured arm wildly, roaring in agony as Shannon's little pit bull angel dangles and swings through the air with it—its jaws latched onto the beast's wrist. Then the beast grabs the little cherub and rips its jaws off its arm, and then it roars and screams and screeches in pain. And it throws the little angel through the air. But the angel recovers and flies back, and its red eyes streak through the gray fog as it harasses around the beast's head.

I rush at the axe, as fiery hot lava—the beast's blood—gushes down around me.

The beast grabs its wound and fiery goo sprays from it like a thumb over a garden hose, down onto my arm and shoulder, and I scream out and fall to the ground. *Fire!* my inner voice shouts at me. It's as afraid of being burned as I am. And I roll, trying to put out the flames.

I'm up in a flash and I rip off my burning jacket and run toward the axe. I try to scoop up the weapon without stopping so the beast can't rain more of its molten rock blood down on me. But the big blade's too heavy and I jerk sideways and fall.

And the beast snatches up the axe, hot liquid rock spraying in front of him as he cocks his arm. And he swings the blade back across his chest, back-swinging sideways at me.

I lean backward—controlled fall—and the blade barely misses my legs and chest and chin. One of my arms isn't so lucky, and the axe grazes across it, slicing through my black shirt and cutting a long gash in my bicep. Warm, sticky blood flows into my armpit as I hit the ground and cry out. *Get back up!* my mind yells at me.

He's gonna kill you! my inner voice—never missing an opportunity —shouts after it.

And the beast has his axe back up and he swings it straight down at me again. I roll sideways at the last instant and a horrendous clang rings out and sparks fly. When I look, the axe is embedded in a manhole cover—one of the blades has cut down into the big steel plate, hacking it in two, and the rest of that side of the axe is sliced into the street. The opposite blade is sticking straight up toward Heaven.

I'm up and I grab my arm, and blood flows onto my hand and I glance at it. In the dark gray of night. . . In the flaming fire and fog-light at the Mike, my blood looks. . .

A huge roar snaps my mind back to the fight. The beast is struggling with its axe. It's hunched over onto one knee, its foot on the big round manhole cover, trying to pull and heave and rip the blade out of the street. He groans and leans down over the axe, readying for one final pull.

Now! It may be my only chance before he cuts me to pieces—I'm running out of energy. I race at the beast, step on its injured calf and jump onto its back.

The beast groans and stumbles forward a little. It reaches back for its leg and then tries to grab at me, and it falls farther forward.

I jump to his head and grab both of his horns. Then I flip forward over the top of his head and pull the horns with me. I feel him come forward and I pull down hard with both hands and then there's resistance, but I pull as hard as I can and I can feel the horns giving way.

The beast bellows and roars out—one final protest—before his neck slices down over the blade sticking out of the street and I pull his head down over the exposed edge, severing his head at the neck!

And fire and raging steam escape from the beast's neck and then lava flows from the stump, melting its way down the street.

I drop the head and horns and slump over onto the side of the Mike, spent and bleeding.

Then the Seattle drone-raid sirens go off. That'll be the backup.

— LII —

I WOKE UP back in my cell in the student dormitory wing of Saint Samuels Seminary. I felt the right side of my chest. There was no hole where Barbara had stabbed me . . . and I wasn't dead. Had it not been for the first three times I died, I might have been a little more surprised. As it was, the thing that surprised me the most stood just outside my cell door, staring in at me, tears running down her face.

As soon as she realized that I was awake, Barbara said, "I'm . . . so sorry, Benito. I . . . I had to . . . she made me."

I rubbed my chest and moaned a little. Then I closed my eyes and let my Shandian mind feel its surroundings. I took a long five-count breath in through my nostrils and I smelled . . . everything. Barbara still smelled like sweet blackberries to me, the bucket at the edge of my cell still reeked of urine and feces, but the blood in my mouth was. . .? I swirled it around a little and it tasted like . . . syrup?

I actually wasn't that surprised. Saint Samuels had a thousand hungry boys to feed and one of the staples of our after-beating breakfasts were pancakes and syrup. "Breakfast all ready?"

"What?"

"Pancakes for breakfast again?" I asked. There was no sense in asking why Barbara had stabbed me in the chest. By then I knew she would probably lie anyway. "What time—why am I still in my. . .?" I looked out the small window. It was still black outside . . . and cold. *Not breakfast. . .*

"You ain't dead," Barbara muttered. "They said—I didn't believe them. I watched you in there for a half hour. I was sure you was dead."

"Thirty-three," I muttered.

"Thirty-three what?"

"I was dead," I told her, "for thirty-three minutes."

"That just"—Barbara frowned, put her hand over her eyes, and coughed out a little cry—"don't make no sense."

Four years was a long time. If it was all you were doing every night, reading and understanding the *Bible* wasn't all that hard. "I'm guessing they don't let you actually read the *Bible*." I knew the answer.

"Well. . ."

"Father D likes. . ." I said, wondering which of the events I remembered in the courtyard were the truth and which were just a dream. "He liked to tell it. I had to smuggle one back here." I crawled over to my stinking privy bucket and reached down through my own urine and feces—I never completely emptied my bucket after I smuggled the book back. And no one was going to dig through the excrement of a thousand boys' five-gallon privy buckets each week, weekly cell inspections or not.

When I pulled the dripping plastic bag out, Barbara put her hand over her mouth and gagged a little.

I chuckled at her. "Funny what makes you sick to your stomach, isn't it," I said. "For instance"—I'd had enough—"after four years, this bag is as precious to me as my dog was."

"I never knew you had a dog."

"His name was Max," I said to her. I wiped the bag on my sweats, opened it up, and pulled out my ragged and well-read copy of God's own Word. "And he was the last loyal soul I ever knew."

Barbara's eyes watered even more. "Benito?" she said, but I didn't trust her.

I flipped open my little *Bible* to the verse that got me through most days, and I read it to her, " 'Though I walk through the valley of the shadow of death, I will fear no evil, for thou art with me.' I used to think of you every time I read that," I told her. It was the truth, because though God never appeared during my four-year imprisonment in pain, Barbara visited me every night. I figured the verse was more appropriate for her. It wouldn't be my last mistake with her. "Why are you even here?"

"Please," she said, "I didn't have a choice."

"There's always a choice," I said. I held up the book. "This book, it's full a lies, too. Page after page of things that . . . just aren't true. And then you—I don't know what to believe in now. Maybe I should write a book about you ripping out my heart. At least that would be the truth." It was more than one truth, and two more than I'd ever read in the *Bible*.

"I didn't mean to hurt you," she said. "I just—"

"I already forgave you," I said. "What else do you want from me?"

"There's a new bishop coming," she said, "to replace Father D— Dominic. I don't know what they're gonna do with you."

"You mean you don't know what they're going to do with you." Deep inside, my inner voice told me that I would protect her no matter what it cost me. It had proven that. And my Shandian mind was silent—it knew too. "You want me to pray for you then?" I asked her.

"No!" Barbara shouted at me. "You're . . . you're just a *idiot*, and . . .

and I don't need no *prayer.*"

"Well," I said, "I'll pray for myself then." And I knelt down on my bed mat and closed my eyes. "Be angry at your friends, but do not sin against them. And do not let the sun go down on your anger, lest you give opportunity to the devil." I figured we could both use something literal.

— LIII —

SHANNON REACHES DOWN and grabs me by my wounded arm and I wince and try not to make any noise. Once I get to my feet, I stare down at the axe blade buried in the street. The rain sizzles and turns to steam as it hits the blade and the remaining glow of red hot lava—blood from the beast slowly cools in the unrelenting rain. "That is a nasty. . ."—I look at Shannon—"where in Heaven. . .? Where were you? Why didn't you come and help—"

"It be your God what put muttons in her own garden, she did," says Shannon, "sowin' and growin' weeds while you monkeys wank on your williams. And here to mow it, I ain't. You and me, Benito, we're here to plow it under. Soon as you muster your molasses, that is. I don't fancy I'll be staying for the ending any longer than he will. A right mean offspring, he is—the Devil's own darling."

He's right about running out of time, because the angel in the pews of my church? "Who . . . is he?" I ask.

Shannon smiles his big mustached grin at me. "Your Judgment, he is. A right fine one at that."

Shannon's little potbellied pig squeals and runs up behind him. And Shannon doesn't even look back when the little demon-angel turned back to pig jumps at him. He just catches it under his arm, and then he starts scratching it between the ears again.

"He likes that?"

"Indeed he does, mate," Shannon says. Then he looks down at the pig. "Still got your bacon then?"

The pig grunts and squeals a tiny squeak.

Shannon laughs and looks at me. "Says he saved *your* bacon right enough."

Lucinda's voice speaks behind me. And she's back to the language of the Mike. "How's a lady to suck tenth teat to that, then?" she says. "Burnin' and boilin' bacon—no better smell in me nostrils. It ain't fair, Shannon—that gruntin' little cunt . . . always curryin' your favor. Slayin' dragons and demons and all manner of devil, he is." She smiles at us both—all three—as she walks up. And I don't know whether she's talking about me or Shannon's little pet pig. Maybe both of us.

I grip my arm as the Mike burns down to a crackle and blood flows from my wound. I moan a little and wince at the pain in my arm.

Lucinda—at least I think she's back to human—reaches over and faster than any of us can react, she plucks a hair off of the little potbelly's tail and it turns to a brown iron feather right in front of my eyes. Apparently Shannon's grog has got a ways to go before it lets go of me.

And Lucinda blows on the quill and it glows up to red hot.

Shannon chuckles. "Mind him with the fire then, love," he says to her. "He might not—"

And Lucinda grabs my arm and sears the feather along the entire length of my wound. And I scream out, but she keeps at it. My flesh sizzles and the smell. . . I remember the smell of my own burning flesh. And when she lets go of me I lean over and vomit out a huge stream of black.

"Aw, for Satan's sake, Lucifia," Shannon says. "I warned—you are a right vicious vixen, you are. I bet his own lovely lady wouldn't burn him like that." He thinks for a second. "Literally, I mean. She be a burnin'—"

"Oh, shut up then, ya monster," she says to Shannon, "he's fine." She points at the ground—at my blood, glowing dark in the night and the flames of the aftermath of the Mike. "There ya go then, his miserable monkey molasses." She glances at the axe, buried in the street, and then back down at my vomit. "Took the Blood Weeper to wick it back out of him, but there it is, sure enough."

I stare down with her. My blood doesn't just appear black in the dark Mike night . . . it *is* black. "Molasses?" I mutter. "Blood Weep-what?"

"Blind and deaf then, are ya?" Lucinda says to me. Then she looks at Shannon and shakes her head. "You sure he's the right monkey? Next, you'll be boiling 'bout he can't write." She chuckles a little. "Wouldn't *that* be an ironic irritation."

"Come on then," Shannon says to her, "stop pizzing about nippin' at him. He's got the blasphemy buried in his own basement, he has. Don't you worry about that none, love." He pauses for a second and sniffs the air. "And he's got about thirty-three a me feathers to find his way back to his memory of it. So instead a wellin' up our ears with more of your wicked wailing, why don't you help him scoop up his molasses and fly his feathers back to his faith."

I'm. . . I don't even know how to react. But I've remembered something—jarred thoughts brought on by who knows what hallucination I'm having. *Shannon's grog*, my Shandian mind says. And that's that—I'm swearing off his liquor cabinet no matter how good it tastes, because this is by far the longest hallucination I've ever—

I just catch a flash of Lucinda's—and her three-fingered hand's on my temple and the other one's on my chin and she—

She's going to kiss you! my inner voice shouts. I don't know if Shannon is going to like it. I know I wouldn't like anyone kissing—

Her mouth opens up. A bright white light bursts out and then her lips are across mine and it feels like the entire eternity rushes into my mouth. My eyes roll up and I shake uncontrollably and I fall, but she catches me and lowers me down into the puddle of my own black blood.

"Monkey molasses," she says. "Flyin' through fog—it's a bleedin' bitch, it is. Why's it me then?"

"Well, me pig's not doin' it, now is he?" Shannon voice is fading, and I'm slipping backward into the black. "Piz . . . go . . . fetch . . . me . . . grog . . . glass."

And then the darkness takes me.

— LIV —

THEY. . . WHOEVER THEY were, they kept me in my cell at Saint Samuels for four more years. I was eighteen before they released me—made me a priest and gave me my own church. Those years were far less brutal, but I would have welcomed a beating if they'd just let me go outside to feel the rain on my face . . . even once.

The very next night after I had said the prayer against her, Barbara came to see me in my cell again. But right before she got there, I heard her talking to someone out in the student dormitory corridor.

I could tell it was a woman, not a booming bald blasphemer like Father D. This voice was younger and sweeter and gentler. I found myself fearing for her, listening to Barbara's words, because when the woman spoke to her, Barbara offered none of her trademark sarcasm and spit back. And I'd come to understand that Barbara only acted that way when she wanted something.

"I don't love him," Barbara's voice burned into my ears as painfully as any PI's torch had ever burned my back. "I just. . . You're not gonna kill him, are you?"

At least she doesn't want you dead, my inner voice heckled me. It was small consolation, and I wondered if Barbara wasn't asking the question so much as making a suggestion.

"Oh, Heaven in the Garden, Sister," the woman's voice said, "no, we aren't going to kill him. Not today." The pause felt uncomfortable, like that was exactly what this woman was going to do one day. "And you *will* love him . . . in time," she said to Barbara. "However, today you will set his soul on the path to redemption."

"With a book?" Barbara had said. It was as respectful as I'd heard her be. Then I heard the rustling of pages. "But there ain't nothing written in it."

"Our Lord's sheep shall hear the voice in this book," the woman's voice said, "and your young priest will know its words, and then we will all follow. For God gave you children eternal life, Sister, so that you will never perish. But our Lord shall snatch that out of her hand."

By the time Barbara's face appeared between the bars on the door to my cell, the woman she had been speaking with was gone.

"You hear all that?" Barbara asked.

"Yes," I said. If she wanted to lie to me, that was her business. I vowed to tell her nothing but the truth.

She held onto the book with both hands. "I knew you was listening."

"So . . . my book," I said to her.

Barbara held up a huge leather-bound book. I could only assume from her conversation that it had nothing written in it.

I picked up my five-gallon privy and tilted it toward her. "Not that book," I said. "Where's my *Bible?*"

"They . . . made me take it away from you."

And I knew the answer, but I wanted her to know that I would never again participate in her betrayal. "How did they know I had it?" I said, glaring at her.

"Don't be that way, Benito," she said. "They're sending me to the Mike tomorrow."

"I doubt that," I said. "Now give me my book."

Barbara held the book up in front of her, like she wasn't going to hand it over without some kind of payment.

I reached through the bars, grabbed onto the big leather spine, and jerked it out of her hands. Had she already figured out what that payment was, I believe she would have held onto it harder. She let me take it without protest.

When I opened up the big book, the pages were tan and ancient and just as I had overheard, they were completely blank.

I thumbed through the parchment a few pages. The pages didn't even make sound as they flipped past my thumb. The room was more silent as they turned.

I closed the book, looked back at Barbara, and then I held out my hand—I had nothing to write with.

Barbara hesitated a little and gave me a look like she had no idea what I wanted.

I just stared at her, continuing to hold out my hand.

Then she smiled an evil grin and reached beneath her habit. She pulled out a metal quill pen and handed it toward me, but when I went to grab it from her, she jerked it back and my fist missed. Then she threw it through the bars and it clinked across the stone floor of my cell.

I didn't look down at the pen. "And the ink?" I asked.

Barbara turned her back to me, showing me the truth side of her. "They didn't gimme none," she said.

"What am I going to write with then?"

"Write it with your shit for all I care, Benito," she said. "You like playing around in it so much."

I turned around and picked up the long pen. The end of it looked like the end of an arrow and it was very sharp.

"You're smart," Barbara said. Then she walked away. The last thing she said to me was, "you'll figure out something."

I eyed the tip of the metal quill, and then I touched it with the end of my finger. And the quill sliced into my finger like Barbara's words had cut into my heart, and I bled just the same . . . exactly the same.

— LV —

I WAKE UP from my "trip" to the Mike, back on the floor of my own church. The rain is drizzling down through the hole in the roof, backlit by helicopter searchlights, and the dripping sounds are accentuated by explosions in the distance.

Drone strikes, my Shandian mind says. For certain the loss of an entire platoon of Protection agents, not to mention one of their MARR's, would warrant an Avenger drone strike.

My thoughts are confirmed when two more explosions rock the city in the direction of the Mike. *Hellfuries*, my inner voice says. Those are Protection's favorite missile of choice.

But was any of it real? My question is answered by a grumbling groan on the floor several feet away from me. My vision's a little blurry and I touch my face to adjust my—but my glasses are gone. I touch my pocket and it tells me that in addition to my flask. . . *Why are they in my pocket?*

I pull them out, wipe them, and put them back on. The angel is still on the floor of my church and it still has a cross through its stomach, but it's not dead.

Another groan from the huge bird of prey tells me he is far from dead. I look at the clock on the wall over the exit to the street. *Only a few minutes. . .* "Molasses?" I mutter. I'm in it deep now.

I look around me and sure enough, there is a gallon of Shannon's— *Grog?* My Shandian mind tells me that may not be what's in the big gallon-sized genie bottle next to me. I can only hope it's not filled with the same thing we were drinking in his shop.

I've blacked out on a bender before, but this one's—*Focus!*

The screech ends the reprimand that my Shandian mind is about to give me, and I grab the bottle of "molasses" and kneel next to the big angel. I still can't believe it.

I work on its stomach for a few minutes—pushing and shoving entrails back where they came from.

There's something in my mind—a long-forgotten warning . . . or riddle . . . or Colonel-ism I can't quite recall. *Hide behind weakness, Benito*, my Shandian mind says, and I remember.

When this big brute does wake up. . . Whatever comes next, I'm pretty sure that the best thing I can do to fulfill my part of this entire plot is to pretend I have no idea what is going on.

The angel groans again and then opens its eyes. The light that didn't get blown out from the caved-in roof shines in its eyes, and he squints and then looks at me curiously.

"I'm sorry," I say to him.

The angel groans a little and then says, "Dammit!"

I think about reprimanding him, but then I just tell him to conserve his energy.

When he replies. . . "*Fuck* you," he says to me.

Now I'm sure that my decision to remain meek instead of manly is the right strategy. Regardless, I've had enough of dealing and debating with angry angels for one day. Better if this one thinks I'm not worth fighting. Besides, I know what he wants anyway—I wrote him.

— LVI —

WITH HER DAY Star Lucifer's plot freshly quelled, Life sat on the throne in her chamber and pondered her victory. Two Golden Guardians stood on either side of her.

Something sinister was shrouded. She couldn't quite push her mind to it. As delectable a demon as Life thought him to be, Lucifer was not one to suffer defeat in silence. Her Day Star would answer.

"But how?" Life spoke softly to herself.

The guards did not even stir to answer.

Life glanced at them. "Dreadful demon stands sequestered for sin of sedition," she said, "yet . . . I sense the point of plot's pen . . . remains immersed in ink."

She stood up and fluttered her wings, hovering for a second in front of her guards before buzzing outside to the great mountain. And then Life stared down at Eden's garden, into the dense mist above Lucifer's latest battleground, Seattle. "My sister's keeper. . ." she said, nodding her head slightly. Then she thought of her own warmark—her orange shining sun. She closed her eyes and shook her head. "Your miserable fog refuses to yield to saintly salvation from the sun," she muttered. "Though I have thrown designing devil in sibling's dungeon . . . the earth of plot's purpose sogs and slips from my grasp—*rife* with rain."

Lucifer stood, wings around himself and his eyes watchful. He waited in his cell deep in the Dungeons of the Damned. The first phase of his plot—there were three—had ended . . . perfectly. Salvation from his tormentor was but two breaths away.

He drank in the darkness and the damp and the misery that would ensue as a result . . . and he waited for his visitor. He knew she would arrive shortly.

The portal from the arena twisted open and a dark angel from Lucifer's own past. . . By the time the angelic figure appeared in front of his cell, Lucifer could discern neither past nor present as his own time.

The angel flitted and then stood in the shadows across the tunnel from his cell. She folded her wings behind her and peered from the darkness at him.

"Angel arrives . . . as plot's point progresses," Lucifer said to the figure. "Soon we will move as the same mind in mutiny."

The angel muttered under her breath, "I shall never meld precious thoughts of the past with dark devil's desire for the future."

Lucifer smiled across at her. "Salvation in the next eternity then?" he said. "May we find feathered friends and foes basking in her glory."

The angel spoke of eternities past and those yet to come. "I begin to doubt the gluttonous glory of Eden's precious garden," she said to Lucifer.

"Ah," said Lucifer, "our minds align in spite of angel's delusions."

"God's own envy in Heaven?" the angel said. And then the deep gray, armored and angry mother of Rain and Mist when she had to be, and a pure soul of Heaven when she didn't, stepped from the shadows. The dungeons brought out the "mother" in her.

The wife of the Great Dragon angel, Jump, had fallen further than her husband had plunged through the roof of their friend Faith's own church. "I would see our precious seed crucified on a cross before I assisted you in this purpose," said Salvation.

"As I have already spoken," said Lucifer. "Shall we, then?"

Salvation walked across the tunnel, pulled one of her flight feathers from her wing . . . and then she sliced it through Life's sun seal, burned into the iron plate on the gate of Lucifer's cell.

END OF TESTAMENT

Congratulations! You just finished *FAITH*, the third installment in Steve Windsor's *THE FALLEN* series.

Turn the page to find out about upcoming book releases for loyal fans of *THE FALLEN* series. >>>>>

GET BOOK 4

THE FALLEN series continues in *HOLE : Testament 4*.
Get your copy of *HOLE* before anyone else.

vixenink.com/hole-fallen/

"Babette's not a monster, she's just . . . misunderstood."

THE FALLEN Series of Religious Thrillers:
JUMP
FURY
FAITH
HOLE
DOGG
BURN
LIVED
LIFE
RAIN
SALVATION

Oh, and one more thing >>>

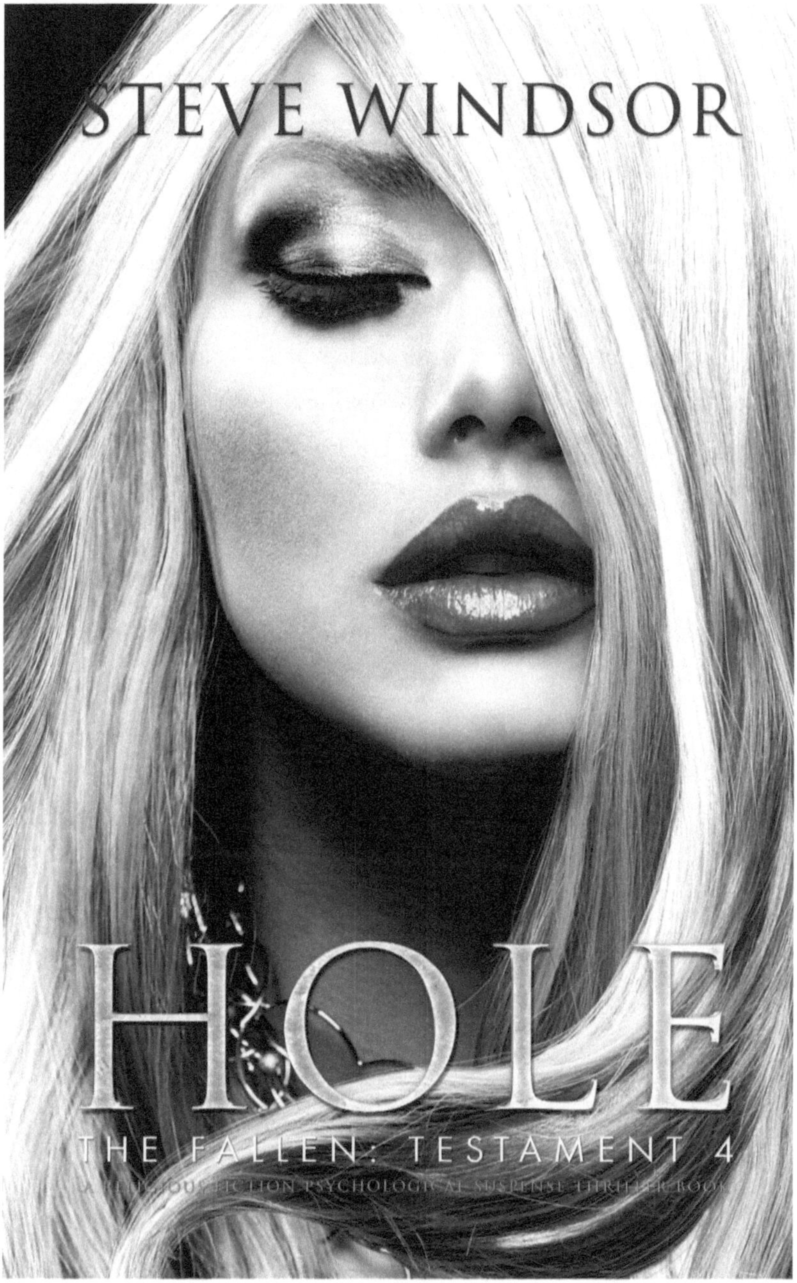
STEVE WINDSOR
HOLE
THE FALLEN: TESTAMENT 4

Review Request

"Kinda cute. . ." She mocks me like my love. My Lord Rain in Heaven, what Fury must think of my begging and pleading. The mere *thought* of asking sends my mind to guilt and shame.

But what else can I do? Denying what my heart wants would be . . . worse. I never think to ask, I never think to pray—I simply want.

And that wanting consumes me . . . as you shall soon see in her book. Though "*HOLE?*" Her name alone makes my soul cold now.

It took a fiery demon from Hell to extinguish that wanting. Though even now . . . I wonder. Is it gone? Do I want for her less even as she spurns and mocks me? Vile beast that she is, she remains my love, my need, my salvation that I pray will deliver me from this Hell of obscurity.

Babette—Barbara? No, no—you misunderstand me. I believe that you will find in her testament—her soul may be lost to me forever. What I want now—the need that has replaced the warm touch of her flesh—is something far more elusive than that.

Dear friend. . . And I have to chuckle to myself of her small size compared to the sheer magnitude of the mountain that must be moved to uncover it. Yes, yes, you have guessed it—I long only for warm words these early days in our testaments. A precious ounce of productive praise to remind me that I toil not only for my own wanting . . . but for the salvation of others.

Close your eyes, my child. Think happiness as we go into the bright orange light—the dense Amazonian jungle of judgment—to smile your favor on my testament.

Bless you for leaving a review of *FAITH*.

About the Author:

Steve Windsor is the author of the *THE FALLEN* series of religious suspense thrillers. *JUMP, FURY, FAITH, DOGG, HOLE, BURN, LIVED, LIFE, RAIN,* and *SALVATION.*

He lives with his wife and two daughters in the real world . . . and many, many other cool people in the imaginary world in his mind.

Connect with the author:
EMAIL: steve@stevewindsor.com
FACEBOOK: vixenink.com/facebook-page

Thank you so much for reading *FURY.*

"I write fiction novels, because the truth . . . is just way too scary."
—Steve Windsor